Sister Circle

Wings Press, Inc.

Agnes Alexander

Sister Circle

The solicitor glanced at Vernetta, took a breath, and said, "I'm afraid not. None of your relatives are willing or able to take in four daughters. But I assure you, you will all be placed with family members who will allow you to stay in touch with each other."

The sisters looked stunned but didn't say anything else.

After Brendon left, Aunt Vernetta told them to go to their rooms and settle down for the night because the trunks would be brought to them in the morning, and they needed to begin their packing. She then left them alone.

When they were alone, Melissa whispered, "Everyone stop in my room before going to yours."

They all nodded, then headed out the door and up the stairs into Melissa's room.

When her door closed and they were alone, she said, "Sister circle."

Once they circled, she said, "I know none of you like the idea of what they're going to do with us anymore than I do, but right now there is nothing we can do to stop them. But my dear sisters, we will not always be young and helpless. I don't know how soon it will happen, but deep in my heart I know we will all be together again someday. We may all be grown, and have houses of our own, but we will be located in the same area, and we'll see each other often. You must believe this with me, and it will happen."

"I believe it," Rosemary's small voice said.

Catherine and Bernadette agreed, then Melissa said, "Then let's say a prayer and ask for God to help us make this happen for us."

After the prayer, they dispersed to their rooms with high hopes, not realizing it would be years before their dream of being together again would come true. Within the next month, all four were sent to their new homes.

What They Are Saying About

Sister Circle

"I just finished reading your novel *Sister Circle*. I absolutely loved it! This is one of the best novels I have read of yours so far.
—DK McLaughlin, author of *Raven* and *Shalome*

Sister Circle

Agnes Alexander

A Wings ePress, Inc.
Western Romance Novel

Wings ePress, Inc.

Edited by: Jeanne Smith
Copy Edited by: Melissa Scott
Executive Editor: Jeanne Smith
Cover Artist: Trisha FitzGerald-Jung
Images Pixabay

All rights reserved

Wings ePress Books
www.wingsepress.com

Copyright © 2024 by: Agnes Alexander
ISBN 979-8-89197-977-2

Published In the United States Of America

Wings ePress, Inc.
3000 N. Rock Road
Newton, KS 67114

Dedication

For my dear friend, Anne Wiseman, who thinks every book I write is wonderful—and I choose to believe her. Thank you for your support, Anne. I hope you like this one as well.
Hugs, Agnes aka Lynette.

One

The Beginning

The four Cardwell sisters had a light meal the church women served after the funeral of their parents. After they ate, their aunt, Vernetta Cardwell Albertson, who had been in charge of everything since their parents' premature death in a freak accident during a thunderstorm, sent them into the informal parlor of the Baltimore house where they had lived all their lives.

Melissa, the oldest child, had been born the second year they had lived in this newly built house. The now sixteen-year-old led the way to the room.

Once in the parlor, the next in line, Catherine, fifteen, looked at the others and asked, "Why do you think we were sent in here and left by ourselves?"

"'Cause the mean old woman who tells everybody what to do told us to come in here, and we have to do what she says, that's why," thirteen-year-old Bernadette answered.

"The lawyer told me she was in charge of everything and there was nothing we could do about the decisions she's made about what's to happen to us," Melissa said. "I don't like it any more than you do, but we can't stay in this house without Mama and Daddy."

The baby, Rosemary, who had turned ten only a month earlier, burst into tears. "I just wish Mama and Daddy hadn't got killed by lightning during that awful storm. They should still be here with us 'cause I miss them."

Bernadette reached over and put her arm around her sister. "We all wish the same thing, Rosemary."

"We sure do," they all muttered as tears welled up in all their eyes.

Melissa wiped her eyes and stood. "Let's make a sister circle and comfort each other like Mama always told us to do when we got upset about something or when we wanted to celebrate something good when it happens."

As soon as the circle formed with the sisters having their arms around each other's waist, it was natural for them to begin comforting each other. Before they finished, the door opened and Vernetta's stern voice asked, "What in the world is going on in here?"

They broke apart and Melissa's voice quivered as she said, "Mama told us to make a sister circle when we were upset, and we would soon feel better, or if we were happy, it would make us happier."

Vernetta frowned. "I've never heard of anything so ridiculous. Now all of you find a seat and be quiet. You need to act like well-bred young ladies, not a group of babies. The solicitor will be here in a minute to inform you of what will be taking place in the next few days. I don't want him thinking you have been brought up with no breeding." She started to the door and paused. "I'll be back shortly, and I expect you to be in your seats when I return. Not standing in a foolish circle. You'll embarrass me if you do such a thing again."

As the door closed, Rosemary hung her head and said, "I don't like her."

Catherine grinned. "My dear little sister, again I'm sure you've said something all of us agree with."

There were nods of harmony and even a giggle or two but as they had been told to do, they all stayed in their seats.

It wasn't long before the aunt and a man who said his name was Wilford Brendon, came into the room. He announced he was helping Mrs. Vernetta Cardwell Albertson settle their parents' estate. He then cleared his throat and added, "I know some of you are old enough to understand, at your age, there is no way for you to remain in this house without any adults living here and both of your parents being deceased. There is no alternative, so the dwelling will be sold, and if there are any proceeds left after your guardian's share is given to them, it will be divided evenly and set aside for each of you to receive when you are eighteen years old."

Catherine, who had always been outspoken, blurted, "Who is our guardian?"

Vernetta butted in. "It hasn't been decided. In the meantime, each of you will be given two trunks. These will be for your clothes and personal belongings. There will be two extra trunks and each of you may select two or three mementos you desire from the household goods. I will have these stored at my home. Someday you may want to display these things in your own homes."

Melissa frowned. "What about the rest of the furniture?"

Mr. Brendon said, "We decided to let friends and family select a piece of furniture to buy if they desire, and what is left will be sold to the public. Of course, the money will go to you sisters to be collected at age eighteen."

"I have a question," Catherine said. "Will we all be living with the same guardian?"

The solicitor glanced at Vernetta, took a breath, and said, "I'm afraid not. None of your relatives are willing or able to take in four daughters. But I assure you, you will all be placed with family members who will allow you to stay in touch with each other."

The sisters looked stunned but didn't say anything else.

After Brendon left, Aunt Vernetta told them to go to their rooms and settle down for the night because the trunks would be brought to them in the morning, and they needed to begin their packing. She then left them alone.

When they were alone, Melissa whispered, "Everyone stop in my room before going to yours."

They all nodded, then headed out the door and up the stairs into Melissa's room.

When her door closed and they were alone, she said, "Sister circle."

Once they circled, she said, "I know none of you like the idea of what they're going to do with us any more than I do, but right now there is nothing we can do to stop them. But my dear sisters, we will not always be young and helpless. I don't know how soon it will happen, but deep in my heart I know we will all be together again someday. We may all be grown, and have houses of our own, but we will be located in the same area, and we'll see each other often. You must believe this with me, and it will happen."

"I believe it," Rosemary's small voice said.

Catherine and Bernadette agreed, then Melissa said, "Then let's say a prayer and ask for God to help us make this happen for us."

After the prayer, they dispersed to their rooms with high hopes, not realizing it would be years before their dream of being together again would come true. Within the next month, all four of them were sent to their new homes.

A strange man who was introduced as a relative of Vernetta's deceased husband came for Rosemary. He said he and his wife wanted a daughter. This wasn't true. He actually owned an orphanage in Shreveport, Louisiana and agreed to take the girl because of the money he'd get for her care.

Bernadette left next. She was sent to help a sickly aunt she had never heard of in Atlanta, Georgia. This was partially true. The aunt had taken the girl because her second husband's flirtatious ways with the women they had hired had made it impossible to keep a suitable companion for his ailing wife.

Melissa and Catherine were both shocked when Vernetta informed them they would be moving to Philadelphia to live with her.

So, the mystery of how they would ever accomplish their wish of someday being together again began.

Two

Melissa

Four years later, twenty-year-old Melissa Cardwell tried for at least the hundredth time to make herself and the two children with her comfortable on the lightly padded seat as the stagecoach rattled across the lonesome Texas prairie. It hadn't been so bad on the train when they first started out, though it was dirty and shaky, and she wondered if the train would be able to get through the snow. But somehow it had and now they were on this stagecoach, which turned out to be worse than the train. When they had arrived in a small town in Texas she didn't remember the name of, she was shocked to learn there was no train going from there to her destination, Bell Haven in West Texas. The only way to get there was by stage. The station manager in the last town they stopped in told her it would take two days to reach Bell Haven, but if the next day was as uncomfortable as this one had been, she wasn't sure she could make it.

She almost wished she'd listened to her aunt Vernetta and refused to take the orphaned children to Ruth Ann's mother-in-law, who lived in the faraway Texas town she'd never heard of. But she hadn't considered it a possibility to heed her aunt's suggestion at the time. In fact, she hadn't let anyone in Philadelphia know she had left on the journey until the train she took had crossed the Mississippi River. She then sent a wire to her aunt and hoped the woman wouldn't take her anger out on her sister, Catherine.

Melissa wasn't used to being as uncomfortable as she was today. Though the Philadelphia home she and her sister had shared with their aunt for the last four years was one of the more prestigious and elaborately furnished on the street where the elite of the city lived, she often felt confined and restricted. At the present time, she couldn't help but long for the comfort of the lavish, well-heated sitting room with its fireplace and large cast iron heater. In her mind she could envision the chairs and settees in the downstairs area with their plush padding and the polished tables holding delicate figurines and crystal lamps. She could even picture one of her aunt's expensive teapots with the imported tea they all loved sitting on one of the marble tables waiting for their usual afternoon tea and cakes. Her mind then wandered to the second-floor bedroom she shared with her sister, Catherine. It was a large room and contained two four-poster beds with soft mattresses and an abundance of pillows so stuffed with duck down she could get lost in them. The seats of the chairs surrounding the table at the window were covered in a pink and green pattern. Her favorite color was pink, and Catherine's was green. There were soft, neutral-colored carpets on the floor. The curtains and the bed covers were made of white silk with pink flowers with delicate mint green leaves. The chairs and the one settee held an abundance of pillows. In the corner of the room was a small heater and when it was cold weather, as it was this time of year, Annie, the only live-in maid, always came in and laid a fire so she and Catherine would be comfortable when they arose to dress.

Though she missed those comforts more than she ever imagined she would, it was nothing compared to the way she still missed the home she had shared with her parents and her three siblings only four years ago. Oh, how she longed to be back in the time when she didn't live with her aunt. Her mind slipped to the warm, but not as elaborate home in Baltimore she and her sisters had once shared with their loving parents. But it was all gone now. Aunt Vernetta had taken charge of dictating the futures of the four Cardwell sisters.

Since Melissa and Catherine lived in her mansion in Philadelphia, they seldom heard from their sisters, though Bernadette, who lived in Atlanta, wrote occasionally. This wasn't true of the youngest daughter, Rosemary. For some unknown reason, their aunt said the orphanage near Shreveport, Louisiana didn't allow outside communication. Later, they learned the orphanage had closed, and the children had all been sent to different institutions. Rosemary ended up in one near the small town of Weatherson in East Texas.

When Melissa and Catherine first arrived in Philadelphia, Aunt Vernetta announced they would be sharing a room and following her rules until she found a suitable mate for the two of them, since they were both nearing the age when a respectable young lady should marry. Of course, she would start with the oldest, Melissa.

Then Weldon Wheaton III came into the picture. He was a railroad man and, though he'd only been in Philadelphia for a year or so, he would have been considered a good catch, though there was something in his background which made his credibility questionable. Melissa wasn't sure what this problem was, but she knew he wanted to marry the *right* woman to give him the status he craved to assure him entrance into Philadelphia's high society. Though nobody had told her, Melissa felt sure he was near thirty-five or forty and she couldn't fathom herself married to a man nearly twice her age, no matter how often Aunt Vernetta sang his praises.

Now, sitting inside this cold stagecoach, she shivered and pushed thoughts of Mr. Wheaton away. Forcing her mind to think of something else, she settled on the weather. There was still snow on the ground in Philadelphia, but she knew if she were there, she wouldn't have to get out in the bad weather, unless Aunt Vernetta made arrangements and insisted she go ice skating with her sister and some of their friends she approved of, or for a sleigh ride around the park with Weldon Wheaton III.

Shaking this thought away, she almost smiled when she remembered how, at times, she'd become bored when living at home in Baltimore with her parents and sisters and would think she wanted to leave and have an adventure. But having an adventure didn't seem as exciting at present because here she sat in the cramped stagecoach bouncing across Texas with little Susie Jenson next to her right side where she'd snuggled and cried herself to sleep, and young David Jenson, who lay on her opposite side with his head in her lap. He was restless and kept moving about, but never came fully awake.

She pushed all thoughts of Philadelphia aside, shifted in her seat, and pulled the blankets more snuggly around the children. She then glanced at the man sitting across from them. He had dozed off and on during most of the trip. He'd let his chin fall to his ample chest, then he'd jerk it upright. Every so often, he'd let out a loud snore or a snort. She didn't understand how the children could sleep through it. She certainly wasn't able to, though she was weary.

Looking down at the children, Melissa shook her head. *How did it come to this?*

Oh, she knew how it had happened, but it was hard to reconcile it with the actual event which had taken place. It had started with a letter from her cousin, Ruth Ann Jenson, in early

December asking her to come to Baltimore because she desperately needed her. Though her aunt didn't want her to go, Melissa insisted she couldn't say no to her widowed cousin. Then, when a couple who were friends of her aunt said they were getting ready to go to Washington to visit their son who worked for the government, her aunt let Melissa accompany them as far as Baltimore. When they arrived, the couple told her they would probably be in Washington at least a week, and she was to stay in Baltimore until they returned to accompany her back home.

Melissa agreed, but when she arrived, she realized she would be staying with Ruth Ann longer than a week. The woman was gravely ill, and Melissa wanted to care for her, since Ruth Ann was not only her cousin, but a special friend.

Ruth Ann had been the only child in her family, and through the years she had gravitated toward the Cardwell sisters because there were so many of them. They all liked and welcomed her into the family, but she and Melissa had grown the closest, though she was three years older than Melissa. This closeness remained through the years. They were more like sisters than cousins.

Her aunt Vernetta allowed this friendship to continue because Ruth Ann's parents had prestigious jobs in the government, and there was nothing Vernetta wanted more than to be connected to prestigious people.

Melissa closed her eyes and recalled the devastating conversation she'd had with her cousin on her first day there. At first, she'd denied the facts, but Ruth Ann insisted it was true.

"I know you don't want to believe it, Melissa, but I'm dying and there's nothing you or anyone else can do to stop it. I have a terrible disease and there's no way any of the many doctors I've seen can help me. I have accepted the fact, and you must do so, too."

"I don't want to accept such a thing, Ruth Ann. You're much too young to die. Besides, you have these two beautiful children."

"I know, and I certainly don't want to die, but I have no choice in the matter. Unless a miracle happens, I will die soon."

"But..."

"Now, let us not talk about it any longer. I asked you to come to Baltimore because there is something I want you to do for me, my dear cousin. The last favor I'll ever ask of you."

"I'll do anything I can."

"When I'm gone, I want you to take my children to Andrew's mother in Texas."

Melissa looked at Ruth Ann in disbelief. "Don't you want your children to live with your parents in Washington?"

"No, Melissa. My parents aren't in Washington most of the time. They're always traveling because of my father's government job. In fact, they left last week for Europe, knowing how sick I was. The doctor told them I probably wouldn't last until Christmas, but they chose not to believe him. Besides, they hated Andrew and never had anything to do with the children until he died."

When Melissa started to say something, Ruth Ann shook her head and added, "I'm afraid when I'm gone, they'll send the children away to a boarding school or let them be raised by servants and nannies. Andrew's mother, Althea, has been more of a grandparent to them than my parents were, though she has never seen the children. She writes to them and to me often. I want her to raise them."

"But all the way to a place called Bell Haven, Texas? I hear there are still wild Indians in Texas, and I'm sure Bell Haven is nothing like Baltimore. Your children will be lost in such an uncivilized environment."

"I don't think so. They always loved the stories their father told them about the things he and his brother did growing up on their ranch. Andrew promised to take them there for a visit someday." A tear came into her eye. "Of course, the accident took him away from us before he could keep his promise." Reaching for Melissa's hand, she went on, "Please, Melissa. Promise me you'll do it. You're the only one in the world I can trust to do this for me, and I want Andrew's mother to raise my children."

Melissa teared up. "I'll do whatever you want me to do, so, yes, I promise to take them. I only hope and pray it'll be a long time before I have to do this."

Three days after Christmas, Ruth Ann Warner Jenson was laid to rest in the church cemetery beside her husband, Andrew. Her uncle on her mother's side handled the arrangements because her parents had sent word they wouldn't be able to come back from Europe because of the weather and diplomatic obligations. The uncle seemed relieved to learn he didn't have to worry about the children. As soon as the funeral was over, he turned them over to Melissa without question.

All of this had happened almost four weeks earlier. Now they were somewhere in Texas and had been for some time. She wasn't sure how big Texas was, though she'd heard it was huge. She only hoped and prayed they'd get to the Jenson ranch soon. She didn't think she could stand much more of this kind of travel.

I only hope Althea Jenson got my letter telling her of our impending arrival and will be expecting us. It'd be awful to arrive at her ranch and she have no idea we were coming, though Ruth Ann assured me she'd welcome her grandchildren under any circumstance.

The sun had set, and it was getting dark when they pulled into what the driver called a way station. To Melissa, it was a shack by the side of the bumpy road. Did they really expect her and the children to eat and sleep in a place like this? Couldn't they at least go to a town with a restaurant and a hotel?

When the stage stopped, she roused the children.

"Are we at Grandma's house yet?" David rubbed his eyes and sat up.

"Where Grandma?" Susie asked.

"She's not here, honey. This is a place where we are going to eat something and sleep for the night. Are you hungry?"

"No. I want Grandma."

"She may not be hungry, but I am, Aunt Melissa," David said.

The door opened, and the driver said, "Climb out, folks. This is our stop for the night. Come on in and get some grub. Then you need to go to bed because we'll be pulling out at dawn."

"Set here all night if you want to, woman. I'm hungry and I'm getting out of here." The man on the seat across from them scrambled out the door.

Melissa didn't think she'd ever met anyone who was as rude, but she didn't say anything. Instead, she turned to the children. "David is hungry, so let's go see what they have to eat."

"I bet it'll be funny," David said.

"What do you mean, funny?"

"All the food we've had to eat is funny."

"I admit it's not like the good meat and vegetables you had in Baltimore, but we must be thankful we have something to eat."

Melissa was surprised to see the driver waiting for her to exit. He offered his hand to her, and she took it. "Thank you."

"Yes, ma'am."

He then reached in and lifted the children to the ground. As soon as Susie's feet touched the soil, she ran into Melissa's arms. David acted more grown up and walked to her.

After taking the children to the privy, they went inside. Melissa asked for a pan of water to wash the children's hands. The rotund woman showed her where they could wash up and then began dishing out food to the male passenger, the driver, and his helper.

Melissa sat the children on each side of her on the long bench beside the rough wooden table where everyone else was seated.

Susie slipped as close to Melissa's side as she could.

David eyed the bowl of food the way station manager's wife sat in front of him. "Aunt Melissa, what is that?"

Melissa smiled at him, though her stomach turned over and she swallowed to keep the bile from rising into her mouth. "It's a stew, David. I'm sure it's good. Let's try it."

He was hesitant, but he finally took a small amount into his mouth. When he took a second bite, Melissa knew he was going to be all right with the meal. She wasn't so sure about herself and Susie.

Surprisingly, Melissa found it tasted better than it looked. Susie didn't complain either. It gave Melissa hope the sleeping arrangements wouldn't be bad.

She was wrong. In the room they were given, the beds consisted of a cot and two small bunks built against the wall. The cover was sparse and didn't look clean. She was glad they'd brought their blankets inside with them. The cover wasn't their main problem. It was the thin straw mattresses thrown on each bed. Melissa had never been subjected to such crude accommodations. She was sure she wouldn't sleep at all well tonight and knew she'd be delighted to get up before daylight to head out of this place. She just hoped the children would be able to get a little rest. David wanted to sleep on the top bunk bed and Susie was glad to sleep on the bottom. Melissa pulled the cot close to Susie's bed, not only to make sure the child didn't roll off, but in case David fell out of the top bunk, at least she and her bed would break his fall.

Her prediction about them getting little sleep was right. When the call to get up came, she was glad to put her feet on the floor. They were served a sparse breakfast of jam and bread. At least the children had milk and she had coffee, though it was much stronger than she was used to. Before the sun came up, they entered the stagecoach to begin the last leg of their journey to the Jenson ranch somewhere in Texas near a town called Bell Haven.

~ * ~

Joseph Jenson, who most people shortened to Joe, came into the ranch house by way of the kitchen. "Something you're cooking sure smells good in here, Ma."

"I'm not surprised you think so. I decided to make your favorite this evening."

"Beef roast?"

"Of course. It should be about done by now. Are you about ready to eat?"

"Got a little more work to do in the barn. Just came in to get the horse liniment Grover picked up in town when he went for supplies this morning. Unless you got it out, he said it was probably still in the box with your order."

"Is something wrong with one of the horses?"

"The one you called Sadie Mae is limping."

"Oh, no. Not Sadie Mae. She's just a baby. Is it bad?"

"I think she'll be all right."

"How'd she hurt her leg?"

"I'm not sure, but she probably stepped in a prairie dog hole in the pasture."

"I didn't put up the supplies, so I guess the liniment is still there. The box is in the pantry on the bottom shelf."

Joe went into the large pantry which was located on the side of the kitchen. It didn't take him long to find the horse remedy. He was about to shove the box back onto the shelf when he saw a paper sticking in the corner. He grabbed it and looked at an unopened letter.

He muttered, "Where did this come from?" Frowning, he walked back into the kitchen. "There was a letter in the box with your supplies. Didn't you see it, Ma?"

"Nope. Didn't look."

He glanced at it. "It's addressed to you."

She reached for it and read the return address. "It says it's from M. Cardwell. I don't know nobody named Cardwell." She stuck the letter in her apron pocket. "I don't have time to read it now. I'll do it when I finish up supper."

"I'll be back in a half hour or so. It shouldn't take any longer to tend Sadie Mae and finish up in the barn."

"The food will be ready, so don't dally."

He went out the door and Althea Jenson went back to the stove. She wondered who had written her a letter, but she wasn't sure she wanted to read it. If it'd had Ruth Ann Jenson's name on it, she'd have ripped it open right away. But she really didn't know anyone with the strange name of Cardwell, and she wasn't sure she wanted to know them. It could be from a strange man. A Matthew or a Michael or even a Mason and right now, she didn't want to know who he was.

In a letter a few weeks ago, Ruth Ann had told her she had something important to tell her. But she hadn't given her any clue at the time about what it was. This worried her a little. She knew Ruth Ann was a beautiful young widow with two children, children Althea thought were probably as beautiful as their mother and as handsome as their father. She would love to see them, but if the news Ruth Ann was going to send her was Susie and David had a new father, she didn't want to read about it from some stranger. On top of this, she knew she'd probably never get to see her grandchildren, and this made her sadder than anyone could ever know.

Althea tried not to resent the fact Ruth Ann might remarry one day. It stood to reason her daughter-in-law would eventually find a new husband and let him raise Andrew's children. A woman without a man had a hard life. She should know. She'd raised two boys alone. But this was different. As Andrew's mother, she couldn't help thinking it was still too soon after his death for Ruth Ann to turn to another man. Her boy had only been gone for eight months. But why else would a stranger write to her?

She pushed the thoughts away and set her mind to finishing up supper. She'd deal with Ruth Ann's new husband later if that was what the letter was about.

~ * ~

When they finally arrived in Bell Haven, Melissa asked the driver if they would be able to continue to ride with him on to the Jenson ranch.

He shook his head and said, "This is the end of the line for the stage. But you can probably go to the livery stable and rent a wagon and a man to take you to the ranch. Most towns have such a service."

"I see. Then, could you give me the directions to the stable?"

"Yes, ma'am. You go down this street for about four blocks and you'll see the livery on the other side of the mercantile."

"What about our luggage? I don't think the children and I can carry it."

"I doubt you could either." He looked around. "Tell you what. See the little café over there on the corner?" She nodded and he went on. "I'm going to go over there and eat a bite. I'll leave the stagecoach here, and when you have a wagon hired, come back and get your things."

"Thank you. We will." She turned to Susie and David. "Come along, children."

They set off in the direction the driver had indicated and had only gone a short distance when Susie said, "I hungry, Aunt Lissa."

"I am, too," David added.

"There's a store down the street. Why don't we stop in there and get a little something to eat before we hire a buggy to take us to your grandma's ranch?"

They did, but they had to hurry because the store was closing. They settled for a few slivers of cheese and bread. "We're not going to take time to eat it now. You can eat it after we hire someone to drive us. I want to get you to your grandmother's house as soon as I can."

They didn't argue and at the livery, though the man wasn't eager to hire out to them, he finally agreed to take them to the Jenson ranch if they'd all agree to sit in the bed of the wagon. "I don't like people from the East asking me questions when it's about dark, 'cause I have to keep my eyes on the road," he said. "Talking to people slows me down."

She didn't tell him she liked his suggestion because she'd already planned to ride with the children so they could eat. Besides, he didn't seem to be a person who would be enjoyable to talk with.

Soon they had collected their luggage and headed out of the town of Bell Haven, if it could be called a town. It seemed to have only a few businesses and would probably not be referred to as a town in Pennsylvania. When they first left Bell Haven, she remembered thinking they would probably get to the Jenson ranch in a short time. She had climbed into the bed of the wagon as close to the back of the driver's bench as she dared. She figured there would be less wind there. The children sat on each side of her. At first, they were excited. They'd never ridden in a wagon like this one. Neither had she, but she didn't find the experience as exciting as they did. All she could think was *I hope it doesn't take long to get there.*

After the children ate and relaxed a little, Melissa sat back, still hoping the ride wouldn't take long. Though she had no idea how far it was to the ranch, she didn't dare ask the cantankerous driver because she was sure he would put them on the side of the road.

It seemed they'd been bouncing along the rutted road for hours, though she knew it hadn't actually been long. But it had been long enough she wondered why she hadn't stayed in the little hotel she'd seen in Bell Haven and headed to the ranch in the morning. She could at least have seen where they were going. But no. At the time, she thought the smart thing to do was get to the ranch tonight. How far could it be anyway? It dawned on her she was going to have to quit thinking things would be spaced in Texas like they were in Philadelphia and Baltimore. She now had to remember she was in a different territory than she was used to.

Her stomach growled and David had told her again he was hungry. She refrained from telling him she was hungry, too. Though she'd given the children all the cheese and bread, it hadn't been enough to fill them. For some reason she'd thought they'd be able to eat when they got to the ranch where the grandmother lived.

Another thing she didn't count on when heading out tonight was the weather being so cold. She never dreamed it would get this cold in Texas. Berating herself, she tightened the blankets around the children and prayed the ride would end soon.

The thought crossed her mind that if her friends back home could see her now, they'd never let her live it down. She didn't even try to imagine what her aunt or her sister, or Weldon Wheaton III would say. As if she really cared what any of them would say.

When the time grew long and the ranch was nowhere in sight, the newness of riding in a wagon wore off for the children. Susie had cried until she finally fell into a restless sleep in Melissa's lap. David had moved away from her and was huddled in the corner of the wagon bed. She knew he had also cried because she heard him snuff back tears several times. He was getting to the age he didn't want anyone to see him cry. Melissa wanted to cry, too, but knew it wouldn't do any good.

She worked up the courage to suggest to the driver they go back to town. In a grumpy voice, he told her they had come too far to turn back. He assured her they would be at the ranch soon. She figured it was because he thought he'd have to return the three dollars he'd charged her to bring them out to the ranch. Knowing there was nothing she could do except hope they'd reach the Jenson place before morning, she sat back in the wagon and thought about home.

Finally, the wagon pulled up to a two-story house with lamplight spilling through a window and falling onto the wraparound front porch. Melissa knew instantly the place wasn't nearly as large as she thought it would be, but it at least looked welcoming.

"This here is the Jenson place. You and the young'uns get out so I can git back to town afore it gits much later. I have to go slow to make shore the horses don't step in a hole and break a leg."

Melissa frowned. "Aren't you going to help us get our luggage out of the wagon?"

"That'll cost you another fifty cents."

She was too tired to argue. She dug into her drawstring bag, got the money, and as she held it out to him, she said, "Here. Now, will you at least put it on the front porch for me?"

"Yes 'em."

Melissa aroused the children. Susie cried again and clung to her.

David mumbled, "Where are we?"

"I think we're at your grandmother's house. Now, let's get out of the wagon, David. The man might take us all back to town if we don't hurry."

David wasted no time. He jumped from the back. "I'm out. You and Susie come on. I don't want none of us to have to go back to town with him."

Because the man didn't offer to help her, Melissa had to climb down with Susie in her arms. She knew she had to be careful because the ground was covered with patches of snow which looked as if it had melted and frozen back. She stumbled and almost fell but was able to grab the side of the wagon to steady herself and to keep from dropping the little girl. The man said nothing more to her and by the time she reached the steps leading up to the porch where he had deposited their luggage, the wagon was pulling away from the house.

The front door opened, and a tall man filled the doorway. "What's going on out here?" he yelled.

Susie whimpered and threw her arms around Melissa's neck. David moved to her side and took hold of her free hand.

Melissa frowned. "Sir, please don't yell. You're scaring the children."

"What children?"

"The children I have with me. Mrs. Jenson's grandchildren."

"Lady, what are you trying to pull? Mrs. Jenson's grandchildren live in Baltimore."

"Who's he, Aunt Melissa?" David whispered.

"I don't know, honey." She squeezed his hand and turned back to the man. "They're not in Baltimore any longer. I brought them here because Ruth Ann wanted them to come to live with their grandmother."

"That doesn't make any sense."

"I don't care whether you think it makes sense or not. Mrs. Jenson is expecting us. I wrote her a letter telling her we were coming. Please inform her we're here."

A woman's voice came through the door. "Who're you talking to, Joe?"

"A woman who says you're expecting her."

"I'm not expecting anyone." The woman pulled the door open, and her face softened. "Well, Joe. Don' just stand there like an unfriendly giant. You don't have to look twice to see this woman and her children are cold and probably exhausted."

"Mrs. Jenson..." Melissa started.

Pushing the rude man aside, the older woman opened the door wider. "Come on in, child, and tell me what has happened. Is your husband with you?"

Melissa again tried to explain. "No, ma'am. I don't have a husband but...."

The rude man interrupted her. "Do you know these people, Ma?"

"Does it matter? They need help." She reached for Susie, but the sobbing little girl buried her face in Melissa's neck. David moved closer to Melissa's side.

Melissa hugged them closer. "You're right, ma'am. We are cold and hungry and would love to come in and sit down."

"Of course. Come right in." She stood aside and held the door open.

Melissa couldn't help noticing, though the room was rustic, it was well furnished with plush chairs, a colorful braided rug, and several tables with oil lamps and accessories. There was a tall rock fireplace on one wall with a mantle made from a roughly honed log. A large wind-up clock sat on it. Two rocking chairs with cushions were on either side of the fireplace and a dying fire, which had been banked for relighting in the morning, glowed inside.

"Joe, stir up the fire and add a log. These folks are half frozen."

He looked as if he wanted to argue, but he moved to the fireplace and threw a log inside.

Melissa wanted to ask him why he was so rude to them, but she didn't get the chance because he turned to her and said, "Now, would you explain why somebody dumped you and your children on our doorstep?"

"Oh, Joe, watch your manners," his mother said. "Go in the kitchen and get these folks something warm to drink." Looking back at Melissa, she asked, "I bet you folks are hungry, aren't you?"

She didn't want to say she was, so she muttered, "The children have said they are."

"Well, my goodness. I bet I can do something about that. There's plenty of left over roast and biscuits you can eat. There's also milk, and after they get some food in them, I might find a cookie for the children. Of course, we have coffee or tea for you."

"I'm sure the children would like anything. We appreciate your kindness because none of us have eaten for a while. A cup of tea for me would be lovely."

"Then, I'm sure Joe will be happy to go get some food and drinks for all of you."

"I don't know a thing about making tea." The man actually sounded as if he growled.

"Oh, all right, Joe. I'll get the food for them. You sit down and talk to them while I fix it." She waved to the chairs, then turned to Melissa. "Please make yourself and the children comfortable and warm yourselves up. I'll be back with the food and drinks in a minute."

Though the man looked at Melissa as if he'd throw her out into the cold night at any minute, she couldn't resist the rocking chair. She crossed the room and took a seat.

Susie stayed in Melissa's arms as they sat. David, who hadn't spoken, moved to the other side of her chair, putting Melissa between him and the man called Joe.

Melissa patted his arm. "Relax, honey. It'll be fine."

They watched the lady as she left the room, but nobody said anything and several minutes passed in silence. Melissa wanted to ask the man if he was Andrew's brother, but she didn't dare. Though they looked a little alike, he seemed to be mad at her for some reason, and she didn't want to give him another reason to yell in front of the children. And yelling was what she thought he'd do if she dared to speak to him.

Nobody said anything for a little while, then Susie broke the silence. Her clear little girl voice filled the room when she asked, "Aunt Lissa, is her my grandma?"

~ * ~

Joe whirled around and looked at the little girl. His face showed surprise. Did he hear her right? Before the woman answered the child, he heard the cups, saucers and glasses clanging together on the tray as his mother entered the parlor with the drinks and sandwiches.

He knew his mother had probably heard the little girl's question, too, so he took a breath and looked at Melissa. "What did the kid mean by that?"

"Yes." Althea put the tray on the table in front of the window. "What did she mean?"

"Are they going to hurt Susie?" David grabbed Melissa's arm.

"No, sweetheart." She patted his hand and turned to Althea. "Mrs. Jenson, I wrote to you telling you I was bringing your grandchildren to you. You should have gotten my letter a week or so ago."

Joe eyed her. *What was this fancy city woman saying?* He knew this couldn't be Andrew's wife. He didn't think a fancy woman like her would ever come to Texas. She'd certainly never mentioned she would come when she wrote Andrew had been killed in some kind of explosion at the plant he ran. What was this strange woman up to? Why was she trying to pass her children off as Andrew's?

"I didn't get a letter a week ago. We don't get our mail until we go into town. Our bunkhouse cook brought a letter today, but I didn't know who it was from, so I didn't take time to read it yet. In fact, I got busy and forgot about it."

Melissa shook her head. "I'm sorry if this is a shock to you, but these are your grandchildren, David and Susie Jenson."

"Don't Grandma Althea want us, Aunt Melissa?"

David had whispered, but Joe heard him and frowned. He got out of his chair and his voice wasn't pleasant, and it was much too loud when he said, "I heard what the boy said and I don't know what you're trying to pull, young lady, but I know you're not Andrew's wife. He told us she had long dark hair and yours may be long, but it's yellow."

"Of course I'm not Ruth Ann. I'm her best friend, Melissa..."

Susie began to cry again, and David hid his face on Melissa's shoulder.

"Joseph!" Althea pointed her finger at him and said firmly, "Don't you dare attack this young lady again. Now set down and let's get to the bottom of this."

"Thank you, ma'am." Melissa smiled at her.

"You're welcome. Now, let me give this milk and sandwiches to the children and pour you a cup of tea. I brought you and me a cup of coffee, Joe."

"Thanks, Ma," he muttered as he took a cup of coffee. He knew he should curb his quick temper and give the pretty little woman a chance to explain herself, but he almost knew she had some kind of scheme up her sleeve. *If I can, I'll keep my mouth shut and let her trip herself up, but it won't be easy,* he told himself.

"Now, dear, please tell me what's going on." Althea sat in the other rocking chair and smiled at Melissa.

"As I said, I wrote to you a few weeks ago explaining why I was bringing David and Susie to you. It was what their mother asked me to do."

"Where is Ruth Ann? Why didn't she come with you?"

"Oh, Mrs. Jenson, I wish you had gotten my letter. It explains everything. I don't really want to tell you everything again in front of the children." She bit her lip, then went on, "First let me tell you, my name is Melissa Cardwell. Ruth Ann and I were cousins and best friends since we were little girls. You've probably heard David calling me Aunt Melissa, and Susie can't say my full name, so she calls me, Aunt Lissa."

Despite his vow to say nothing, Joe couldn't control himself. "What did you say your name was?"

"Melissa Cardwell."

He frowned. "Ma, what was the name on the letter you got?"

"I don't remember, but it might have been it."

"Have you read the letter?"

"No, son. I haven't."

He stood. "Where is it?"

"I left it in my apron pocket. It's hanging on the pantry door."

He went into the kitchen and retrieved the letter. Glancing at the address, he saw it was from M. Cardwell. *Could she be telling the truth?* If so, why had Ruth Ann sent the children instead of bringing them herself? Did she want to get rid of Andrew's kids because she had found another man? He started to open the letter, but knew he had no right to do so. He hurried back to the parlor and handed it to his mother. "I think you should read this now, Ma. Maybe it will tell us what's going on."

Althea nodded. He watched her facial expressions change as she read the letter. As she folded it, tears appeared in her eyes. She handed the letter to Joe and turned to Melissa. "Thank you for bringing the children to me. They're beautiful. Of course, I knew they would be."

"Yes, they are, and they're wonderful children, too."

Joe concentrated on the letter. It was hard to accept what was written there. *Was it the truth? Did Ruth Ann actually want his mother to raise her children?* Most women would want to leave their children with their own mother. He went on and read the account of his sister-in-law's death and how Melissa was heading to Texas while it was still winter, and she had his brother's two offspring with her.

He folded the letter and glanced up at the woman and the children. Susie did have dark auburn hair like Andrew said his wife had and the little boy had the black tresses just like all the Jenson men.

He noted the little boy had moved from the other side of the chair to stand in front of his grandmother. He was giving her a shy smile. The little girl was still on Miss Cardwell's lap, but she was sitting to the side and looking at her grandmother as if she might speak to her soon.

"I have to ask you," Joe looked at Melissa. "Why did she want Ma to raise her kids instead of her own mother? Is her mama not still living?"

"Oh, yes. Both of her parents are still alive. Her father has an important government job, and his wife often travels with him. Ruth Ann wanted Mrs. Jenson to raise them because she didn't want their upbringing left to boarding schools or a nanny. She knew your mother would do a wonderful job because of the way Andrew was raised."

Tears came into Althea Jenson's eyes. "Oh, I'm so proud. That's a wonderful tribute from a woman who I know must have been a good wife who really loved my son."

"Is Grandma sad, Aunt Melissa?" David asked.

Before Melissa could answer, Althea said, "No, sweetheart, Grandma isn't sad. You know when women get old like me, they sometimes cry when they're happy."

David laughed. "Mama told me that one time."

"Well, she was right. Now, why don't you all finish your food and I bet Grandma can find a big fat cookie in the kitchen for you."

Susie took a bite of her sandwich and said with her mouth full, "I like cookie, too."

An hour later, Althea asked Joe to drag the four trunks and all the valises into the house. Then she put the tired and sleepy children in the bedroom he'd shared with Andrew when they were small. Though he'd often suggested they should set it up as a guest room, for some reason his mother had kept the two beds the boys had used as they grew up. The other spare room was used as storage. The only other two bedrooms in the house were his mother's and his. He wondered where his mother planned for the woman to sleep. When his mother and the woman came back into the parlor after putting the children to bed, he found out.

"Joseph," his mother addressed him when she entered the room.

He knew she was serious when she used his full name instead of Joe. Doing so always told him she would entertain no argument. He couldn't help giving her a smile. "Yes, Ma."

"Go to your room and get what you'll need in the morning. You'll be sleeping in the bunkhouse with the hands tonight."

He frowned, but before he could speak, she went on, "Melissa needs a bed to herself, so she will be sleeping in your room."

He opened his mouth, but she gave him the look which always told her son they'd reached the end of the discussion.

Shaking his head, and without saying anything else to her, he headed to his room. She didn't know it, but he was cussing under his breath as he climbed the stairs because he didn't like giving up his bed. Not so much because he didn't want Melissa sleeping there, but because he never slept well in the bunkhouse. A couple of the hands almost raised the roof from the building because they snored so loud, especially the one called Bear, because he not only snored, he growled.

~ * ~

Since it was cold in the room she was given to sleep in, Melissa took a quick sponge bath. Althea had filled the ceramic pitcher sitting in the matching bowl on the rustic bureau with warm water for her. Digging in her trunk, she slipped into a soft pink cotton gown and tied the darker pink ribbons encircling the neck. She didn't take time to put on her slippers as she hurried across the room and climbed into the high-backed bed. She leaned over to blow out the lighted lamp and noticed the table matched the bureau, the bed, and the huge wardrobe in the corner. It was massive, manly, and rustic, but there was a beauty about it. With the right curtains, spread and a few other decorations to soften it up it would be a handsome ... no ... it would be a lovely bedroom.

She giggled. *What in the world made me have such a thought? The gruff man who sleeps here would never allow anything which looked the least bit feminine in this room. What's the matter with you, Melissa? You were silly to think such a thing in the first place.*

Snuggling down in the soft feather mattress, she couldn't help noticing the smell in the room. It wasn't the sheets, because Althea had insisted on putting clean sheets on the bed before Melissa retired. She thought part of the odor came through the pillowcases from the feather pillows. It was a masculine smell. Kind of like spice, leather, and wood. It had to be his smell. The arrogant, rude, hateful, unlikable, cursing, Joseph Jenson who happened to also be the most intriguing, devastatingly handsome man she'd ever seen. He also had the most captivating dark eyes of any man she'd ever looked into. Of course, she hadn't looked into many men's eyes.

She turned over and jerked the cover to her chin. *Melissa Anne Cardwell, what are you thinking? Aunt Vernetta would have a fit if she knew you'd had such a thought about some uneducated, overbearing cowboy. She'd tell you Weldon Wheaton III would never propose to you if he knew.*

Shaking her head, she muttered, *get yourself in control and go to sleep. In the morning, get up and help Susie and David get acclimated to their new home, then, as fast as you can, get yourself back to Philadelphia where you belong. You've been gone long enough, and if you don't get back soon, another woman could become Mrs. Weldon Wheaton III instead of you, even if deep down you know you don't want to end up married to him, no matter how often Aunt Vernetta says it'd be a good thing.*

She turned over again, and her next thought was *but would marriage to him be so bad or should I hold out for a man who is more like the one my imagination keeps telling is out there? One who is much more romantic and handsome than Weldon. Of course, Weldon has plenty of money and I would always live the life Aunt Vernetta tells me I was meant to live. The kind I have grown accustomed to living with her. Maybe I could be as happy with him as she says I will. Or would I? Should I settle for a man*

I know I don't love because his wealth will assure me I'll always have anything money can buy? Or do I want to hold out for real love?

You need to put these foolish thoughts out of your mind, get yourself home and in time, all of this will be behind you. You'll never again have to think about how intriguing Mr. Joseph Jenson is behind his rough exterior or how this room smells like him. You are probably destined to become Mrs. Weldon Wheaton III. Everyone, except Catherine, tells you he's perfect for you. Now turn over and go to sleep.

She decided to give it a try, though she thought it'd take her a long time to go to sleep with those thoughts tumbling around in her head. But she was wrong. Exhaustion took over and in minutes she gave in and fell into a deep slumber.

~ * ~

The next morning, a rested Melissa came down the stairs, but before she entered the kitchen, she heard Joe saying, "But, Ma, I've got to have it. I didn't think to get it last night. Can't you slip in and get it for me?"

"No, Joe. I don't want to disturb Melissa. She was exhausted last night, and I feel she needs to sleep as long as she can this morning. In fact, the children were so worn out, they are still asleep, too."

"What do you think of the kids, Ma?"

"Oh, son, they're wonderful. Little David is so much like Andrew was when he was a child. I feel God sent that little boy here to ease the loss of my youngest son. And little Susie must be like her mother. Melissa told me I'd have loved my daughter-in-law if I'd ever met her. She even said Ruth Ann and Andrew planned to visit us last summer, but he was killed in the factory explosion in the spring before they could make plans to come. I wish I could have met Ruth Ann, and I so wish I could have seen Andrew and told him how much I loved him one more time."

Melissa knew tears must have come into her eyes because Joe said, "Please don't cry, Ma. I know learning of Andrew's death was one of the hardest things you've ever had to handle. It was hard for me, too."

Melissa couldn't help noticing his voice was soft and gentle when he spoke with his mother. Not the loud hateful voice he used when talking to her.

"Yes, son. I know how close you and Andrew were." Althea sighed and added, "Losing your father and my son were the two worse days of my life."

"I miss them both, too. Especially my brother, but I know he would've wanted us to honor him by raising his children the way he would have. I want to make them happy and for us to give them a good life here on the ranch."

"But you know Andrew didn't want to be a rancher, Joe. I'm sure he expressed this feeling to his wife. Why do you suppose Ruth Ann really thought her children would be better off with us than with her mother and father?"

"I don't know why, Ma, but she must have thought it, or she wouldn't have had them brought here. Why don't you ask Melissa. Maybe she could tell you why."

Melissa wasn't prepared for the tingle she felt when he used her given name. All he'd ever called her was Miss Cardwell. Swallowing and biting her lip, she hurried into the kitchen. "Good morning."

"Good morning, Melissa." Althea turned and smiled at her.

Joe nodded. "I need to get something out of my room." When Althea shot him a look, he added, "I hope you don't mind me going in there this morning?"

"Of course not, Mr. Jenson. Help yourself. It's your room, after all."

He didn't answer but turned and headed out of the kitchen.

"I'm surprised you're up, Melissa. I figured you'd sleep until noon as tired as you were when you got here last night."

"I thought I would have, too, but I guess I'm used to the fact that once I wake up, I get up because I can never go back to sleep."

"Then have a seat at the table and I'll get you a cup of coffee and fix your breakfast. Or would you rather have tea?"

"Coffee is fine. I usually drink a cup in the morning." She pulled out a chair. "Have the children stirred yet?"

"Not yet. Like you, they were exhausted, so I figured they'd sleep late."

"They were awfully tired, but they made the trip better than I thought they would."

"It was wonderful of you to bring them to me, dear."

"The aunt I live with didn't want me to come, but I had promised Ruth Ann, and there was no way I was going to break my promise to her."

"I know cousins can be close, but you and Ruth Ann seem to be extra close."

"As I told you, she and I were almost like sisters. Ruth Ann lived next door when I lived in Baltimore with my parents and my three sisters. Her father worked for the government and after she was married, her mom and dad moved to Washington. She chose to stay in Baltimore."

"I see. So, you kind of grew up together?

"In a way, we did. She was an only child. Her mother was my father's sister, so we were not only cousins, but we became best friends."

"Then you must have known Andrew."

"I did. He was a wonderful husband and father. Ruth Ann loved him more than anything. If it hadn't been for Susie and David, I don't know if she could have made it without Andrew."

Tears sprang into Althea's eyes. "I'm glad he was loved so much."

"He loved her the same way. Your son was a good man, Mrs. Jenson."

"So, you liked him?"

"Oh, yes. Very much. He often invited me to join them for special occasions. When my aunt allowed me to visit them, he made me feel as if I was a member of his family." Melissa reached out and touched Althea's arm. "You would have been proud of him and the way he loved his wife and was raising his children."

"I have always been proud of both my boys, though they were very different."

"I see Joseph is nothing like Andrew, but Andrew often spoke highly of his brother. They must have been close."

"They were. There was only a two-year difference in their ages, and as I said, they had different personalities. Each one respected the other for the way they felt, and their differences never interfered with their friendship."

"That was wonderful."

"As you probably know, they went to college in the East, and when he finished his first year, Joe couldn't wait to get back to the ranch. He says it's in his blood. Andrew, on the other hand, found he was more suited to the Eastern business world. Besides, he'd fallen in love with Ruth Ann. He came home and tried to be the rancher his father wanted him to be, but he was miserable. After a few months, he went back to the woman and the life he loved."

Joe's voice interrupted them. "Look who I found coming down the hall."

David led Susie into the kitchen in front of Joe. They were still in their pajamas. Susie let go of her brother's hand and ran to Melissa. "Hold me."

"My goodness, sweetheart. You're freezing." Melissa wrapped her arms around Susie.

"The room's cold." David looked at his grandmother and gave her a shy smile.

"Well, why don't I go get you some clothes and let you get dressed right here in this warm kitchen?"

Susie nodded.

"Well folks, it looks like the kids are in good hands now and I need to get to work." Joe glanced at Melissa then turned to his mother. "I'll be back by early afternoon. Don't worry about a midday meal."

"Are you sure? It's awfully cold out there and you'll need…"

"We'll be fine. Grover is going with us, he'll have food for us, and he'll keep hot coffee going all day."

"Be careful, son."

He nodded, glanced at Melissa but didn't say anything as he went out the door.

Althea turned back to Melissa. "Let's get these two dressed and then I'll dish up breakfast for all of you."

"Good. I'm hungry," David said.

"I hungry, too," Susie added.

~ * ~

Joe shook his head when he got outside. What in the world was wrong with him? The minute he'd stepped into his room, he'd felt the overwhelming presence of the woman. He walked to the bed and almost laughed. The spread was crooked, and it hung almost to the floor on one side. He knew she'd probably never made a bed in her life. Then he saw her nightgown on the pillow. He felt compelled to pick it up and hold it to his nose. Her soft lilac sent hit his nostrils like a bullet. He dropped the nightgown as if it were a hot branding iron and rushed to the wardrobe to get the belt he needed. For a reason he didn't understand, he felt the need to get out of the room before her presence overpowered him.

He crossed the back yard, which was covered in the light frosty snow which had fallen during the night. He knew they had to move those cows to the other pasture before a big storm hit and he didn't remember a January when there hadn't been a large storm. So far, there hadn't been a big snow in this part of Texas, but he figured they couldn't count on one not coming. But whether it snowed or not, moving the cows was what was important now.

Not the fact he'd been stirred when he'd seen his bed and knew it had cradled Melissa's beautiful body last night.

The bunkhouse door opened, and Ned Langston walked out. "'Bout ready to go?"

"Yeah. Had to get the belt to hold the extra ammo. We're likely to need it out there. We may run into all kinds of wild animals looking for food. I don't want one of us or one of our cows to end up as a wolf's supper."

"I agree." Ned pushed his hat back. "When you came to the bunkhouse last night, you were a regular old grouch. If you don't mind, what did you argue with your mama about to get thrown out of your house?"

"Didn't argue with her about a thing."

"Then why'd she throw you out of the house?"

Joe shook his head. "Needed my room for the guest."

"You have a guest?"

"Yeah. Andrew's wife died a while back and a woman brought their children to Ma."

"So. Why'd you have to give up your room?"

"You're sure being nosy this morning, Ned."

"Sorry." Ned chuckled. "I can just see some old hag running you out of your bed."

"You don't know how far from the truth you are."

"What do you mean?"

"Our guest is ... What are you looking at?"

"The beauty who just came out on your back porch."

Joe turned. Melissa was getting an armload of wood from the stack near the back door.

Guilt spread through him. "Dang. I forgot to fill the wood boxes this morning."

"Is she your visitor?"

"Yes. She brought the children."

"Now I understand why you were in such a bad mood last night. If she was in my bed and I wasn't there with her, I'd act like an old, wounded bear, too."

"Get on to the barn and saddle up for us both, Ned. I'll join you as soon as I fill the wood boxes for Ma." Joe headed for the porch.

Clomping up the steps, he said, "Go back in the house, Miss Cardwell. I'll get the wood for you."

"Thank you. I am getting cold."

He wanted to tell her if she'd let him fold her in his arms and hold her against him, she'd be more comfortable, but he bit his tongue and said instead, "You shouldn't be out here without a coat."

She nodded and darted into the house.

He followed when his arms were full of firewood. "Sorry, I didn't do this..." He stopped when he realized he was talking to an empty kitchen. Shrugging, he dropped the wood in the box by the stove and went for another load. It took three armfuls to fill the kitchen box, then he went for a load to start filling the box by the fireplace.

Stepping through the parlor door, he could hardly believe his eyes. His mother sat in one of the rocking chairs and little Susie was on her lap. David sat at her feet and Melissa had taken the other rocker. "Well, looks like you're all getting to know each other."

"Why don't you join us, son? I'm sure your niece and nephew would like to get to know you, too."

"Can't do it, Ma. Before I go out on the range, I have to get a couple more loads of wood or you'll be sitting by a fireplace with no fire in it."

David almost whispered, "Do you want me to help you get the wood?"

Joe started to say no. He knew he could get the wood faster himself, but not only was his mother giving him that look, but

Melissa's eyes looked at him as if she didn't think he'd bother with the boy. "Sure, David. Grab your coat. It's cold out there."

David jumped up. "Where's my coat, Aunt Melissa?"

She looked at Joe in surprise, then stood. "I'll get it for you. It's hanging on the hall tree."

"Never mind, Miss Cardwell. Come on, David, I'll get it for you."

The boy looked a little hesitant but stood and followed Joe into the hall. After getting David into his coat, they went through the parlor without speaking to anyone. It was when they were near the woodpile when David said, "Did you know my daddy?"

Joe was startled but managed to hide it. "Sure, I did. He was my brother."

"Did you like him?"

"I not only liked your daddy, David. I loved him just the way you love Susie."

"Sometimes Susie makes me mad. She cries when she wants something. She throws my toys when she gets hold of them, too."

"But you love her, don't you?"

"Sure. She's my sister. I have to love her."

Joe smiled. "Hold out your arms and I'll fill them with wood for you to carry in."

David did and in a matter of minutes his arms were full. Joe then filled his and they went inside.

On the third trip to get wood, David automatically held out his arms. "What should I call you?"

"Well, my name is Joe and I'm your uncle so why not Uncle Joe." David frowned and Joe added, "But if you're not comfortable with that, you can call me Joe."

David nodded.

As Joe deposited his armful of wood in the box by the fireplace and turned to empty David's arms, David said, "Guess what, Aunt Melissa."

"What David?"

"This is my Uncle Joe, and I'm gonna call him that."

"Does he want you to?"

"Sure. We talked about it, didn't we, Uncle Joe?"

"We sure did." Joe laid the last stick of wood in the box and turned to smile at David.

David looked at his uncle. "Can Susie call you Uncle Joe, too?"

"Of course she can. I'm her uncle, too."

"Hear that, Susie? We've got an uncle now."

"We got Grandma," Susie said.

"Yes, and an Aunt Melissa."

Susie giggled.

"Well, you folks have a good day. I've got to get out on the range. We're got to move cows today. It looks like there might be a storm and I want to get it done before it hits."

"Can I help you, Uncle Joe?"

"I'm afraid it's not a job for a boy, David." He then saw the hurt in the boy's eyes and added, "Even a boy as grown up as you, but there is one thing you can do."

His eyes brightened. "What's that?"

"You know you're not in the city now. You're on a ranch. And out here there always needs to be a man at the house."

"Why?"

"Because the women might run out of wood, or they might need something from the smokehouse and it's up to a man to get it when it's cold outside."

David nodded. "I know how to get the wood, but I don't know how to get something at the smokehouse."

"Don't worry. I've already brought everything inside your grandma needs to cook today. I'll show you how to do it later."

The little boy relaxed. "Good."

Joe headed for the door and was surprised when Melissa stood and followed him. When he reached the kitchen door, he turned. "Is there something you want, Miss Cardwell?"

"Two things. One, I want to thank you for the way you seemed to have taken David under your wing. He's been a lost little boy since his father died. They were close and there hasn't been a man in his life since Andrew's death."

"I see a lot of my brother in him. He's a fine kid." He took his hat off and ran his fingers through his hair. "Now, what was the other thing you wanted? I'm kind of in a hurry."

"It can wait."

He frowned. "No. You have my curiosity up. Just tell me now."

"If you insist. I was going to ask you to call me Melissa instead of Miss Cardwell all the time. The children are used to my first name, and I don't want them any more confused than they are already. I was also going to inquire if I might call you Joseph."

He stared at her for a few seconds, then nodded. "All right, Melissa, I'll use your first name, but don't call me Joseph. Ma uses Joseph when she's mad at me or wants to make sure I get the point of what she's saying. I'd rather you call me Joe."

She smiled. "Then I'll do it. Thank you, Joe."

He looked into the liquid pools of her sky-blue eyes and was about to tell her how beautiful they were. He caught himself and said, "Now that's settled. I've got to go." He opened the door and stepped outside without giving her time to answer. He didn't want to hear anything else from her soft voice or see her beautiful smile. A smile that went straight to his heart and a voice which made him feel warm all over, even with the temperature as low as it was today.

Ned was headed toward the house leading the horses. "It's about time you got here. We've been ready to go for ages."

"Then let's not waste any more time. We've got to get those cows switched." He was glad to have something to think about except Melissa's smile, her soft voice, and those beautiful blue eyes. He knew he had no right to think about any of her gorgeous features in the first place. She would be going back to Philadelphia soon. Which would be a good thing, because he knew the longer she stayed, the harder it would be to hide his attraction to her.

~ * ~

Melissa sat beside the fireplace and watched the children playing with their toys. Susie sat on a quilt rocking her doll back and forth. David pushed the two toy trucks across the rocks on the hearth. Both children had sad smiles on their faces.

"Do they not like their toys, Melissa?" Althea whispered.

"Oh yes. They love them. These were the gifts their mother gave them for Christmas. I'm sure they're both remembering the last day they spent with her. Ruth Ann left this world the day after Christmas."

"I'm so sorry. Was Christmas a sad time for them?"

"Not at all. Ruth Ann felt the best she'd felt in weeks. We decorated a tree with the children helping us, then we had hot chocolate and cookies before we all went to bed. Everyone got up feeling good on Christmas morning and we had a real celebration. Ruth Ann spent the whole day with her children and went to bed happy."

"Mommy is an angel now, Grandma. Aunt Lissa said so," Susie said.

Althea smiled at the little girl. "Your aunt is right. I'm sure your mother is watching after you right now."

Susie looked at them. "We didn't play with toys in 'Delphia. Aunt Netta wouldn't let us."

Althea cocked an eyebrow. "You went to Philadelphia?"

"Yes," David said.

"I took them there so I could pack for this trip to Bell Haven," Melissa explained.

"I see." She turned back to the children. "Well, you don't have to worry about playing with your toys here, sweetheart. You can play with them anytime you want. I might even be able to find some of your daddy's old toys. You might like to play with them."

David's eyes grew bright. "I'd like to have Daddy's toys."

40

"That would be wonderful, Mrs. Jenson."

"Oh, Melissa, why don't you call me Althea? Everybody around here does."

"I call you Grandma," David said.

"Yes, you and Susie should always call me Grandma. I meant for grownups to call me Althea."

"Can Uncle Joe?" Susie asked.

"Well, he is my son, so it's best if he calls me Ma." Althea stood. "Speaking of your uncle Joe, I'm sure he'll be in to eat supper soon. I better put it on the table. Would you like to help set the table, Melissa?"

Melissa was surprised. At Aunt Vernetta's house she'd never been asked to help with anything to do with putting a meal on the table. The maid or the part-time butler always served her and her sister and her aunt after they were seated. Even when she was with Ruth Ann, there was a maid waiting on them. This was going to be a new experience, but she didn't feel she could refuse. She stood and followed Althea to the adjoining eating area of the huge room.

It wasn't long until Joe came in. He nodded to everyone, then moved to the sideboard and washed his hands.

"We always have a blessing before we eat," Althea explained as they gathered at the long wooden table. She sat on the side at her son's left. The grandchildren elected to sit on either side of their grandmother. Joe took his place at the head of the table and Melissa was left to sit alone on the long bench facing Althea and the children.

Althea said a short prayer, then Joe took a piece of chicken from the platter then passed it to his mother. She took a piece for herself and placed a drumstick on each of the children's plates. They both grinned at her.

When all the plates were ready, Althea broke the silence. "I've been thinking about something today, Joe. I think it's time we cleaned out the extra bedroom down here."

"Why?"

"You've been telling me for some time to do it and I didn't see the need. I think we have a need now."

"What need is that?"

"I think it will make Susie or me a perfect room. I know it's fine for her to share a room with her brother now, but I'm sure they'd like their own place as they get older so they can store their toys the way they want to."

"I'm guessing David will be staying in mine and Andrew's old room."

"I thought he'd like to sleep in the room his father used as a boy."

David nodded.

"Are you asking me to clean out the room for Susie or for you?"

"Eventually for Susie. But I thought until she was older, I might sleep down here."

"That's thoughtful of you, Althea," Melissa said.

She smiled at Melissa and turned back to Joe. "If you don't have time, you could let one of the hands help."

"I'll take care of it when we get all the livestock settled." He turned to Melissa and changed the subject. "How have you fared today?"

"I've done fine."

"Good. I was afraid since you've never experienced anything except city living, being on the ranch might have been hard for you."

Althea laughed. "She might be a city woman, but she's helped me today. She told me a lot about the children and their lives back in Baltimore and about her relationship with Ruth Ann and Andrew. She also told me about her sisters and her Aunt Vernetta in Philadelphia."

"I don't like her," David said with a mouthful of chicken.

"You shouldn't say that, David," Melissa admonished him.

"Well, I don't, Aunt Melissa. She's not nice like you and Grandma."

"I couldn't play with dolly." Susie looked at her grandmother and grinned. "You nice."

"Thank you, sweetie."

"I admit Aunt Vernetta doesn't understand children. She's always been a little strict."

"Sounds like she was more than strict if she wouldn't let a little girl play with her doll." Joe's voice was stern. "How long did you live with her anyway?"

"My sister Catherine and I moved in with her when our parents died."

"I guess the two of you were too old to play with dolls."

Melissa felt she should defend her aunt, but it was hard to find the right words to use. "We were, but she was good to us. She taught us all the things a lady should know so we could grow up and take our rightful places in society."

Joe laughed. "I guess that's all a woman like you would need to know."

Melissa bristled. "What do you mean by that?"

"It's simple. Only in the city could you survive. Out here we like real women. Not some piece of artificial fluff."

She didn't understand why his words not only made her mad, but they hurt more than she ever thought they would. She bit her lip and looked down at her plate to keep from saying anything. She didn't want to upset the children by starting a fight.

"Joseph, you have no call to talk to our guest in such a way. You can at least try to be a gentleman while she's here."

"Let's just hope she won't be here long. I'm tired of sleeping in the bunkhouse."

"Don't you like Aunt Melissa, Uncle Joe?"

Joe looked at his nephew and felt a little guilty. "Your aunt is a nice lady, David. She's just not the kind of woman who can live the type of life we have to live on the ranch. She will be going back to Philadelphia soon."

David frowned. "I thought we were a family. Mama said Aunt Melissa and Grandma would always be here for us. She didn't say nothing about you because she didn't know you."

Althea reached over and patted his arm. "Now don't you go to worrying, David. Your Aunt Melissa will always be here for you no matter where she is. Your Uncle Joe and I will be here, too."

"Good." David turned back to his food.

Melissa didn't say anything. She couldn't. Though it angered her when Joe pointed out her faults, she knew he was almost right. She didn't know anything about living in these primitive conditions, but she wasn't completely helpless. Her determination would help her to survive anywhere. It just so happened she wasn't brought up or didn't think she'd ever have to survive in a place like this. She wanted to go back to the comfort of her life in Philadelphia where she would probably marry Weldon Wheaton III or someone like him, then live the way she'd been taught she should for the remainder of her life. But she didn't understand why this last thought didn't make her happy.

"Well, guess what, children, "Althea changed the subject.

"What," they said in unison as they looked at their grandmother.

"Do you know what a month from today is?"

"What?" Susie asked.

"It's Valentine's Day. It's a day everybody shows how much they love one another by doing something special."

"How, Grandma?" David asked.

"Well, we can cut out paper hearts and we can say nice things to each other. We can even write notes. I'll probably bake some heart shaped cookies and if the weather will permit, I bet Uncle Joe will let you go with him to give the horses a special treat."

David's eyes lit up. "I've been wanting to see a horse."

"I tell you what, David," Joe said. "After supper, I have to go put liniment on a colt who hurt her leg. Her name is Sadie Mae. How would you like to go meet her?"

"Great." He threw down his fork. "Let's go."

Joe chuckled. "I think we can finish our supper first."

"I go," Susie looked at him.

Joe looked a little doubtful, but said, "If Grandma will come with us, I don't see why you can't come, too, Susie."

Althea laughed. "We'll see. Grandma needs to wash the dishes. Maybe Aunt Melissa will go with you."

~ * ~

After they finished supper, Joe helped David into his coat as Melissa bundled up Susie. He wondered if the child would suffocate the way she was wrapping the scarf around her neck. "It's a little messy out there in the snow. I think since Susie is so small, I'll carry her."

"I walk."

"Do you really want to walk, Susie?" Melissa looked at her. "Uncle Joe is big and strong, and you'll be safe in his arms."

"Will he carry David?"

"I'm too big to be carried, Susie. I'll walk."

"I walk, too."

Joe couldn't help remembering Andrew had been the same way when they were young. He always wanted to do whatever his big brother did. Shaking the thought away, he opened the back door. "If everyone is ready, we'll go."

They stepped out on the porch and started down the steps. Joe and David went first to make sure there weren't any hidden objects the ladies could step on and fall, Joe had explained.

On the second step, Susie balked and jerked Melissa's hand. "What's wrong, honey?"

"Carry me, Uncle Joe," Susie's voice sounded near tears. "It scary."

Joe turned around and scooped Susie up in his arm. "It is a little scary, Susie, but we'll light a lantern as soon as we get in the barn, and it won't be so dark."

She flung her arm around his neck. "You teck me?"

He chuckled. "Yes, pretty Susie, I'll always protect you."

"Don't be such a baby, Susie." David sounded disgusted.

"She's just a little girl, David. Everything's new to her here and it'll take her a little while to get used to it. Since she's so young, maybe you could help her adjust."

"I'll try, Uncle Joe."

"Good. She's not so citified yet. She's not like some women. She's still young enough to learn." He glanced at Melissa to see if she heard his barb, but she was busy trying to hold her skirt high enough to keep it from dragging in the muddy snow and wasn't paying him any attention. He shook his head, turned, and put his free hand on David's shoulder, then headed to the barn, leaving Melissa to get there on her own.

In the barn, Joe stood Susie on a pile of hay. "Let me make us some light and I'll pick you back up if you like."

"Uh-uh."

He lit the lantern and saw Susie holding her hands out to him. He picked her up and led the children to the stall in the corner. "See the little horse. Her name is Sadie Mae."

Susie grinned. "Her pretty."

"She is pretty, Uncle Joe. Could I touch her?" David looked up at him.

"Sure. I'll open the stall and you can rub her nose. She'll like that."

"I touch her, too." Susie wiggled and he let her down.

"Are you sure they're safe touching a horse?" Melissa asked.

"Of course they are. I'm watching them." Joe lifted an eyebrow. "Would you like to come over here and see Sadie Mae?"

"No, thank you. I'll just wait here." She looked around. "It's a little smelly in here. Is it always this bad?"

"It's a barn, Miss Cardwell. What do you expect it to smell like? Some fancy Philadelphia drawing room?"

"Of course not," she snapped, then lifted her chin and looked at the hayloft above.

Joe was glad she had shown her true thoughts about the ranch and about the family who lives there. Now he could put the stupid thoughts he'd had about the possibility of her being in his life out of his mind. He decided then and there he was going to make sure the children felt at home as soon as he could. Then she could get her shapely little butt on a stage and get away from them before he did something stupid like ask her to stay longer or worse, take her in his arms and kiss her and never let her leave.

~ * ~

As the next few days passed, the children grew more accustomed to their new home. David went to the barn almost every night with his uncle. Occasionally Susie would join them. She was also following her grandmother around and having a good time learning to help in the kitchen, if it were only folding the napkins and putting them on the table.

Melissa knew it was time she began thinking about going home. There was no question but that the children would be fine without her, and the Jensons certainly didn't need her around. Her feeble attempts to help had consisted of keeping Joe's room somewhat tidy, setting the table, and gathering the eggs. She had only washed dishes twice and Althea told her not to bother again. She knew it was because the first time she had broken a cup and the second time she broke a plate and cracked another one.

Her relationship with Joe hadn't changed. Though there was still an undeniable attraction between them, it seemed they both fought it becoming more than thoughts in their minds. They had somehow come to some type of unspoken truce that when they had to talk to each other, they only used short and somewhat terse phrases.

She knew when she left, the kids would miss her for a little while. But their lives were here now, and they'd soon almost forget the way they had lived in Baltimore. She would miss them more than they'd ever miss her, but she doubted she'd ever be able to forget the life she lived in Philadelphia. She was raised for such a life, not for living the almost primitive way women married to ranchers lived.

She made up her mind she would leave shortly after the Valentine's Day celebration because she wanted to see the children enjoy a holiday which wouldn't be followed with a tragedy as their Christmas had been. She also wanted to see if Joe would desert the family and go to the dance in town everyone on the ranch had been talking about. She noticed he'd said he probably wouldn't go when his mother mentioned it to him at supper a couple of nights ago. She hoped he meant it. Of course, she knew there was no hope he would ask her to accompany him, though deep in her heart there was no way she could stop the jealousy she felt when she thought of him dancing with some other woman in his arms.

On February tenth, four days before Valentine's Day, Melissa put the children to bed. She kissed each of them goodnight, then went to the room she slept in. Changing into her nightgown, she decided she didn't want to go to bed. Instead, she decided she'd slip downstairs and have a cup of tea. The water in the kettle should still be hot and though Althea had banked the fire in the fireplace before she went to bed, it would still be warm enough to sit there and drink it.

She grabbed her robe, slid her feet into her slippers, and headed down the stairs. She was halfway to the bottom when the voices below floated to her. She sat and listened.

"I know she's a pretty woman, Ma, but you've got to admit she's useless."

"Now, Joe, you shouldn't talk about Melissa in such a way. She has been receptive to learning since she's been here."

He laughed. "It would take her years to learn how to live on a ranch and you know it."

"I think you're wrong, son. She's a smart and lovely woman. I'm sure she can do it."

"I admit she's beautiful to look at, but she's as out of place here as you or I would be in her fancy Philadelphia home."

"Andrew didn't have any trouble fitting in Ruth Ann's world."

"That's different. While we were in college, he really liked the area, and he knew right away he wanted to live the rest of his life in the East. He began integrating himself in their ways and their society, but I hated the place. I couldn't wait to get out of school, so I could come home. You don't know how happy I was to see this ranch again."

"I do know, son, and you're right about Andrew. He wrote how Ruth Ann loved him enough to overlook his bumbles at first. You know love covers a lot of mistakes."

"Look, Ma. If you're insinuating, I'm in love with Melissa Cardwell, you're dead wrong. As I said, the woman looks tempting, but if and when I ever marry, I want a woman who will come to this ranch ready and willing to work beside us. And she will have to understand I'm including Susie and David in the deal. Since Andrew is gone, I intend to be the best substitute father those children could ever find."

"You will be, Joe. They already love you, and when you marry and have children, they'll all be like brothers and sisters to them."

"That's what I want to eventually happen. But it don't have to happen right away. I've got plenty of time."

"Have you given any thought as to who the mother of those children could be?"

"Sure, I've thought about it, especially since they've taken to me." He sighed. "Megan at the diner in town has let me know she could be interested in me. Our neighbor Shad keeps telling me his daughter has reached the marriageable stage. There are a couple of others."

"Oh, Joe, I hate to think you'd choose a wife the way you would pick out a new horse for the ranch. A man should fall in love with a woman before he thinks of marriage, or at least he should think he'll fall in love with her when they become man and wife. I can't see you falling in love with either of those women."

"Maybe love isn't so important."

"You're wrong, Joe. I'm going to say it right out plain. Love is the most important basis for any marriage. It was in mine, and I want it to be in yours."

"Then it may be a long time before I get married because I'm sure not in love."

"I have to disagree with you, son. I've been watching the two of you and I'm not sure if you're in love yet or not, but I know for sure you're falling in love with Melissa Cardwell, though you're fighting it as hard as you can. I'm also sure she feels the same way about you."

He chuckled. "You couldn't be more wrong, Ma. As I said, Melissa's a beautiful woman and her looks would make any man's head spin, but she's sure not wife material for a man like me. She'll go back to Philadelphia and marry some slimy tenderfoot and let him pat her on the head like a trained puppy instead of really loving her. She'll then have teas and gossip sessions with her snooty friends and brag about having the most wonderful husband in the world. As far as I'm concerned, as wife material she's worthless and always will be."

"I wish you wouldn't say such things. Melissa is a wonderful girl."

"I've heard all I want to hear about Melissa Cardwell, Ma. She's going back east soon. And the faster she gets her butt out of here, the better it will be for all of us. Now, I'm going to get out to the bunkhouse. I've got a lot of work to do in the morning. We have some fences down and they have to be repaired. Good-night, Ma."

"Son..."

The back door slammed, and Melissa wiped the tears off her cheek. She knew she had to hurry, or Althea would catch her sitting on the steps. As quietly as she could, she turned and slipped back into Joe's room. She fell across the bed and sobbed. So she'd been right. He thought she was worthless. Just a trained puppy for some man in Philadelphia. The sad thing was, she knew his words were truer than she'd realized until she heard him say them. But did she want to be some man's trained puppy?

After a good cry, Melissa sat up. She knew what she had to do. She moved across the room to his desk. Taking out a piece of paper, she began to write. When she finished the letter, she placed it in an envelope, wrote his name on the back and propped it against the lamp on the table beside the bed, knowing he wouldn't find it for a few days. She then packed her valise. She didn't bother with her trunk. After all, she had plenty of clothes in Philadelphia. She got dressed, took a seat in the chair by the window and waited for the first signs of daylight.

~ * ~

Althea was worried, but she knew she couldn't let the children see her concern. It was getting close to suppertime and Joe would soon be in to eat. This would take their mind off their aunt. How was she going to tell them Melissa got up sick and in pain and asked if somebody could take her into town to the doctor? Maybe she was sicker than anyone thought since she was staying so long. And where was the bunkhouse cook, Grover? Surely, he wouldn't leave Melissa in town and come home alone.

Susie walked around the table throwing napkins on each plate. "Where Aunt Lissa?"

"I told you earlier, honey. She had to go to town this morning. She'll be back later." Althea smiled at her.

"Do you want me to get some wood, Grandma?"

"That'd be sweet of you, David. I'm sure Uncle Joe would appreciate it." Althea knew he could only carry in a few sticks of wood at a time, but it would keep him busy and his mind off his aunt's absence.

David went for his coat, buttoned it up and stepped out onto the porch. In a matter of minutes, he returned followed by Joe. They both had an armful of wood. "Found this boy out here working and thought I'd give him a hand."

"Great. Go ahead and fill the wood boxes, then wash your hands and let's eat. It's going to get cold."

When they sat at the table, Joe frowned. "Where's Melissa?"

"Doctor," Susie said with her mouth full of roast.

"Doctor?"

"She got up sick this morning and asked Grover to take her to town to see the doctor. She should be back soon. Would you like some more gravy for your potatoes, Joe?"

She knew he got the idea she didn't want to talk about Melissa's absence, so he lifted an eyebrow and said, "Sure, Ma."

After supper, Joe spent time in the parlor with the children while Althea did the dishes. She smiled to see how he was relating to them. They were beginning to love their uncle, and she knew it wouldn't be long until they thought of him as their second daddy.

But what about Joe? He needed a woman in his life. One who would love the children as much as he did. One who would love him for the rest of his life and would eventually give him his own children. No matter what he said about it, in her way of thinking, he needed Melissa Cardwell.

After putting the children to bed and promising she'd have their aunt come kiss them good night as soon as she got home, she joined her son in front of the fireplace. "All right, Joe, ask your questions."

After she told him again what had happened this morning, he frowned. "But, Ma, the wagon was in the barn when I rode in. Grover had to have brought it back."

"Then, where's Melissa?"

"I don't know, but I'm going to find out." He stood and rushed toward the back door.

"Come back and tell me."

"I will." He slammed his hat on his head, put on his coat, and hurried out the door.

~ * ~

The men looked up when Joe came into the bunkhouse and let the door bang against the wall. "Is Grover here?"

"Right here, boss. What you need?"

"Did you take Miss Cardwell to town this morning?"

"Shore did. Poor little thing was as sick as she could be. I was afeared she was gonna die afore we got to town."

"But she didn't."

"No, sir. I put her valise in the wagon and drove as fast as I dared on the snowy roads." He shook his head. "Strange, though, as soon as we got to town, she seemed to get better."

"Did she go to the doctor?"

"I let her out there and she told me to wait. She came back a while later and said for me to go on home 'cause she was gonna stay in town."

"Did you take her to the hotel?"

"Nope. She told me to go on and she'd walk to the hotel."

"And you just left her there?"

Grover looked frightened. "Yah. Did I do somethin' wrong?"

Joe shook his head. "No. I guess there wasn't anything else you could do."

He turned and started out the door.

"They's one more thing, boss."

Joe turned around. "What is it, Grover?"

"She give me this here letter and told me to give it to you. I was waitin' till you come in for the night, but I might as well give it to you now." He picked up his coat and began searching in the pockets. "Here 'tis."

Joe took the letter and nodded. "Ma was worried about her, so I better go tell her what happened. I'll see you guys later."

Outside, Joe took a deep breath of the winter air. He opened the note, but it simply said, *I'm too sick to ride back to the ranch. Will stay at the hotel tonight.*

He wasn't sure what Melissa was up to, but he had an idea, and he didn't like what his thought indicated. Yes, she should go back to Philadelphia because she belonged there. Yes, she would never fit in here. But, in spite of all the reasons why he shouldn't, he wanted her here.

~ * ~

The next morning at breakfast, David looked at his grandmother. "I know it's Valentine's Day. Will Aunt Melissa come home today?"

"I make her card," Susie said with a mouthful of egg.

Joe decided to go against his hunch and said, "Don't worry, kids. I'm sure she'll be here before the day is over."

"Good," David said.

"Son, are you sure?"

"Of course, Ma." Joe wiped his mouth and stood. "I'm going to my room and get another shirt, since I noticed a tear in this one when I washed up this morning. I'm sure Miss Cardwell won't mind."

Going straight to his wardrobe, Joe pulled out a warm blue shirt, removed the one he had on then slipped the clean one over his head. When he turned to go, he noticed the letter propped against the lamp on the table beside the bed. Frowning, he moved over and picked it up. He was surprised to see his name written across the envelope.

Still frowning, he ripped it open and began to read.

To Joseph Jenson: Because I know you think I'm worthless and am no good for this household or for anyone who lives in your home, I am relieving you of having to pretend to like me in front of the children. I'm sure you and your mother will take excellent care of them, and they will soon forget their Aunt Melissa. I will never forget them or their parents. Please take extra care of David. His father's death hit him hard because they were so close. Of course, Susie needs special care, too, but she's young and doesn't understand what's happened.

Please try not to feel too harsh about me, Mr. Jenson. I tried as best as I could to fit in on your ranch. It was a life I'd never seen or been a part of. You were right when you said I was worthless there. I do want you to know I felt welcomed by your mother, and I tried to help as I learned what and how to do the things required. As for you, though I know you never liked me, I couldn't help appreciating the way you treated the children. You're a good man and I can't help telling you after meeting a strong man such as you I could never be satisfied to be the wife of the silly man my aunt has picked out for me. It may mean I will never marry but I want to be more than some man's trained puppy.

Blessings to the Jenson family.
Melissa Cardwell

Joe read the letter again, then crammed it in his pocket. How could he have been so stubborn and stupid? In an instant, it was as if a fog lifted, and everything became clear to him. He knew exactly what he had to do. First thing, he'd enlist his mother's help, then he'd set out to make things right on the Jenson ranch.

~ * ~

It was daybreak when the stagecoach pulled away from Bell Haven. Melissa sat in the corner with her head turned toward the window. Besides her, there were three male passengers, but only the man in a blue checked suit who sat across from her had tried to start a conversation. But she didn't want to talk with him or anyone else. She gave him one-word clip answers and turned her head. She wasn't up for idle chatting, and she knew he nor anyone else could say anything to make it easier for her to go back to Philadelphia. Even the constant tears hadn't helped make her like her decision to go. But after crying through the night in the small hotel room, she had no more tears. All left now was the sadness which had seeped so deep it had invaded her soul. She realized this feeling would continue into her future. Oh, she'd be physically comfortable in her aunt's lavish home, and her sister, Catherine, would be delighted when she returned, and as for her friends, she'd smile at them and drink the tea they served when she visited. But marrying Weldon Wheaton III or any other man like him was out of the picture now. After seeing what a real man was like, she decided another woman could have Weldon and all the rest of the available men she had met in town. Melissa only hoped when she was an old lady, leaving the West today wouldn't leave her as bitter and uncaring as Aunt Vernetta.

It was nearing noon when the stagecoach gave a sudden jerk and began to slow down. Melissa pulled back the sash and saw they were nowhere near what looked like civilization. With another jerk the stage stopped.

In a moment, the door yanked open, and the driver stuck his head in. "Ma'am, step out here please."

Being the only female passenger, Melissa knew he was talking to her, but she could only stare at him and wonder what he wanted.

"What in the world do you want her for?" One of the fancy dressed men asked.

"This don't concern you. Come on, ma'am. Your husband is here to get you."

Her eyes grew large. "Husband?"

"Yes. Now come along and talk to him."

"There's been a mistake. I have no husband. I'm..."

"Go talk to him, lady. Holding the door open is making it colder in here," a passenger said and took her arm, propelling her toward the door.

The driver reached in and took her hand to help her out.

"I don't understand why..." Her voice floundered when she saw Joe Jenson standing behind the driver.

He looked at her and shook his head. "How could you do this to us, Melissa?"

She stared at him. Was she dreaming or was she having a nightmare?

"Little Susie and David are all upset because you left without even saying good-bye to them. We're a family, Melissa. How could you run out on us just because life hasn't turned out like you thought it would here in the West?"

Her heart began to pound. "I don't know what you're talking about."

"The children need you. Ma needs you and no matter what you think, I need you, too. Please come home."

"I'm going home to Philadelphia."

"But you'll be so far away the children might never get to see you again. Don't you love them at all?"

"Of course, I love them, but I know they're better off with you and your mother than with me. You'll be there for them always and I've been told I'm worthless."

"You're not worthless. You just have a lot to learn about living on a ranch."

The door to the stage opened and the man stuck his head out. "Damn it, woman, go home to your husband and children so we can move on."

"He's not..."

The driver intervened. "The man's right. I'll throw your bag down and you go on home with your husband."

"He's not my husband." She almost screamed.

"If he's not your husband, are there no children?"

"Yes, there are children, but..."

"No buts. This line don't believe in helping a woman run away from her family. Now go on home where you belong." The driver climbed back on the stagecoach and tossed her valise to the ground.

"Wait..."

The driver ignored her. "Better step away, lady. Don't want to run over you." He then snapped the whip over the horses' backsides and the stagecoach began to roll forward.

"No. You can't leave me here." But the stage moved away, leaving her standing in the light snow.

She whirled toward Joe. "What is the meaning of this?"

"I got your letter."

"So?"

"Do you want to stand here until we freeze, or do you want to ride back home with me?"

"How? I only see one horse."

"It'll only take one." He picked up her valise, hooked it over the saddle horn then mounted. Before she could say anything, he reached down, scooped her up with one arm and settled her in his lap.

"Why in the world did you kidnap me, Joseph Jenson? It's cold out here and I was trying to do the right thing. I know the children will have a good life with you and their grandmother and you made it clear I wasn't needed or wanted on your ranch."

He seemed to ignore her and reached behind him and pulled a blanket from behind the saddle. "Here's a blanket. Wrap it around you and put your head against my chest. You'll be warmer that way."

The horse plodded down the snowy road in the opposite direction. Melissa felt she should make or at least try to make Joe take her back to the stage and explain to the driver she wasn't his wife, and David and Susie weren't her children. But it felt so good sitting here in his lap with his arms around her. The only thing marring the scene was the fact the sun went behind the clouds and in a short time it began to snow.

It took her a little time to work up the courage to speak to him again. Finally, she muttered, "Why, Joe?"

"I found your letter."

She thought for a minute. Then said, "So you said, but you weren't supposed to go into my room until you came in from work tonight. You should have found the letter then and I would have been far enough away you couldn't catch up with me."

"I believe it's my room, too. I have a right to go in there any time you're not using it."

"It is, but..."

He interrupted. "Why didn't you leave on yesterday's stage?"

"I planned to, but I missed it."

"I'm glad you missed it."

"Why?"

"Because I didn't have to go as far in this awful weather to stop you, which means if you sit still and quit distracting me, we'll be home by dark." He reached up, turned up the collar on his coat and pulled his hat down over his eyes.

Melissa was confused. In one way she was still upset he'd stopped her trip, but in another she was pleased he had. Glancing up at him, she saw the snow on his nose and eyelashes. He had to be cold. Without thinking it over, she took the blanket from her shoulders and spread it across the front of both of them.

"Thanks," he muttered and used one hand to unbutton his coat. He then pulled her against his chest and pulled the coat as far as he could around her.

"I'm sorry I left without telling anyone,"she whispered.

"Doesn't matter now. You're going back."

"Joe, I know you can't stand me, so please tell me why you want me to go back to your ranch."

"It's simple, Melissa. You belong there."

She was stunned. *What did he mean? Did he want her there because of the children? Or did he want her there himself?* Again, she asked, "What makes you say I belong there?"

"I said it because you do. Matter of fact, I told Ma to make sure the preacher was there when we got home."

"Why?"

"Honestly, Melissa do I have to explain everything?"

"Yes, you do."

"All right. The preacher will be there because I plan to move back into my room tonight."

"Where will I sleep?"

"You'll sleep where you've been sleeping."

"But ... Joe Jenson, are you saying ... do you...." It then dawned on her he had mentioned the preacher. Without finishing her sentence, she sat up and stared at him. "Are you asking me to marry you?"

"I guess I should have asked instead of telling you we're getting married. But it wouldn't have mattered. We're getting married this evening either way."

She huffed. "It would have been nice to have a choice as to whether to marry you or not."

"I didn't ask you, Miss Melissa Cardwell, because I knew a hard-headed woman like you would say no, then we'd have to waste a lot of time arguing about it. It was easier for me just to tell you we're getting married tonight and get on with it. The kids will have the parlor all decorated with valentines and Ma is making a big celebration supper. I wouldn't want to disappoint them. Would you?"

She dropped her head against his chest again and was quiet a moment as happiness she'd never known began to fill her entire being. Without taking time to think about her action, she snuggled closer to him. "I don't want to disappoint them either," she whispered.

He let out a big breath, leaned down and kissed the side of her cheek. "That takes a load off my mind. I was afraid I'd have to gag you and tie you up for the ceremony. Now stop talking. I need to concentrate on this road. We may be running into a blizzard, and I want to get us home while I can still see where we're going. If Thunder steps wrong and throws us, we could freeze to death out here, and then we'd miss all the wonderful years of marriage we have ahead of us."

Melissa leaned up, kissed his chin, then molded herself against his chest and bit her lip to keep from speaking. A big smile had crossed her lips. Joe was right. They were going to have many wonderful years. What a wonderful celebration this Valentine's Day was turning out to be.

Three

Catherine

As her aunt stalked into the room without knocking, a surprised Catherine Cardwell whirled around on the light green cushioned stool at her dressing table on her side of the room she shared with her sister, Melissa. "Is something wrong, Aunt Vernetta?"

Shaking a letter toward her niece's face, Vernetta said, "I should say it is. Why didn't you tell me about this?"

Catherine was confused. "Tell you about what?"

"You know what. I'm sure you knew she planned to do this when she took those orphans to Texas against my advice. I can't believe Melissa would do such a thing! I knew she was headstrong, but I never suspected this."

"I'm sorry, Aunt Vernetta. I have no idea what you're talking about."

"I'm talking about what your ungrateful sister has done." When Catherine only stared at her, the sparse white-haired woman continued. "The little twit has disgraced me, and after all I've done for her. I had everything arranged for her to marry Weldon Wheaton III as soon as she returned from Texas so he could get what he wanted, and she could take her rightful place in Philadelphia society. Now she's saying she has married some uncouth rancher. How could she do such a thing to me? How could she want some nobody cowboy instead of the wonderful Mr. Wheaton as a husband?"

Stunned, Catherine gasped. "Married? Melissa can't be married."

"She says she is." She flung the letter at Catherine. "Read it for yourself, then finish getting ready for church. You should go and pray about deceiving me about this," she shouted in an angry voice and stalked out of the room.

Still bewildered, Catherine watched her aunt leave her room, muttering about how she would be ruined in Philadelphia society when word got out about Melissa and the cowboy.

Knowing she didn't have to reply to her aunt, Catherine bent and gathered the letter and the envelope from the floor. Because it ended on top, she looked at the envelope and her mouth flew open. It had been addressed to her. She knew immediately her aunt had opened her mail. Why would she do such a thing? Mail should be private.

Furious, she started to get up and confront her aunt but curiosity about what was in the missive got the better of her. She decided to sit and read what Melissa had written before she talked to her aunt. Unfolding the letter, she began to read.

My dear sister, Catherine. I hope this letter finds you well and enjoying the spring weather which I'm sure is beginning to surround you in Philadelphia.

I'm also sure you, as all you sisters will be, were shocked to see my new name on the envelope of this letter, but please let me begin at the beginning to relieve you of your confusion.

As you may have suspected, getting Susie and David Jenson to Texas and to their grandmother was no easy task. The train was dirty and uncomfortable, though I would now consider it good transportation, compared to the stagecoach we had to ride for the last leg of our journey. But the hardships we suffered were forgotten as soon as we arrived at the Jenson ranch. The children's grandmother, Althea Jenson, welcomed us with open arms. Her son, Joseph, warmed up quickly to the children, but I could tell right away he wasn't pleased with, and I'm quoting him the way he described me, 'a hifalutin city woman who needed to get herself back to Philadelphia as quickly as she can because she'd never be any good to anyone in his family or in all of Texas.'

This hurt my feelings at first and I didn't understand why I was immediately attracted to this man. But attracted I was, though I knew he couldn't stand the sight of me, or so I thought.

I won't go into the details of how he pulled it off, but suffice it to say, when I decided it was time to return to Philadelphia and the kind of life I'd known there, he stopped me. He said he knew it was crazy, but he loved me and wanted me to marry him and live on his Texas ranch with him for the rest of our lives. I didn't fight him because it was what I wanted, too. We were married on Valentine's Day with his mother, the two children, and his ranch hands as witnesses.

And believe me, Catherine. I have never been happier. It is so much more wonderful than I could have had with Weldon Wheaton, III or any other man in Philadelphia. I now have a love and a happiness I never dreamed was possible. It is what I wish for all my sisters to have for themselves someday.

Please write and let me know how Aunt Vernetta takes the news I'm not coming back to Philadelphia and I'm definitely not going to marry Weldon. I'm sure some other single woman will be pleased by this news because others have made it plain they like the man, and they can have him with my blessing.

Just know I love you and hope you can visit me here sometime in the near future. I will be writing our sisters basically this same letter because I want all of you to know how happy I am. I also want you all to know this is the kind of happiness I wish for all of you. Please write to me as soon as possible. I love you dearly and I know I will have your love and support.

Until we can meet again, and you can meet Joe, I'll always be...

Your loving sister, who is using this letter as our Sister Circle to share my news with you until we are together again to form our circle in person.

With all my love,

Melissa

Folding the letter, Catherine sat back with a smile. Though she was shocked at the news, and she missed her sister terribly, she couldn't help being pleased Melissa had found such wonderful happiness.

It flitted across her mind she was almost glad her aunt had opened her letter. At least the older woman now knew Melissa's news, therefore, she wouldn't have to tell her. Confronting the aunt about opening her mail would have to come later. Right now, she wanted to think of how to begin a letter to Melissa and tell her how happy she was for her, and to ask her to write again and tell her more about her husband and her new style of life.

With the smile still on her face, she returned to her dressing table. She knew it would be an uncomfortable day at church, but thank goodness, her aunt had informed her earlier she planned to spend the afternoon with a friend who had invited her to lunch. Catherine then knew when she got home from church, the first thing she would do was write to her sister. It would take a while to finish, but when she did, she'd put it away and tomorrow, she would go to the post office and mail it because she didn't trust her aunt or their one maid, Annie, or the part-time butler to do it.

~ * ~

Annie Fillmore, the only live-in servant in the household, stood on the back stairs and listened to the irate woman screaming at her niece about Melissa's marriage. She couldn't help smiling. At first when the two sisters moved into the Albertson household, she thought of them as just two more of the silly high society ladies who would be a lot of trouble to take care of. But they had fooled her. Instead, she found them to be rather quiet and standoffish, and they seemed to be more interested in spending time together than taking part in their aunt's society functions, which she insisted they attend often.

In fact, they'd been so cooperative it surprised her when Melissa defied her aunt and went to Baltimore to take care of her cousin and her children. She was even more surprised today when she heard about the woman's marriage to a Texas cowboy.

Annie had expected Melissa to go along with her aunt and marry the wishy-washy, no-good Wheaton man. But the Cardwell sisters had more gumption than Annie dreamed they had. Especially Melissa. She still wondered about Catherine.

When she knew her boss's tirade with her niece was about over, the maid hurried down the stairs. She didn't want Mrs. Albertson to ever find out she had a habit of sneaking around the house to gather all the information she could about what was going on in the mansion. Information she hoped to use to her advantage later.

~ * ~

Though things seemed strained when her aunt had come home last night, nothing more was said about Melissa's letter and knowing her aunt had lunch plans with one of her ladies' groups on Monday, Catherine went to bed early.

The next morning, she plastered on a smile and headed downstairs. She was happy to find her aunt so absorbed in what to wear to her upcoming meeting she didn't seem to care if her niece planned to go out, too. In fact, she seemed pleased by it. The only thing surprising Catherine was the fact her aunt didn't mention her outburst on the previous day, nor the letter from Melissa, or the fact she had married a man in Texas.

So, Catherine decided she wouldn't mention it either. Not at this time, anyway.

After the almost silent breakfast, each of them went about their own plans for the day. Catherine couldn't wait to get into town and send her letter.

It was a windy day, and as often happened, the wind gave Catherine a slight headache. After posting her letter, she went to the library, but she didn't feel up to staying as long as she usually did. She decided she didn't feel well enough to go anywhere else, so she headed home.

Knowing her aunt would probably still be out, she decided she'd go to her room and take a nap. Napping often helped make her feel better, and she hoped it would this time. If her aunt was still out, the house would be empty with the exception of Annie, who most always stayed near the kitchen. Therefore, she knew it would be quiet and she'd be able to doze off quickly. Then maybe the evening meal wouldn't be as strained as breakfast had been and she'd confront her aunt about opening her letter.

As she approached the stately home, she noticed a buggy parked in the driveway. Frowning, she wondered who this could be. Unless Aunt Vernetta had left the luncheon early, her carriage shouldn't be at home. If she was home, her buggy should be in the carriage house, not outside.

Catherine decided the best thing to do was to slip in quietly and try to avoid anyone who happened to be here. She didn't want to be drawn into a conversation with her aunt or any of her friends until her head felt better.

The front door was unlocked, so she eased it open and stepped inside. Now if she could just make it to the winding stairs and up to her room, she knew she'd be fine. She was at the first step when she heard her aunt say, "I'm leaving the office door ajar because if Catherine happens to come home early, I'll hear her come in. She's always rushing and doesn't slip in quietly as a lady should. But just in case, I certainly don't want her to hear what we're discussing."

Catherine froze. Undoubtedly, her aunt had somebody in her office she didn't want her to know about. What could be going on?

A man answered, "I understand, Vernetta. It's best she doesn't know what you're up to until it's too late for her to do anything about it."

She recognized his voice and knew her aunt was talking to Weldon Wheaton III.

Her heart began to pound. *What in the world could they be talking about, and why would they care if she heard their discussion?*

Her aunt went on. "I have already apologized to you because things didn't work out with Melissa. But please let me apologize again. I don't know what possessed the girl to marry some uncouth cowboy in Texas when you were so willing to marry her."

"I told you, I forgive you, Vernetta. Maybe it was a good thing she and I didn't marry. She was a little impulsive and I want my wife to be seen and not heard, as they say."

"I do admit, Melissa didn't hesitate to speak her mind. But I thought marriage to you would settle her down."

"Well, it can't happen now." He chuckled. "As I also told you, I have no intention of demanding you return the ten-thousand-dollar payment I gave you for her. I will just let it be the down payment for Catherine, or one of your other nieces."

"I appreciate it, Weldon. But I think you should only concentrate on Catherine at this time. Especially since you haven't met my other nieces."

Catherine was stunned. *What in the world is going on? Is Aunt Vernetta actually selling one of us to this man?* She started to storm into the office and demand an explanation, but her aunt's next statement stopped her.

"Catherine is as pretty and as smart as Melissa. Plus, I don't think she's as headstrong as her older sister and it makes her easier to get along with. She'll be more apt to go along with most any plans you have. I know she'll be an asset to you. I also know she'll not fight marrying you quickly. In fact, I'm sure we can pull off a summer wedding."

"I suppose you're right. Of course, I hear your nieces, Bernadette and Rosemary are pretty, too. Either one of them would probably do." He chuckled. "I do think Rosemary is a little young, but strange things have happened at times. A lot of pretty girls get married before their sixteenth birthday."

"I don't think marriage to Rosemary would get you the prestige you're seeking, Weldon. People would wonder why you wanted a mere child as a wife."

"You're probably right, my dear. I was only letting you know I won't give up until I'm married to one of the Cardwell sisters, no matter how long it takes."

"I understand. But I know if you pursue Catherine, it will work well for both of us."

"That's why I came to you in the first place. You need the money and I need a name like Cardwell secured to mine so I can travel in the circles you do. Though I'm now a wealthy man, the upper class still often sees me as the son of Elroy Weldon Wheaton Jr. and the three Boston prostitutes he murdered. Even dropping Elroy from my name after all the publicity and shame, hasn't kept many of them from labeling me as the murderer's son when they look into my background. I suppose they think his bad blood will show up in me someday."

Vernetta added, "And you believe if you have a wife who is a respected Cardwell, and the niece of a well- to- do Cardwell woman who married a wealthy Albertson, they will not continue to treat you in such a manner."

"I know so. Why else would I pay you thousands of dollars for one of your nieces?"

Catherine had heard enough. With her mind reeling, she slipped back to the front door and stepped outside. Taking a deep breath to settle her nerves, she made as much noise as she could as she swept in the front door.

Her aunt came immediately into the entranceway to meet her. "Catherine, I'm surprised to see you. What are you doing home so early?"

"Oh, Aunt Vernetta. I have a fierce headache. It must be the wind. It often makes my head hurt. I couldn't complete my errands because it's hurting so bad. I even thought I was going to throw up because of the pain."

"I'm so sorry. What can I do for you, dear?"

"I want to go to my room and lie down. If I sleep a little, I'm sure it'll be better when I awake."

"Shall I have Annie get some tea or something for you?"

Catherine covered her mouth with her hand. "Oh, no. The thought of food makes me sick."

"Then go to your room, and take a nap, dear. I'll warn Annie not to disturb you. I'll come check on you later to make sure you're feeling better."

"Thank you, Aunt Vernetta. You're very kind." Catherine hurried up the stairs before she lost control of her emotions and confronted her aunt the way she wanted to.

~ * ~

After a long afternoon and night of thinking and planning what she should do, Catherine came up with what she thought was the perfect plan. Now she only had to remain calm to make it work. She went down to breakfast the next morning determined not to let her aunt know she had any idea what was going on. Entering the dining room, she said in as happy a voice as she could muster, "Good morning, Aunt Vernetta. It's looks like it's going to be a beautiful day, doesn't it?"

"My goodness, Catherine," Vernetta put her silver coffee pot down and looked at her niece. "You seem to be a completely different person this morning."

"I feel like a different person. Once I went to sleep, my head eased off and I slept like a baby. In fact, I had a beautiful dream."

Vernetta gave Catherine one of her rare smiles. "Have a seat, dear, so Annie can serve us. Then you can tell me all about it."

Annie appeared with coffee for Catherine and a tray of breakfast food for both.

When they were alone again, Catherine said, "This looks good. I'm hungry."

"I'm sure it'll be tasty as usual." Vernetta picked up her silver knife and buttered her bread. "Now tell me why you're so gay this morning."

"It's probably because of my dream. It was wonderful. In it, I was at a lovely garden party with you and your friends. All of my friends were there, too. I had on a beautiful dress, and everyone complimented me on it. I think it was a soft pink or white. I'm not sure. But I know there was beautiful music, amazing food, and we were all dancing, and having a fantastic time. It was like we were celebrating some special event but I'm not sure what it was." She paused and took a bite of her poached egg.

"My goodness." Her aunt smiled again. "You did have an extravagant dream."

"I know." She took another bite of food and changed the subject to see if she could push her aunt a little further. "When is your birthday, Aunt Vernetta?"

Vernetta raised an eyebrow. "Why in the world do you want to know in what month my birthday occurs?"

Catherine smiled. "I thought if it was this summer, we could have a garden party to celebrate. I know it wouldn't be as elaborate as my dream, but I'm sure it would be a wonderful thing for us to do and I'm sure all your friends would enjoy it. Don't you agree?"

Shaking her head, Vernetta said, "I'm afraid we can't do that, Catherine. It happens my birthday is in February, so even if I wanted to celebrate the event, a garden party would be out."

Catherine shrugged. "Oh, well. Maybe somebody else will have a party and invite us."

"True. You never know what will come up this spring or summer to celebrate with our friends."

Catherine didn't miss the smug look on Vernetta's face. She knew immediately the woman was thinking about her niece's marriage to Weldon Wheaton III. She wanted to throw her breakfast in her aunt's face, but instead she said, "You're right. I'm sure something will come along. It's still cold around here but it won't last forever."

They ate in silence for several minutes, then Vernetta said, "I'm sorry to say this when you're in such a good mood, Catherine, but I feel we need to discuss something."

She felt it was about the letter from Melissa, but she asked, "What?"

"What do you think about your sister's marriage to a cowboy."

It was what she had expected her aunt to bring up. Catherine put her spoon down and sighed as she had planned to keep her aunt from knowing what she really thought. "I don't know what to think, Aunt Vernetta. At first, I was upset because you opened my letter, then I realized I was glad you did because I'm pleased you knew about the marriage before, I did."

"I had a feeling it might contain bad news. That's why I opened it."

Catherine nodded and forced another sigh. "After I thought about what the letter said, I couldn't understand what Melissa was thinking. How could she give up all the advantages and luxuries she has here with us and tie her life to a man who will require her to live her life in some primitive land without any friends or family?"

"Why, Catherine. I never dreamed you were so mature and levelheaded. I'm glad you now understand why I was so upset with Melissa's letter."

"I'm sure it was part of why I had such a headache yesterday."

"It probably was, my dear, so we'll drop the subject. You can then concentrate on a possible garden party for this summer."

"Oh, that would be fantastic. I'll spend my morning thinking about a beautiful dress to wear. Maybe I'll even be able to have a new one made."

"To keep you in such a good mood, I'm going to reward you with a surprise."

Catherine forced a smile. "A real surprise?"

"Yes, dear. I'm going to give you a note to take to Mr. Hammons at the bank and tell him to let you draw money from your account to have a dress designed for a summer party. You can then take it to the dressmaker and see what you can find you like."

"Oh, Aunt Vernetta. You're wonderful. I could hug you for doing such a sweet thing."

"That's not necessary. But I don't want you to make a decision about the pattern for your dress until I have the time to go with you to help you make the final decision. It must be perfect for the occasion." She wiped her mouth with the napkin and laid it aside. "I have my church ladies' luncheon today and a meeting with my lawyer tomorrow. Then I plan to have a guest for dinner with us on Friday. But I might be able to be free by the first of next week to go to the dressmaker."

"Fine, Aunt Vernetta. I'm looking forward to it." Catherine again praised her aunt for her actions, then stood because breakfast was over. She went to her room and wondered why she didn't throw up because of all the lies she'd told her aunt this morning. The encounter had left her with an upset stomach. But with her aunt out for most of the afternoon with her ladies' group, she didn't have time to get sick. She had to commence carrying out the plan she'd thought of last night. After all, it was Tuesday already, and her aunt had informed her Mr. Wheaton was the guest who would be coming for supper on Friday.

~ * ~

It wasn't as hard to get all of her money out of the bank as Catherine thought it would be. She was grateful her aunt hadn't put down a limit on the amount she could withdraw. Acting as innocently as she could, she told the banker she'd learned her aunt was having some financial difficulties and she wanted the money to relieve her relative of the burden. When she saw he was about to refuse, she went on. "I'm so lucky to be living with my aunt and I want to help her all I can. Of course, I know she would never take my money, so I've decided to pay some of her bills without her knowing it until it's a done deal. I don't need to keep saving money. I know she'll continue to provide a good home for me until I marry, then it'll be my husband's responsibility to take care of me."

When she saw him weakening, she added, "Mr. Hammons, I know I can count on your discretion not to let Aunt Vernetta know what I'm up to. I'm afraid she'd feel obligated to try to stop me. I just want to help, and I know you probably want the same for her."

He agreed. "You are a wonderful niece, Miss Catherine. I'll get the money for you."

Thanking Mr. Hammonds, she left the bank with her money with a smile on her lips because it had worked so well. Her next stop was at the dressmaker's shop her aunt always used. Knowing how devious Vernetta was, she chatted with the woman about a future garden party because she felt her aunt would check to be sure she'd gone by there.

Though she hated to spend the two dollars she gave Miss Colleen, it was to assure her place in line to return to pick out a pattern and choose material for her new frock at a later date. Although she knew she'd never return, she felt certain this would satisfy her aunt if the woman checked up on her, which she more than likely would do.

Her next stop was the train station. After studying the schedules, she found out there was a train leaving early on Friday which would take her to Memphis and connect with one going to Texas on Saturday. She didn't try to find one to Bell Haven because she didn't know if it was near any of the cities the schedule said the Texas train stopped. She only knew Bell Haven was in West Texas where Melissa now lived. She'd search out the exact location later. Now, it was imperative she get out of Philadelphia before her aunt married her off to Mr. Wheaton.

She arrived back at the house before Vernetta, and this gave her time to begin sorting her clothes to see which ones she would take with her. It wasn't going to be easy because she knew her aunt often looked in her wardrobe. She decided she'd say she was picking and choosing what she would wear for the dinner party her aunt had planned for this weekend.

When she finally chose four of her gowns to take, she hung them together in the wardrobe along with three skirts and shirtwaists to match. She then turned to her bureau and selected underthings, two nightgowns, stockings, and a robe. She knew the space in the valise was limited, but she couldn't go to Texas with nothing to wear. She just had to be careful to see nobody caught on to what she was up to.

~ * ~

Annie Fillmore wasn't the dimwitted and faithful servant she pretended to be. In fact, this ruse had not only kept her working, but it had helped her to make her escape plan and to stash back much of her cash in the four years she had worked for Vernetta Cardwell Albertson.

But she had put things on hold when she learned of Vernetta's plan to sell her niece to Weldon Wheaton III. She also knew about the ten thousand dollar down payment and her curiosity made her stick around to see if Melissa Cardwell would be naive enough to go along with the evil plan.

She was glad to find out the woman had gumption. Not only had she thwarted her aunt's plan by taking her cousin's children to Texas, but she had married a man there and had no intention of returning to Philadelphia and becoming Mrs. Wheaton III.

Now by chance, she found out about the new plan for his marriage to a different Cardwell sister. Would Catherine Cardwell fall for it? Would she agree to marry the silly man? In the few things Annie had been able to overhear, she was beginning to think she would. Then something happened to change everything.

She'd gone into Catherine 's room to put away the newly folded laundry and her sharp eyes saw some of Catherine 's underclothes were missing from the drawers. Frowning, she looked around the room and couldn't understand what had happened to them. She knew she'd put them in the chest of drawers only a day or so ago.

Then she opened the wardrobe and knew at once what was happening. Catherine had a valise tucked in the back corner and it contained the missing garments. She then saw the four gowns and the casual clothes which were kind of separated from the others. Annie smiled.

The woman wasn't the quiet little mouse she pretended to be. She wasn't going to be used by her devious aunt any more than her sister had been. In fact, Catherine Cardwell was planning to run away.

Leaving the room, Annie decided it was now time to pack her own bag and get out from under the threats Vernetta Albertson held over her head. But first, since Vernetta was out, she was going to make a stop in the woman's office. It was a good thing she'd been able to find the code to open the safe. There was something there she wanted besides the money she was owed, and she intended to get it.

~ * ~

On Thursday evening Vernetta received word from a neighbor her friend Harriett Bruster's husband, Claude, had fallen down the back steps of their home and broken his neck. He had died instantly. It was too late in the evening for her to go to be with her friend, but now it was Friday morning, and she was in a quandary as to what to do.

Harriet had been wonderful to her when Gaither had died, and she knew she should go and support her friend in her grief. But she had invited Weldon Wheaton III to have supper with them tonight and she wanted to make sure everything was perfect when he arrived. It could be the first step in getting him and Catherine closer to the altar.

Catherine entered the dining room. "You look upset, Aunt Vernetta. What's wrong?"

"Oh, dear. I don't know what to do. You know I've invited Mr. Wheaton for supper tonight and I've already laid out the menu for Annie to cook. I was so looking forward to him having a relaxing meal with us. He is such entertaining company and I wanted you to enjoy it."

Annie appeared with their breakfast and Catherine had a quick thought. "Well, Aunt Vernetta, I'm sure Annie has everything ready in the kitchen and I'm sure I can be ready before you return from your friend's house. So, why don't you plan to visit her this afternoon? I'm sure you would be able to get home before Mr. Wheaton arrives."

"Well..."

"Since Annie will be in the kitchen most of the day, I'm sure she wouldn't mind preparing something for you to take to your friend." She looked at the maid. "Would you be able to do that, Annie?"

"Of course, Miss Catherine."

"See, Aunt Vernetta. I'm sure you know something your friend is especially fond of. Maybe Annie could make the dish."

"She does rave about Annie's lemon pie every time she has eaten it here."

"Would a lemon pie be too much to ask you to make, Annie?"

"No, Miss Catherine. In fact, I'll make three. I want to make sure Miz Bruster has all the pie she wants, and then there will be one for the meal tonight. Then you'll have your choice of the lemon pie or the chocolate cake you asked for."

Vernetta nodded. "Then I'll do it. I'm sure I can trust you to handle the kitchen and Catherine to take care of everything else here." She turned and smiled at her niece. "I now remember, you said you needed to go buy something you needed for tonight. Could I pick it up for you while I'm going through town? Then you wouldn't have to leave here."

"Oh, I meant to tell you I changed my mind about buying the broach I saw in the window at the dress shop and thought it'd look pretty on my blue dress. I had a better idea, if you don't mind helping me out."

Vernetta frowned. "What was your new idea?"

"I thought of your beautiful cameo pin. The one you wore to church last Sunday. I wanted to ask you if you would permit me to wear it tonight. It will look so much better on my dress than the one I saw at the shop."

"You amaze me at times, my dear niece. I never dreamed you had noticed my pin. It was a gift from my beloved Gaither one Christmas." She gave Catherine a smile. "I'd be delighted to let you wear it for our special supper tonight."

"Oh, thank you, Aunt Vernetta. I think you're wonderful."

~ * ~

After leaving the dining room, Annie let a big grin cross her lips. *Honestly, Catherine Cardwell, I'm beginning to think you're as good as I am at pulling the wool over your aunt's eyes. I was beginning to think you'd given up on leaving here, but I was wrong. You planned to use the trip to buy the pin to get out of the house and to the train station this afternoon. Now, you don't have to have an excuse to get out since your aunt will be visiting her friend at the time you need to leave. I'm going to have to stay on my toes to keep up with your thinking.*

When she got out the makings for the lemon pies, she thought, *I may just make four pies. One might taste good when we're rolling down the tracks between here and Memphis.*

~ * ~

At twelve-fifteen, Vernetta pulled her buggy out of the carriage house and headed to her friend's place with two lemon pies. Catherine hurried to her room, changed into her dark rose-colored traveling suit skirt and white ruffled shirtwaist top. She hung the dress she'd been wearing in the wardrobe, then checked around quickly. The last thing she did was toss her hairbrush, toothbrush, and a few other personal items into a small bag. She slipped her arms into the jacket of her suit, placed her hat on her head, threw her cape around her shoulders, gathered her luggage, and left the room.

Stopping by her aunt's room, she placed the note she'd written on the dresser and laid the cameo pin on top of it. She didn't want the woman to think she'd stolen it.

Hurrying down the stairs, she hoped she wouldn't run into Annie as she left the house. She liked the woman, but she sometimes felt the maid watched her a little too closely. She often wondered if her aunt had Annie spying on her.

But this didn't matter now. She was out of the house and on the street. She hoped there would be a carriage to hire on the next corner because she didn't want to have to walk all the way to the train station carrying her luggage. But she would if she had to. She couldn't worry about her comfort now. All she had to do was drop the letters in the mail to her sisters, then get away and so far, things had worked in her favor. She only hoped her luck would hold until the train pulled away from the station at two o'clock. She then knew she could take a deep breath and relax, because it wouldn't matter what time her aunt came home. She wouldn't find anyone except Annie at the house, and hopefully neither the maid nor her aunt would have any idea where she had gone or when she'd be back.

~ * ~

Vernetta Albertson parked her buggy in the stable and practically jumped out. She was in a dither because she had gotten home much later than she had planned. But it had been hard to get away. Harriet Brewster had clung to her as if she were her only friend. It got to the point Vernetta wished she hadn't gone to the woman's house. But at last, another friend arrived, and Vernetta was able to say a quick good-bye and slip out.

Now she knew she had to rush to make herself presentable for this important evening. She only hoped things would go well tonight. Of course, she never doubted Catherine would do what she said she would do. She was much more dependable than Melissa ever had been.

Going through the back door, she almost yelled, "Annie, forget about tending to the horse for the time being. We need to get ready for..."

She stopped and looked around the silent room. Something was wrong. Annie was nowhere to be seen and there were no cooking smells emitting from the stove.

Vernetta's eyes widened. "Annie! Where are you?"

There was no answer and Vernetta walked over to the stove. Jerking the oven door open, she saw the still mostly raw roast sitting in the pan with no vegetables around it. Neither were there any pots nor pans on top of the stove where other food should be cooking.

Frowning, she checked the fire box and saw only a few red embers. The fire had almost gone out. Stunned, she turned and ran out of the kitchen as she began yelling Catherine's name.

The only response she got was an eerie silence.

Rushing up the stairs to Catherine 's room, still calling her niece's name, she opened the door and hurried inside without knocking. The room was in its normal pristine condition.

"What is going on here?" she cried. "This can't be happening to me. Not tonight of all nights."

Though her logical mind told her she would get no answer, she once again yelled, "Catherine, where are you?"

~ * ~

Shortly after the train left the station, Catherine jumped when there was a tap on her shoulder. She looked around and was shocked to see Annie Fillmore standing beside her seat. A jumble of thoughts crossed her mind. *What is she doing here? Did Aunt Vernetta send her? Did she come to take me to my aunt's house?*

Finally, she stammered, "What ... Why ...?"

"Don't get upset," Annie said. "I know you're surprised to see me, but I want to explain my presence to you. May I sit down?"

Catherine could only nod and mummer, "As long as you're not here to make me go back to Aunt Vernetta."

"I assure you, I'm not." Annie put the basket she had in her hand and her valise beside Catherine's, then sat in the seat next to her. "I'm doing the same thing you're doing. I'm running away from Vernetta Albertson, too."

Catherine frowned. "I don't understand. Are you telling me the truth when you say Aunt Vernetta didn't send you to bring me back?"

"I assure you, Miss Catherine. I'm not here to make you go home, and unless your aunt is home by now, she doesn't know either of us have left. As I said, just as you are, I'm running away. In fact, I've been planning my escape from her for some time. I was about ready to go when I realized you were leaving. I decided to wait and leave when you did."

Still not sure of what was going on, Catherine said, "I don't understand."

"Here comes the porter to check our tickets. I'll explain as soon as he's gone."

Catherine nodded as the porter called out, "Get out your tickets, ladies and gentlemen."

The ladies obeyed and when he got to them, they held their tickets to him. He took Catherine's first, then took Annie's. "I see you are both going to Memphis. I assume you're traveling together."

Before Catherine could answer, Annie said, "Yes, sir. I'm Miss Cardwell's maid."

"It's wise when a lady has a companion to travel with her." He punched Catherine's ticket and moved on.

"Now, Annie. Please tell me what's going on."

"It's actually very simple. The woman has been blackmailing me into working for her ever since her husband died, and I've been planning to get away from her since then."

"I don't understand."

"I was about ready to leave when Miss Melissa married her cowboy and didn't return. I was afraid your aunt might suspect I was planning to escape, so I decided to wait a while. Then your aunt decided you would make a good substitute wife for the man. At first, I thought you were going to go along with it, but as I watched you, I realized you had no intention of ever becoming Mrs. Weldon Wheaton III. I stuck around to see what you planned to do and when it became clear, I decided it would be wise for us to leave at the same time. As the porter said, it's safer if women travel together."

"I'm still confused. How did you know when I was leaving and where I was going?"

"I followed you into town. When you bought your ticket, I bought one, too. I've watched when you packed your clothes, then I did the same. Today, I actually left the house before you did. I waited and watched until you arrived and got on the train, then I followed you. I waited until the train pulled out to let you know I was aboard because I was afraid you might panic when you saw me."

"I almost did."

Annie laughed. "I admit, I was a little nervous, too. I thought I had everything planned out well, but I admit, sometimes you fool me in the way you act."

"I've caught you watching me around the house."

"And I didn't think you noticed. You're a brave, clever woman, Catherine Cardwell."

"If you could see how frightened I am inside, I don't think you'd ever call me brave or clever, Annie Fillmore."

"I'm frightened, too, so let's try to relax. Maybe it'd help if we thought about how confused and upset Miz Vernetta Cardwell Albertson will be when she comes home and finds a raw roast in the oven and no cook to finish it."

In spite of herself, Catherine giggled and added, "Or no niece in her room putting on her prettiest dress to greet the man who her aunt thinks will be her niece's future husband."

~ * ~

Hurrying from Catherine 's room to hers, Vernetta threw her purse on the bed along with her jacket. She turned to put her hat on the dresser and spied the pin. Frowning she picked it up along with the note under it.

She read the short note, and her anger flared. But before she could react, there was a loud banging on the front door. "Oh, no," she muttered and stuffed the note in the pocket of her skirt. "He's here already. What am I going to tell him?"

The knocking continued and grew louder as she hurried down the stairs and opened the front door.

"Where were you, woman? I've been knocking for ages."

Vernetta thought fast as she stood aside for him to come inside. "Oh, Weldon. I'm so glad you're here. Something terrible must have happened."

"What are you talking about?"

"Catherine is missing."

He frowned. "What do you mean, missing?"

"I must sit down." She headed for the parlor.

He followed. Throwing his coat on a chair, he glared at her. "What's going on?"

Sticking her hand in her pocket to make sure the note didn't fall out as she sat, she said, "Everything was being readied for your visit, so I went to call on a friend whose husband died last night. I was delayed longer than I expected and when I got home, I found the house deserted. Catherine was nowhere to be found."

"Did you look for her?"

"Of course I did."

"Did you check with the maid?"

"She is missing, too. Something has happened to both of them. I'm so worried." She touched her pocket, making sure the note was still inside. "I think we should get in touch with the authorities, don't you?"

Weldon glared at her. "Why would you think that?"

"Because I can't find her. Somebody must have broken in here and kidnapped her." A strange look came into his eyes and it frightened Vernetta, though she didn't know why.

There was silence for a few seconds, then he said, "What do you have in your pocket?"

"Nothing," she stammered.

He stood and moved to loom over her. "Give it to me."

"I don't have anything." She was about to cry.

He grabbed her arm and twisted it.

She screamed.

"Now, are you going to give it to me, or do I have to break your arm and take it?"

Tears ran down her cheeks as, without a word, she retrieved the note and handed it to him with a shaking hand.

He took the note and read it aloud. *Aunt Vernetta, I know you don't like me, but I can't believe you'd be so heartless as to sell me to the repulsive Weldon Wheaton III. You need not turn to Bernadette or Rosemary because I've warned them to have nothing to do with you or him. As for me, by the time you read this, I'll be where you'll never be able to find me. Catherine.*

He turned to her with hate in his eyes. "So, you let her know you'd sold her to me."

"I don't know how she knew. I never said a word."

"It doesn't matter now." He looked at the note again. "You've made things impossible for me to ever marry a Cardwell. You're going to have to pay for it."

"I'm sorry, Weldon. I..."

He took hold of her arm. "Let's go to your office. I want my money back."

She didn't want him to know she'd already spent most of the money, so she tried to think of something else to tell him. "Oh, Weldon..."

But he was already pulling her toward the study.

Once inside, he demanded she open the safe. "Please, Weldon. I'll help you think of..."

"Shut up, old woman, and open the safe. I want my money."

Knowing there was no need to argue with him, Vernetta opened the safe. Then, she decided to pretend she'd been robbed. "It's gone."

"What do you mean, it's gone?"

"The money is gone."

Fury spread across Weldon's face as he shoved her around to face him. Then without a word, he placed his hands on her neck and squeezed until she stopped screaming and fell to the floor at his feet.

He looked down at her and said, "I'll get in touch with the authorities now, Vernetta Albertson. It's such a shame I came to your house and found your niece missing and you murdered. I'm sure they will assume it was done by some unknown intruder."

He looked at the note again and laughed. "Nobody is ever going to see this note, my dear Catherine. I intend to track you down. You shouldn't have called me repulsive. I won't let you get away with it. I still intend to make you my wife, whether you want to marry me or not. I'll be in control of you then, and you'll do whatever I demand in the future."

A voice sounded from the front of the house. "Vernetta, I was walking my dog and thought I heard screaming. Are you all right?"

Without waiting for the person to come inside, Weldon ran out of the office, through the kitchen and out the back door. He knew he had to get away before anyone saw him there.

He didn't stop to realize they not only had seen him fleeing, but they'd already recognized his carriage in the yard.

~ * ~

They had been on the train for a few hours when the porter announced they would be making a stop. He said the passengers would have about forty-five minutes to get off and walk around, find something to eat, or to simply relax.

Catherine looked at Annie. "I am a little hungry, but I don't want to get off the train and take a chance of not getting back on before it pulls out."

"You don't have to worry about being hungry, Miss Catherine. I packed a basket for our supper. We can either eat it in here or we can go out on the platform and find a bench to partake of the food."

"Wonderful, Annie. I only have one request. Please stop calling me Miss Catherine. You were my aunt's maid, not mine. I prefer you call me Catherine from now on."

Annie gave her a funny look. "Are you sure?"

"I'm positive." She stood. "It would be good to get out of this seat for a while. Let's see if we can find a bench close to the station. We don't want to miss the train."

Annie grabbed her basket and followed.

They did find a bench and Catherine was delighted with the food Annie had packed. Especially the lemon pie. Laughing, she said, "I can't believe you brought the pie Aunt Vernetta wanted you to serve at supper."

Annie grinned. "I didn't. I made four pies. Two for Miz Bruster, one to leave for Vernetta, and one for us."

"Wasn't that a lot of trouble?"

"Not really. I only stuck the roast in the oven, and I didn't bother to cook anything else. I decided if they ate tonight after discovering we were gone, pie would be all she'd have to serve."

Catherine laughed again. "And you called me devious. I think you can give me a race for the title, Annie Fillmore."

"Why don't we just agree we're two women who are smart enough to control our own lives and live it the way we want to."

"Sounds good to me." Catherine finished off her pie. "Now if you don't mind, tell me where you plan to go from here to start the new life you want to live."

Annie's face became serious, and she hesitated before muttering, "I don't know."

Catherine frowned. "What do you mean, you don't know?"

"All I had on my mind was getting away from Vernetta. I knew I'd find a place to settle down once I was out of her house."

"What about kin? Do you have people you can contact?"

"Not that I know of. As I said, I just knew I had to get away." She took a deep breath. "Besides, it may take you a while to find your sister in Texas, and I figured you needed somebody with you."

Catherine looked at her for a minute, then said, "You're right. Besides, it'll be nice to have someone with me and I'm sure when I find my sister, she'll welcome you, too." Catherine stood. "Let's get back on the train. I don't want to take a chance of missing it since we've got this far."

~ * ~

Since he'd had nothing but bad luck since leaving the fort, Chet Randell wondered again if he'd made a mistake by resigning from the army and heading West to claim the ranch his uncle had willed to him. When he first got the news, he'd thought it was the right thing to do because all the memories he had of visiting the place when he was a boy were fun and exciting. He even had good memories of when he'd lived there for a couple of years as a teenager.

But now, the whole idea of it being the place he wanted to spend the rest of his life began to fade in his mind. What if his uncle had let the ranch run down? What if the hands all quit? Could he manage to run the place on his own? Probably not, since the time he was there all he had to do was what he was told needing doing.

Besides those doubts, he'd had nothing but trouble on the trail. The old horse he'd been able to buy from the nearest town wasn't able to outrun the outlaws who jumped him outside of the same town. Not only did he have to fight the two men, but when one of them came at him with a knife, Chet had shot him. Explaining all of this to the town's sheriff hadn't been easy and he'd had to spend a night in jail until things were straightened out.

Then in another area, he'd stopped in for a meal in a saloon. The food wasn't bad, but he thought he was going to have to fight the little redhead who tried to lure him to her room. His instinct told him all she'd wanted was to get him drunk and take his money—the money he'd been sent from his uncle's estate and the money he'd saved while in the army. He did consider it lucky he'd never been a heavy drinker and was able to get away without trouble enough to land him in jail.

Now here he stood on the edge of the ravine with the ten-dollar horse who had managed to step the wrong way, land his right front foot in a gopher hole, and break his leg. Knowing the horse was suffering and wouldn't be able to go on, he knew what he had to do but he dreaded it.

Though he'd tried his best to hide it, Chet had always been tenderhearted. Especially where animals, children, and helpless women were concerned. So, after unsaddling the animal, he gave it some oats, let it drink water, then led it to a shaded area in the meadow they were crossing, and put it out of its misery. He was glad there was nobody around to see the mist gathered in his eyes.

After completing the deed, he wished he had a shovel to bury it, but he didn't. There was nothing he could do now except pick up his saddle, work his way to the road and hope a stagecoach or some good-hearted farmer would come by and give him a lift to the next town.

~ * ~

After changing trains several times, going first north, then south, but always inching closer west, Catherine and Annie learned they had come to the end of the track and had to get seats on a stagecoach for the rest of their journey. Though the trains hadn't been enjoyable rides with the smoke and the dust and the loud passengers, the stage was much worse. As it bounced, throwing them from side to side along the dusty road, Catherine glanced at Annie, who was seated beside her. "Reckon we'll get to the next stop in one piece?" she asked.

"Your guess is as good as mine," Annie said. "I wasn't sure we'd make it on the train, now here we are. I guess if others have lived through it, we will, too."

The only other passenger was a man who had introduced himself as Luther Pascale. He sat on the seat in front of them. Though he didn't look much over thirty-two or thirty-three, his brown hair was beginning to gray at the temples, and he wore a brown checked suit. With a slight grin, he asked, "Have you ladies ever ridden in a stagecoach?"

"This is our first time," Catherine said. "Have you ridden one before, Mr. Pascale?"

"Oh yes. Many times. I'm working on getting my own wagon, but until I do, I go from town to town peddling my wares because it's the best way to travel when you're in the West."

"What do you peddle?" Annie asked.

"I mostly sell to housewives. Things like scissors, needles, and other sewing needs. I also sell kitchen gadgets. A new can opener they've come up with has sold well lately." He grinned. "Would you ladies be interested in one?"

"Not at this time," Catherine said. "Maybe later."

"I'll keep it in mind." He frowned.

"Is something wrong?" she asked.

"No. I was just wondering why we were slowing down. As far as I know, we're not near the way station."

Before she could ask him what a way station was, the stagecoach came to a complete stop. There was some talking outside, then the door opened. "Got a new passenger for you," the driver said.

A tall dark-haired man threw his saddle on top of the coach. He stepped inside and took a seat beside Luther.

Catherine noticed he was dressed in black pants, a blue shirt, a black vest, and wearing a gun in a holster on his hip. He was the perfect picture of what she'd always thought a cowboy should look like.

"Howdy, folks," he said as he tipped his black hat toward the ladies.

Catherine wasn't sure how to react, so she simply nodded. So did Annie.

Luther introduced himself and stuck out his hand. "If you don't mind me asking, what were you doing out here in the middle of nowhere?"

"Don't mind at all telling you. I cut across the country instead of using the road, and my horse stumbled and broke his leg, and I had to put him down. Been walking along here hoping somebody would come along. Glad it was a stagecoach." He glanced again at the women. "My name's Chet Randell."

"Luther Pascale."

They both looked at the women, so she felt she had to say something. "Catherine Cardwell and this is my friend, Annie Fillmore."

"I'm pleased to meet all of you. But please don't think me rude if I go to sleep. I've been in the saddle for two days and I was looking for a campsite when I lost my horse. I may pass out at any time."

There was a little more conversation, then Chet Randell was as good as his word. He leaned back in the seat, pulled his hat over his face and in a few minutes, he was emitting a gentle snoring sound.

Soon, Luther was nodding, too.

Catherine looked at Annie and shook her head. She didn't understand how these men could sleep with the way the stage swerved, rocked, and often hit holes in the road and bounced. Maybe only somebody who was from the West could do it.

"I'm glad we've become friends, because it looks like it's just you and me entertaining each other now," Annie whispered, then giggled.

"Looks that way." Catherine giggled, too.

"It's kind of hard to believe the two of us have become such good friends so quickly."

"Why, Annie?"

"I figured when I joined you, you would treat me as your maid. Which, by the way, I wouldn't mind being for you. You've always been nice to me."

Catherine shook her head. "You might as well get the word maid out of your head. Even if I wanted to hire you as one, I couldn't. I don't have enough money. Besides, I prefer being friends."

Before Annie could reply, the stagecoach sped up and there was the sound of gunfire.

Luther rose up and pulled a gun from somewhere inside his coat.

Chet sat straight up, grabbed his gun and said, "You women get your heads down. Sounds like we're being attacked."

"Maybe we can hold them off." Luther sounded scared.

"If you ladies have a lot of money in your purses, you might want to put it inside your dress or cram it in your shoe or something," Chet said to them. "Just make it snappy. I'm sure the stage will stop in a minute."

Catherine didn't want to lose the money she had with her, so she grabbed her purse and took out the dollars she had in it. Seeing the men were busy looking out the windows, she pushed it down the neck of her dress because it was easier than putting it in her shoe. She saw Annie doing the same thing.

The shooting had let up and the stagecoach rolled to a stop.

Chet crouched at the door and whispered, "Try to stay calm and maybe we can get out of this alive."

The door jerked open, and Chet's gun went off. The man at the door flew backward from the impact as the bullet went into his shoulder.

"They done shot Ira," another man shouted. "I'm getting' out of here."

"Don't you dare ride off," a second voice said, but it was too late. The horse was galloping away.

For a minute, all was quiet, then the man yelled, "Come out of there with your hands up."

"Don't say anything," Chet whispered.

Shortly, a bullet slammed into the side of the coach.

Chet raised enough to put his gun out the window. He then fired back.

The next thing they heard was the horses running away.

In a few seconds, he said, "I think it's all over now."

"Oh, thank goodness," Catherine said. "I was so frightened."

"You did good." He opened the door. "I'm going to check on the driver."

In a minute he returned. "If you folks want to get out, it's safe now. They're gone."

"How is the driver?" Catherine asked.

"He was hit in the arm and lost his gun, but he'll be all right." He reached up his hand to help her out. Then he helped Annie.

Luther followed them. "You sure did a good job, but where's the man you shot?"

"I hit his shoulder. He rode off with his partner."

"We were sure lucky your horse died on you," Peters, the driver, said as he climbed down and joined them. "We couldn't have got rid of them the way you did."

"I'm glad I could help. I guess it was my army training."

"You're in the army?" Catherine asked.

"I was. Just got out a while back and learned I'd inherited a ranch in West Texas. Thought I'd try civilian life for a while."

"We're lucky he happened to be with us, aren't we, ladies?" Luther asked.

"We sure are," Annie said. "I definitely appreciate what you did."

He smiled and nodded at her.

"Well, folks," Peters said. "Maybe we should get on our way. We're only a few miles out of a town called Frederville. We were slated to stop there for the evening. I'll send a wire to the home office when we get in. They'll put us up for the night and send another stage tomorrow."

"It sounds fine to me," Catherine said. "I've had about all the excitement I can stand today. Besides, you're bleeding heavily, and you probably need to see a doctor."

"I agree with Miss Cardwell," Chet said. "In fact, I figure I'll ride up front and help you. I know how hard driving a stagecoach is and you could hurt your arm more if you try to do it."

He protested, but Chet won the argument.

Catherine couldn't help thinking Chet Randell probably won most of the arguments he entered into as she climbed back onto the stagecoach. She then wondered what the town of Frederville, Texas would be like.

~ * ~

The next morning, Catherine and Annie, who had shared a room in the small hotel, got dressed and headed to the café down the street. When they went in, they saw Chet sitting alone at a table near the side of the room. He waved to them.

As they walked up to him, he stood. "Would you ladies do me the honor of joining me?"

Annie nodded and smiled, and Catherine said, "Thank you, Mr. Randell. We'd love to."

He held chairs for them. Annie sat across the table and Catherine sat to his right. "Have you seen Grover this morning?" Annie asked.

"I did knock on his door and told him I was coming here for breakfast."

"You didn't want to eat at the saloon?" Annie asked.

He shook his head. "I didn't mind sleeping there because the hotel was full, but I didn't want to eat there."

"May I ask why?" Catherine asked.

"I happened to get a look at the kitchen and the cook, and decided I'd rather come here."

She smiled at him. "I assume it wasn't as clean as it should be."

He chuckled. "That's putting it mildly."

The waitress walked up with the coffee pot and two cups. "I assume you women want coffee." Her voice wasn't friendly.

Both nodded.

At the same time, Luther walked in. Chet waved to him, and he hurried across the room to take a chair at their table.

The waitress frowned. "Are there any more people coming to join you?"

"No. This is it," Chet said.

"Good." She walked off without taking their order.

"She's not very friendly, is she?" Annie muttered. "She looked strangely at Catherine and me when we sat down."

Luther laughed out loud. "It's not because she's unfriendly, Annie. At first, I'm sure she thought Chet was this handsome cowboy sitting here alone, and she was interested. Then two beautiful women joined him, and it made her angry because she knew he wasn't going to be flirting with her. Then when I came in, she's wondering why the four of us showed up at different times."

Catherine didn't say anything, though she did glance at Chet.

Chet didn't say anything about Luther's explanation. He only smiled and said, "I think I'll have ham and eggs with a side of potatoes this morning because I don't know when we'll get to eat again. What about you folks?"

They all ordered the same thing and as soon as breakfast was over, they each paid separately. This seemed to confuse the waitress even more. None of them took it on themselves to explain anything to her.

Outside, Chet said, "I see a mercantile down the street. Why don't you ladies go there, and I'll go check on the stage and Peters?"

"Maybe Mr. Peters will be able to take us further this morning," Luther said.

Chet shook his head. "I'm not sure he's going to be able to continue his route, so if they're not sending others to take over, I'll see if there is some other way we can continue our journey today."

~ * ~

Catherine had never been in a store like Mack's Emporium. She was fascinated by all the strange things which could be bought at one place. Not only were there clothes and dry goods, but there were tools and animal feed, as well as eggs, bacon, medicines, jars of candy, and even jewelry, among a variety of other things. The proprietor was friendly and didn't seem to mind as she and Annie kept looking around.

Catherine didn't want to spend much of her money, but she felt she should buy something. She ended up buying hairpins and a chocolate treat. She loved chocolate and she hadn't had any since the last chocolate cake Annie had served in Philadelphia.

Annie was conservative with her money, too. She bought a pack of needles and a spool of white thread. She said she needed them because she had a skirt needing repair.

It wasn't long until Chet returned without Luther. After buying a dozen cigars, he ushered them out of the store.

Outside, he said, "Luther is waiting at the livery stable for us."

Catherine frowned. "Why there?"

"He's there because you have two choices." She raised her eyebrow, and he went on. "You can catch the stage that'll leave later today or tomorrow because they're sending a driver to take over for Peters, or you can stay here in town until there's another one, which will be at least three or four days from now. Or we can get a buckboard to accommodate the four of us and our luggage and head for the next town where a different company has a regular stop."

Catherine glanced at Annie. "What do you think?"

"I'm not sure."

She turned to Chet. "What do you think we should do?"

He looked surprised she had asked the question, and he said, "It's up to you. That's why we're meeting at the livery. If you want to try the wagon, we'll get it and a team of horses. If you want to stay here, I'm going to get a horse and be on my way. Luther said he'd make up his mind about what he wants to do by the time we go back. I think, since he's been traveling with you, he feels a little responsible for you ladies and he's waiting to see what you decide to do before he makes up his mind."

At the same moment, another stage came down the main street and Annie grabbed Catherine's arm and whispered, "Did you see the man at the window?"

"I did." She looked up at Annie. "I think our minds are made for us, don't you?"

Annie nodded and Catherine said, "Let's go get the wagon. We'll pay our share."

~ * ~

Less than an hour later, the luggage had been brought from the hotel and was covered with the tarp Chet had bought to protect it and the basket of food Annie had collected. Now, the wagon was on its way to West Texas. Chet drove the team and Luther sat on the wagon seat beside him. Catherine and Annie were sitting in the wagon bed on a mattress Chet had bought for them to sit on during the day and to sleep on at night if they chose to continue in the wagon.

Annie looked at Catherine and said in a soft voice, "I think we made the right decision to come with them, don't you?"

"I know we did. Though we don't know them very well, both of them have already proved they're much nicer than Weldon Wheaton III."

"How in the world do you think he knew where we were? I was sure we got out of Philadelphia without anybody knowing."

"I thought so, too, Annie. But with a man like Weldon, you never know. He's as devious and as underhanded as Aunt Vernetta. People like them have their ways of finding out things."

"I know. But as you said, Chet and Luther are much better company than Weldon. I think if either of them had meant us harm or wanted to rob us, they would have had ample time to do so before now."

Catherine smiled. "I guess they realize we don't have enough money to fool with attempting to rob us."

Annie returned the smile. "I think Chet might be the only one with any money to speak of. Otherwise, he wouldn't have insisted on paying for this rig and everything else himself, even though we all offered to pay a share."

"He did say if he couldn't use it on his ranch, he'd sell it. Maybe he could sell it to Luther. He did say he wanted a wagon to use to peddle his wares."

"I don't know," Annie said. "I'm beginning to wonder if he's as interested in his selling job as he said. I've noticed he hasn't mentioned it lately."

Catherine smiled. "You've noticed a lot about Luther, my friend. Is there something special going on between you two?"

Annie blushed. "Of course not. I hardly know the man. Besides, what about you and Chet? I've noticed glances happening between the two of you since he joined us."

"Don't be ridiculous, Annie. The only thing I'm interested in is getting to my sister."

Annie sighed. "At least we managed to avoid Mr. Wheaton."

"And I'm thankful. I just hope he doesn't decide to follow us."

"But as you said, knowing him, he probably won't give up until he finds you."

"That's what has me worried."

It wasn't long before the conversation died down and Annie kept nodding. Soon she stretched out on the mattress and went to sleep.

Catherine busied herself looking at the bleak terrain and wondering why Annie had said what she did about her glances at Chet. She had been sure nobody had noticed the quick looks she had cast on the handsome cowboy. She knew now she was going to have to be more careful with her actions, because very little got by without Annie's noticing it.

~ * ~

Weldon Wheaton III stared at the man in the Western town. "What do you mean, she hasn't shown up for the next stage out of here?"

"Just what I said, mister. When the stagecoach came here after being attacked, we told the passengers they were guaranteed seats on the next one as soon as it and the new driver got here. Though none of them have shown up to catch it yet, it'll be leaving in a couple of hours."

"Have they been contacted to let them know the driver is here?"

"Of course. I personally sent word to the hotel and a man who stayed at the saloon came by here to check."

"I went to the hotel, and they said Miss Cardwell had checked out."

"Then, sir, I suggest you check the café and maybe the stores to see if you can find her. Otherwise, all you can do is wait here and see if she shows up before the stagecoach leaves today."

Without answering, Wheaton whirled around and stomped out of the office.

The station manager just shook his head and turned to his work.

Weldon was furious. After all of his searching, he was sure Catherine would head to her sister in Texas and he intended to find her and force her to marry him before she got there, if she wanted to save her pretty little neck.

Through his fury, he had to smile at how he'd been able to get away from Philadelphia. When he'd heard a neighbor coming to the door, he'd managed to scamper out the back. He knew he had to get out of town because it wouldn't be long until the law was after him. He didn't think the neighbor had seen him, but he was sure they'd seen his buggy, and they would tell them he was there. Of course, they'd say he was the one who killed Vernetta.

He had now had time to think of something to tell them if and when they caught him. He was sure they'd believe he'd walked in, found Catherine and the maid killing Vernetta, and they'd forced him at gunpoint to get them out of town. This was what he'd say if she refused to marry him. If she would agree to be his wife, he could tell them a stranger had forced their way in, killed the woman and kidnapped Catherine and the maid. All he had to do now was find his future bride and carry out one of those plans.

~ * ~

Sitting on the wagon seat, Chet glanced at Luther. "The women have quit whispering. Look back there and make sure they're all right."

Luther did look, then he chuckled. "Annie has laid down and gone to sleep. It looks like Miss Catherine is taking in the scenery."

"Good. They've acted kind of skittish ever since we left town."

"I noticed. But there ain't nothing we can do about it." Luther changed the subject. "Tell me about this ranch you've inherited from your uncle."

"It's been years since I've been there, so I don't know much about it. The lawyer said my uncle kept it in good shape. He also informed me there were two hands who agreed to stay and keep it running until I got there and decided what I wanted to do with it."

"Have you ever run a ranch?"

"I was in my teens when my folks died, and I lived with my uncle for a couple of years and learned a little about it. My brother was in the army, and I decided I'd join up. Found out about the inheritance and decided I'd had enough of army life." He guided the horses around a deep rut in the road.

"Is your brother still in the army?"

Chet shook his head. "He was killed last year on maneuvers."

"Sorry about that. Was he your only family?"

Chet nodded and changed the subject. "What about you, Luther? You always been in the sales game?"

"I lived on a farm in Kansas with my grandpa until he died. His son got the place and decided he didn't want a kid around, so he put me in an orphanage. After I got out, I knocked around a bit and tried different things until I met this drummer who had some interesting tales to tell. I decided then I was going to be a salesman so I could tour the country like he did." He chuckled. "To tell the truth. The job is not the fun I thought it'd be. There're times I don't have enough money to buy a meal and I've had to make do with anything I could find. Lately, I've thought about giving it up and seeing if there's not a job out there, I'd like better."

"Maybe if I decide to keep the ranch and try my hand at running the place, you'd be interested in working there."

Luther looked at him. "You have just given me something to think about. Working on a ranch couldn't be the worst job I've ever had."

~ * ~

Luther didn't say anymore, and Chet let his mind wander. If he did keep the ranch instead of selling it, and Luther would come to work for him, at least there'd be somebody on the place he knew. He'd like to have somebody there and from what little he'd learned about the man, he felt he could trust Luther.

After all, it was probably time he thought about putting down roots, as his mama used to say, and this ranch in West Texas might be just the place for him to do it. He might even consider getting married, since the lawyer had suggested he find a wife or somebody to do the cooking and cleaning since the woman who worked for his uncle had left. If he did marry, he might even think about having a couple of kids. He instantly thought of the pretty Catherine who was riding in the wagon bed behind him.

This thought made him chuckle. Why in the world would a woman like her want to marry him? He had left the army, though it was his idea to leave, not theirs. He'd never held a job for long and though he had a little money, he wasn't a rich man, and he could tell from the way she looked and acted, she was a lady of breeding who could have any man she wanted. She was not a woman looking for any husband she could find.

A huge deer leaped out of the woods and into the path of the wagon. The horses reared, and the wagon jerked. Catherine screamed and for a few seconds it felt as if the wagon would turn over. It didn't, though, but when it came to a stop, it was leaning to the side and a back wheel was twisted and looked as if it would fall off at any minute.

Both men jumped from the front bench and hurried to help the women out of the back where they'd been thrown to the side.

"Are you all right?" Chet asked.

"I think so," Catherine muttered.

Annie was crying. "I thought I was going to die."

"Not if I can help it," Luther said and reached for her.

As soon as they settled down, the men checked the lopsided wagon wheel. "Looks like we lost the linchpin," Luther said.

Chet nodded. "And there's no going on without one, is there?"

"Afraid not."

Luther returned to the women and explained the situation.

It wasn't long until Chet unhitched one of the horses and headed to the next town to find the items needed to fix the wheel. Luther guided the women down to the creek to wait for him.

~ * ~

As Chet entered the tiny town of Boo, Texas, he hoped it would have a blacksmith. Or at least a place where he could find a linchpin. He rode his horse down the main street and was surprised to see a small station near the end. He wondered if he should stop and find out if the women would be able to make a connection here for their destination. Without giving the idea too much thought, he stopped his horse at the hitching rail and dismounted.

He walked up to a counter and said to the station manager, "Had some trouble down the road a piece and I know you use linchpins. Would you happen to know where I might find one and the equipment to fix a wagon wheel?"

"I sure do."

A stagecoach pulled in and an obvious Easterner jumped out and hurried to the platform. Without a greeting, he said, "Has a pretty blonde and another woman been through here lately?"

The station man frowned. "Can't say as they have."

The man snorted. "They have to be somewhere. I know they were headed this way."

The driver got off the stage and walked up. "I'm Hagger. The company sent me with a new stagecoach to take over for Peters back in Frederville."

"Welcome, Hagger. What can I do to help you get on your way?"

"Make sure the passengers are ready to leave here in about five hours. I'm tired and need to eat and get a little rest."

"Sounds good," the station manager said.

The driver turned to the only passenger. "You heard what I said. If you want to keep going, be here in five hours." Without waiting for an answer, the driver walked off.

Interested at what had been said, but ignoring the passenger, Chet said, "Sorry to interrupt, but how about the linchpin?"

"Of course," the station man said. "There's a guy name of Wilson who does work for us. He's down the street in the general store. He has a sort of blacksmith shop in back of his place. He might even be willing to go out and help you if you didn't break down very far away."

"I had a run-in with a deer a couple of miles back and the wheel was damaged."

"I saw a wagon on the side of the road as I came by. The driver probably would have stopped to help but didn't see nobody around. He said he figured you'd come to town," the Easterner said.

"I was telling the man where he could get it fixed," the station man said.

"Is some broken down wagon more important than the woman I was asking about?"

"Why are you so interested in this woman? She your runaway wife or something?" Chet asked.

"Not that it's any of your business, but I intend to marry the woman just as soon as I catch up with her."

"Don't she want to marry you?" the man behind the counter asked.

"Doesn't matter whether she wants to or not, she's going to."

Chet raised an eyebrow, and asked, "Maybe she doesn't want to get married and decided to run away."

"When I catch her, she'll be sorry she left."

Chet said no more to him and turned to the station manager. "Thanks for the information." He then glanced at the man. "I wish you well with your woman. In the meantime, I need to get my wagon wheel fixed."

Before either could answer, he got on his horse and headed to the store the man had told him about. For some reason, he had a strange feeling the man looking for a woman was talking about Catherine, but he wasn't going to tell him he knew where she was. He wanted to talk to her first and find out what was going on. He felt she would tell the truth.

~ * ~

Since Mr. Wilson had gone with Chet to fix the wagon wheel, it didn't take long to get the job done. After paying and thanking him, and watching him leave, he turned to Catherine. "Do you mind if I have a few words with you alone before we head out?"

She looked surprised, but said, "Of course not."

"Why don't we take the canteens and get some fresh water from the creek," Annie suggested to Luther.

"Sounds like a good idea."

When they were alone, Chet said, "Something happened in town, and I need to ask you about it."

"What happened?"

"A man came up while I was at the stagecoach stop. He said he was looking for a blonde who he intended to marry. For some reason, I felt he was talking about you."

"Oh, no!" she cried as she covered her terror-stricken face with her hands. "How did he know where to find me?"

Confused, Chet said, "So you don't intend to marry him?"

"No! I can't stand the man."

"Then why...."

"It was something he and my aunt arranged. He bought me from her, but I managed to get away. You can't let him get me. Please."

"Calm down, Catherine. You're safe with me. Now, tell me what's going on."

"You won't make me go back to him, will you?"

"Not if you'll explain to me what's so terrifying about this man."

"I will, but I need to sit down first."

Chet led her to a downed log where she took a seat. He sat beside her. "Now, please tell me the reason you're afraid of this fellow."

~ * ~

Catherine knew telling Chet the entire story was her only chance to get away again, so she took a deep breath and began. She started with how her sister Melissa had managed to avoid marrying the man and how she had learned he had chosen her next to be his wife and why he needed one. She then explained how she'd found out he had paid her aunt ten thousand dollars for her hand. She told him how she'd managed to convince her aunt she'd go along with the marriage while all the time she was planning her escape from the coming nuptials. The only thing she couldn't tell him was how Weldon Wheaton III had found out she had run away and had followed her because she had no idea how he knew where she was.

When she finished her story, she looked up at him and whispered, "Will you help me get away from him?"

He nodded and smiled at her. "Yes, Catherine. I'll help you."

Without thinking it through, she threw her arms around his neck. "Oh, Chet. Thank you."

He folded his arms around her. "It'll be my pleasure, ma'am. I don't intend to see an innocent woman hitched to a man she doesn't want to marry."

"All I can say is, thank you. You're wonderful." It then dawned on her she had thrown her arms around his neck and his arms were around her. She pulled away, blushed, and muttered, "I'm sorry. I didn't mean to throw myself at you."

He laughed. "You can throw yourself at me anytime you want to because you felt good in my arms." He winked and let her go.

She blushed again, but didn't say anything and he added, "Now, let's tell Annie and Luther we're ready to leave. I want to get you away from here before he comes this way."

Catherine felt better after confessing to him, but she blushed again when he offered his hand to help her up. But it didn't stop her from taking it.

~ * ~

When the stage was ready to pull out, Weldon got on. He was the only passenger, so he sat back and pondered how he'd somehow missed Catherine. *How did she manage to get out of town? Or was she still here? No,* he discarded the thought. *She couldn't be. I looked everywhere and nobody knew anything about her whereabouts. Is it possible she was further ahead of me than I thought she would be? Is she already in the town near where her sister lives? Should I just relax until I get there?*

He then sat up straight with a jerk as the remembrance of the stranger he'd run into at the stage stop flitted across his mind. *He seemed to be interested in why I was asking about Catherine. Did he know her, and did he know I was after her before I told him? Did he know where she was, or could he have helped her to run away from me again?*

"No," he muttered. "She doesn't know I'm after her, so how could she get anybody to help her escape from me. Besides, he'd have no reason to help her, unless he was one of those stupid men who thought he was put on earth to help people."

Weldon quit muttering and thought, *Of course, the man could see how beautiful Catherine is and decided he wanted her himself.*

This idea infuriated him, and he cursed as his thought turned to *it doesn't matter what he wants, I'll catch up with them and when I do, she'll be sorry for going with him and he won't get the chance to be sorry. He'll be dead.*

~ * ~

The sun was going down when Chet said, "Folks, it's still several miles to the next town and it doesn't look like we'll be able to make it before nightfall. Besides, the horses are getting tired. What do you think about finding a spot to camp for the evening?"

Everyone seemed to be thinking over his suggestion, then Catherine muttered, "I've never camped out."

Everyone laughed, and Annie said, "I didn't think you would have, but you may find it's not so bad."

"Then what do you say?" Chet asked.

"It's up to the women," Luther said.

Chet nodded. "While you ladies are deciding, let's all look for a good place to stop. I suggest we get off the road in case the stage left town early. If the man Catherine is afraid of is on it, I don't want him to see us."

This was enough to make Catherine agree to her first camping trip.

Thirty minutes later, Luther pointed out a cropping of trees surrounded by wild bushes. "Think it would do?"

Pulling the horses to a stop, Chet said, "Stay here with the women and I'll walk in there and see if it would be good enough."

He wasn't gone long, and when he returned, he said, "Looks like Luther found a good place. I can pull the wagon in there behind some trees, and it can't be seen from the road. There's a creek below the hill where we can water and feed the horses. There are also some grassy spots where they can graze."

"Where will we sleep?" Annie asked.

"You and Catherine will sleep in the wagon. There are some soft looking spots on the ground, and Luther and I will sleep there.

I have a couple of blankets in my bedroll. You ladies can have one."

"Sounds good to me," Luther said. "I've slept on the ground before and at times, I didn't even have a blanket."

After they pulled to the spot, they set up their camp, and broke out the basket of food Annie had bought. They then gathered around a downed log to enjoy the bread and cheese.

Looking at Catherine and realizing a lady like her was certainly being gracious about roughing it like the others, Chet wished he could make her more comfortable. He blurted, "I'm sorry we can't have a fire, ladies, but I don't think it's wise to announce our presence here."

"I don't mind," Catherine muttered. "It's a pleasant evening."

After they finished their cheese and bread, Annie took out a can of peaches for dessert.

"Oh, my," Luther said. "You're a woman who has done stole my heart. I love peaches."

"I figured you'd like them, but I never dreamed it was a way to attract your heart." She giggled, glanced at Catherine, and said, "I bought two cans in case you want to steal some man's heart."

Catherine simply blushed and began gathering up the remains of the food they'd had. She had no idea Chet was thinking *she doesn't need peaches. I think she already has my heart and the last thing I need in my life at this time is some woman. Especially a proper woman like her.*

As they ate peaches, everyone relaxed and chatted about different things, Chet announced he wanted to get an early start in the morning. "It's about twenty-five miles from here and I'd like to get into Bell Haven before dark."

An excited Catherine jumped up and stared at him. "Did you say Bell Haven?"

"Yes. My ranch is near there."

"I'm headed there, too. It's the town my sister, Melissa, lives near."

Chet grinned. "Then I won't have to put you out so I can go to my new home. I'll even help you find your sister's place."

Catherine turned to him. "I'm so excited. I could hug your neck for getting me to her."

"A man can't refuse an offer like that," Chet said with a grin and wondered why he couldn't keep his mouth shut. He didn't need her hugging him again.

Luther stood and reached his hand to Annie. "I have something I want to talk to you about, so let's go for a walk before those two do something to embarrass us."

Annie laughed and took his hand. "Maybe we better go."

Chet and Catherine ignored them as she threw her arms around his neck. "Thank you again, you wonderful man. I can't believe your ranch is near the same town as Melissa and Joe's. This means I'll get to see you again."

He felt warm inside and knew he had to do something to defuse the situation. "It'll be good if the spreads are close enough to each other."

"They should be. Melissa said she lived near Bell Haven, and you said your ranch was near there. They'd have to be close together, wouldn't they?"

"Not necessarily. One could be north or east of town for several miles and the other for several miles south or west or whatever. Either way, both would depend on Bell Haven for supplies and other things which can only be bought in town."

She frowned. "Does that mean I won't see you?"

"Now, don't worry. I'll make sure we won't lose touch with each other. I've kind of got used to you being around."

She nodded. "At least those words tell me you like me a little bit."

He chuckled and winked at her. "Yes, Catherine. I like you a little bit."

"That's good to know."

Before he could pull her into his arms and tell her how he really felt about her, he said, "Now, let's get things ready to settle in for the night. I want to get an early start in the morning."

~ * ~

Later, as they lay on the mattress in the bed of the wagon, Annie said, "There's a couple of things I want to tell you, Catherine."

"Sure. What are they?"

"Before we ran away, I opened Miz Vernetta's safe and took a couple of things."

"What did you take?"

"She owed me fifty dollars, so I took it. I also took the papers she had been using to blackmail me into working for her."

"Did you take anything else?"

"No. I was tempted to take what money was left there, but I didn't. Do you think I did wrong for getting my things?"

"I don't see why it would be wrong, since the money was yours and whatever was in those papers is something nobody needs to know,"

"I kind of want to tell you what they said."

"You don't have to, Annie."

"I know, but it would be a load off my mind if somebody besides me knew. I trust you."

"Then, I promise not to tell anyone."

Annie bit her lip. "I saw her mix the poison she used to kill her husband. Unfortunately for me, she saw me watching and gave me a sinister smile. She took me in her office and made me sign a paper saying I was the one who killed him."

"Why in the world did you sign it?"

"I had to, Catherine. She had the poison concoction in her hand and said she'd pour it down my throat if I didn't sign it. After I put my name on it, she put it in the safe and every so often, she'd remind me it was there."

"Oh, Annie. You need to destroy the paper."

"I'm going to, but I want to show it to Luther first."

"Why are you going to show it to him?"

"That's the other thing I wanted to tell you. Luther asked me to marry him, and I said yes."

"Oh, Annie. Are you sure you want to marry him?"

"I'm positive."

"But he'll be traveling to sell his wares and you'll end up alone while he's gone."

Annie giggled. "He's going to quit peddling. Chet offered him a job on his ranch and he's going to take it. He wants us to marry and live there."

"What if Chet's ranch turns out to be a terrible place? What if Luther changes his mind? What if ...?"

"There are always what ifs in life, Catherine, and sometimes you have to take a chance to get what you want. What if you hadn't left your aunt? You would still be there and maybe getting ready to marry a terrible man. But look what's happened since you took a chance and left. Sometime tomorrow, you'll be in the town your sister lives near. If you hadn't taken a chance and run away, it would never have happened."

"I guess you're right."

"I know I am. Leaving worked for me, too. I've never wanted anything more than to meet a good man, fall in love with him, get married and have my own home. Luther is the answer to my dream."

"You're right, Annie, and I'm happy for you. And if you want to tell Luther about the blackmail, I'm sure he'll understand."

"Thank you, my friend. You'll find the same happiness someday. I'm sure of it."

"When do you plan to get married?"

"We figured there'd be a preacher in Bell Haven. I told Luther I wanted you to be there, so I thought we'd marry before you go looking for your sister."

"I'm glad you want me there." She reached out and squeezed her friend's hand. "I've been this long waiting to see Melissa again, I can sure take time to see my friend get married."

"Thank you, Catherine. You may not realize this, but you're the only friend I have."

Before the words could sink in, the sound of rushing horses filled the air.

"Oh, no. It must be the stagecoach. I pray they don't see us," Catherine whispered.

"Don't worry. They won't," Chet said beside the wagon.

This startled Catherine, but she didn't answer him.

In a matter of minutes, the sound of the passing stagecoach began to fade in the distance, and she took a deep breath.

"Relax and go to sleep now, girls," he said, and moved away before she could answer.

It took Catherine a while to go to sleep. She couldn't get over the fact Chet had stood by the wagon to protect them, and she hadn't even known he was there. It began to dawn on her more and more what a special man he was. The kind she'd wanted to have in her life someday.

~ * ~

When they pulled into Bell Haven the next day, Catherine wasn't surprised to see it was a small town, but not as tiny as many they had seen on the way from Philadelphia. Since Annie said she and Luther wanted to get married before they went on to Chet's ranch, she asked him to let them check into a room at the small but inviting hotel so they could get baths and dress.

"I thought you'd want to find your sister right away," Chet said.

"I've taken all this time to get to Melissa, so a little more time won't matter. Annie wants me to attend her wedding and I wouldn't think of not going."

He smiled at her and for some reason she thought this had pleased him. But she didn't dwell on it. "Then, I'll go see if I can't get things finished with the lawyer they told me to contact when I got to town. Afterward, I'll make sure to get the groom ready for his wedding."

"It sounds like a good plan to me."

He laughed. "Besides, I'm a little hungry. How about we get something to eat before we do anything else?"

They all concurred, so they had a quick meal, then she and Annie checked into the Bell Haven Hotel and were shown to a neat room with starched curtains and a matching spread. She realized this would be a nice room for Luther and Annie to share while Chet took her to find Melissa. Putting her valise on the chair at the window she asked, "What do you plan to wear to get married in, my friend?"

"I only have one other clean dress. It's nothing special but it'll have to do." She pulled out a green checked dress made like the blue checked one she was wearing.

Catherine shook her head. "No, Annie. You have to have something special for today."

"But I don't have anything else, and I can't afford to buy anything fancy."

"I understand." Catherine opened her valise and took out two dresses. One was yellow and the other, pink. "Which one do you like best."

"I can't take your dress, Catherine."

"Why not? I don't have any other wedding present to give you, and it would be an honor if you'd take one of these dresses as my gift to you."

Tears came into Annie's eyes. "I can't believe you'd want to give one of your beautiful dresses to a person like me."

"What do you mean, a person like you? You're one of the most special people I know. Besides, other than my sisters, you're my very best friend."

After a few more tears, and a few hugs, Annie said, "If you're serious, I've always wanted a pink dress but have never had one."

"Great. Pink will look wonderful on you with your dark hair. Now, let's shake out the wrinkles and see about getting our baths. You know the men went to the bathhouse to clean up and get ready. We don't need to keep them waiting, so let's get ready for this wedding."

"You're right." Annie reached for the pink dress and shook it vigorously.

As she shook the yellow one, Catherine was pleased her friend had chosen the pink because the yellow had always been her favorite.

~ * ~

When he and Luther collected the women, Chet couldn't believe how beautiful Catherine was in her pretty yellow dress. To him, she looked more like a bride than Annie, but he didn't voice this. He simply grinned at her and helped her into the wagon to sit on the mattress beside her friend. He then joined a nervous Luther on the wagon seat. "You look jumpy, my friend. Not about to change your mind about this, are you?"

"Not on your life. I can't wait to marry Annie." He looked over at Chet. "Did you get everything settled about the ranch?"

"Sure did. It only took me signing some papers."

"Now, what about you? You should think about marrying so you'll have a helper on this ranch of yours."

"Where in the world am I going to find somebody to marry in a strange town where I don't know anybody?"

"Don't be stupid, Chet. There's a pretty woman sitting right behind you who is all decked out like a bride and from what I can tell, she wouldn't mind being the bride for you."

Before Chet could answer, he saw a man step out of the tobacco shop on the left side of the street. Recognizing him as the man at the stagecoach stop before, he said quickly, "Duck your head, Catherine. I see Wheaton."

"Oh no!" she whispered as she dropped her head to her knees. Annie did the same.

The wagon kept moving and nobody said anything for a few minutes, then Chet spoke. "You can get up now. He only glanced at us, so I'm sure he didn't see you."

"Oh, Chet. Thank you, again."

"Don't worry. Let's get these two married, then I'll get you to your sister and they can protect you from him."

"All I ever say to you is, thank you."

On the edge of town, they pulled into the yard of a white clapboard house beside a small white church.

Luther helped Annie out of the wagon first, and they headed toward the front door, but waited on the porch for their friends.

Chet took Catherine 's hand, and he didn't know where the courage came from, but he said, "You know, if you were married, you'd be safe, and you'd never have to hide from Wheaton again and there wouldn't be a thing he could do about it."

"True, but who in the world could I marry?"

His courage almost failed him, but he pushed it back and whispered, "Me."

Catherine stopped and stared at him. "Are you serious?"

"Dead serious. Would you consider marrying me?"

There was a long pause, then she whispered, "You better be serious, Chet Randell, because my answer is, yes, I'll marry you."

Stunned, and almost not believing he'd heard her correctly, he took her hand, and they went up the steps to the porch. Before anything was said, the front door opened and the man said, "Hello there, folks."

"We've come to get married if the preacher will do us the honor," Luther explained.

"Well, what a happy day," the tall man with gray hair said. "Come on in and I'll be glad to perform the ceremony."

"Thank you," Luther grinned and took Annie's hand.

The preacher called, "Mildred, get your Mama, and come in here. You don't want to miss this. It's the first time in all my years

I've been asked to perform a double wedding, and I get to do it before we leave town."

Luther started to correct the preacher, but a grinning Chet interrupted him. "Don't argue with the man, Luther. Catherine said yes."

Four

Bernadette

Hiding in the attic, where she often took refuge when Henry Goddard, her aunt's present husband, was in one of his drunken states, Bernadette Cardwell was finally able to take the crumpled letter from her chemise to read in the dimming light. She had intended to read it when it first arrived but as soon as the postman left the porch, her aunt Elsa started screaming. At the time, all she could do was cram the letter in her chemise and hurry to the room where the invalid was confined.

"What's going on, Ginny?" she asked the day maid.

"When I came in, she started yelling about getting up to cook supper. When I tried to calm her down, she started fighting me. Maybe you can do something."

"I'll see if I can." Bernadette turned to the shriveling woman in the bed. "Now, Aunt Elsa, calm down and let's decide what you want to cook tonight."

It took a while, but they finally got her settled, gave her some medicine, which made her doze off. They then left the room. On the way out, Ginny said, "I don't know how much more I can take of her strange actions, Miss Bernadette. She's wearing me out."

"Oh, Ginny. Please don't quit on me. You know the cook walked out a couple of weeks ago and Henry hasn't found another one, though he tells me he's looking. I know it's hard for us to have to prepare what we eat, and to take care of Aunt Elsa with no help from Henry. But I could never do it without you."

"Don't worry. I'll hang in here for a while longer." Ginny changed the subject. "Weren't you supposed to meet your friend, Julia, for tea this afternoon?"

"I was, but maybe I should stay here. I can send her a note and apologize."

"You'll do no such thing. Go put on a pretty dress, sweep up your hair where a few strands have come loose, grab your bonnet, and go meet your friend. Your aunt is not going to wake up for hours."

"Are you sure you don't mind if I leave?"

"I don't mind at all."

Bernadette did as Ginny suggested. She met Julia at the tearoom on one of Atlanta's quiet streets. It was a lovely outing and she needed it, but when Julia stopped gushing about her new husband, Willard, and started bragging about her visiting brother, Drake, it made Bernadette wish she'd been able to read the letter from her sister, then maybe she'd have somebody to brag about, too. But she hadn't read it, though she knew she'd do it as soon as she got home.

But it didn't happen.

Ginny left shortly after Bernadette arrived at the house, then Henry came home. Bernadette knew right away he was drunker than usual. She only hoped this time he wouldn't act and talk to her the way he'd been doing lately.

Yes, he had a hard life being married to a woman confined to a bed and who didn't know who she was half the time. But he wasn't the only person in the world who had a hard time. It didn't give him a reason to whine about it and say things she could only hope he didn't mean. Things such as, "Oh, Bernadette, how I wish I was married to a woman like you," or "Don't be so shy when I try to hug you, sweet Bernadette. A man needs to be close to a woman now and then," or what he said tonight which scared her, "I can't wait for the old bitch to die. Maybe we should go ahead and kill her, then I can tell you how I much I want you."

He had then grabbed her and tried to kiss her on the lips.

Bernadette became not only scared but infuriated. She might not have been able to get away if he hadn't been so drunk. As it was, she managed to push him off her and he stumbled against a table and fell. She didn't stop to see if he was all right. She fled the parlor and left him on the floor.

Now here she sat in the corner of the attic where she knew she'd stay until sometime later tonight. If all stayed quiet downstairs, after a while she'd slip into Elsa's room to make sure the woman was sleeping. That way, she wouldn't have to see Henry again tonight and she wouldn't venture down from her room until she was sure he was out of the house in the morning.

Sighing, she put her hand on her chest and felt the letter in her chemise. A smile crept across her lips as she took it out and whispered, "It's now time to see what you have to tell me, Catherine," she muttered and ripped open the missive. "I only hope it's good news."

~ * ~

Carl and Martha Rafferty sat in the sunroom of their house in one of the better sections of Atlanta with their visiting son, Drake. They were waiting for their daughter and her husband and their other son and his wife to show up for the family supper to welcome

Drake, who lived in Texas and worked as a ranger, home for a visit.

Carl glanced at his wife then looked across the wicker tea table at his son. "Drake, it has been almost two years since you've been home, and you don't know how much this visit means to us. But I don't understand why you feel you have to leave on Saturday. You'll only have a week here."

"I'm glad to have this much time to spend with you and Mom, Dad. I only hope I'll be able to come more often in the future. Since I had a lull in my cases, I grabbed the chance to visit this time. But spring is here, which means I'll probably be pretty busy for a while. Bad guys seem to act up more when the weather is nice."

"I wish you'd give up chasing outlaws and decide to come back to Atlanta. You could find yourself a good wife and settle down close to your father and me like your brother and sister have done." His mother sat back in the high-backed chair and sipped her tea. "I'd love to have you live close to us and not in the wilds of Texas."

"Martha's right, son. Julia is happy with Willard Bingham, her lawyer husband. Michael, and his wife, Diana, are thrilled with their new baby. If you would consider moving back home, I'm sure your brother would be happy for you to help run the family business. It keeps growing and it keeps him busy. I even go in and help him sometimes."

Drake took a breath and drank his coffee. It wasn't the first time his parents had put pressure on him to give up his job as a Texas Ranger and move back to his hometown. He didn't want to hurt their feelings, but he liked his job and the freedom and independence it gave him to live his life the way he wanted to live it. He could never see himself living in a city like Atlanta again. He loved the openness of Texas. He forced a grin and said, "Now, you both know I've got too much cowboy in me to come back to this city to live. I'd be an embarrassment to you and your society friends."

"I don't believe that for a minute," Carl said.

"Neither do I, son. You know you would never embarrass us," his mother said. "Why, in no time, I'm sure you'd fit right back in with your old way of life and our friends. All of them like you and ask about you often."

"Your mother's right. I learned the other day, there's a house only a couple of blocks over which I know could be bought cheaply. It's the perfect place for you to move right in and start a family of your own. You could raise your children with your siblings and their spouses, and you could be here for all our family gatherings."

"And Letica James often mentions you. I'm sure she'd make you a wonderful wife."

He almost told his mother Letica James was the last woman he'd ever marry because, not only he but most of his friends had already tasted her favors. But before he could say anything, there was a noise in the hallway and his sister-in-law came into the sunroom with a whimpering baby in her arms. "Hello, everyone. I'm sorry to burst in on you like this, but Michael had some business to take care of before we could leave the house."

"Where is Michael? He didn't just let you and the baby out of the carriage and drive away, did he?" Carl asked.

"Oh, no. He's putting the carriage in the back. Bobby was getting fussy, and I wanted to get inside as quickly as possible. He let me out so I could feed him and get him settled down."

Martha stood. "Julia and her husband haven't arrived yet, so come with me, Diana dear. We'll go into my sewing room where you can have privacy to feed little Bobby."

"Thank you, Mother Martha."

Drake had to smother a laugh. He couldn't help thinking how strange it would sound if his mother's name was Mary and Diana insisted on calling her Mother Mary. He didn't voice this, though.

He knew the rest of the family didn't have the warped sense of humor he did.

It wasn't long before Michael came into the sunroom and joined the men. "Have a seat, son. Your wife is feeding the baby and Julia and Willard haven't arrived yet. It means you're in time to help me convince your brother to give up his life in Texas and move back to Atlanta where he belongs. I was telling him he should get married and join the rest of the family here. I even told him I was sure you wouldn't mind him working with you in the family business, so he wouldn't have to try to find a job."

"Of course I wouldn't," Michael muttered. "Are you considering moving home, Drake?"

Drake could tell by his older brother's eyes he had no intention of welcoming him into the family firm. He saw his brother relax when he said, "Not at all, Michael. This is all Dad's idea. I'm perfectly happy being a Texas Ranger and I have no intention of giving it up."

In a matter of minutes, the maid brought coffee for Michael and refilled the other men's cups. When she left, they fell into general conversation, but it wasn't long before Drake was wondering why he'd said he'd stay in town until the next Saturday. Though he loved his family, he didn't know if he wanted to spend a week with them and listen to their continual pressuring him to move back home. Though he felt a little guilty for wanting to get away, he couldn't help it. He was already anxious to head back to the wide-open spaces of Texas.

~ * ~

Still hiding in the attic, Bernadette unfolded her letter from Catherine and began to read.

My dearest sister, I didn't believe in coincidence until recently, but after the things that have happened to me, I can't say I don't believe any longer. You'll understand when you read further in this letter.

Since I wrote and asked you not to get in touch with me until you heard from me again, I'm not sure if you know anything about Aunt Vernetta's death. The authorities may have contacted you, but if not, don't be shocked when I tell you what happened. After living with the woman, I realized she wasn't the upstanding citizen she claimed to be. Melissa will back me up on this. Going behind our backs, our aunt had sold first Melissa, then me, to the unscrupulous Weldon Wheaton III for ten thousand dollars down with more to come after the nuptials. Not because of her desire to see either of her nieces in a happy marriage, but because of her greed and the need for money to maintain the lifestyle she lived and wanted to continue. Anyway, when her maid, Annie, and I ran away, I was afraid she'd turn to you next, and try to get you to marry him, since he seemed determined to marry one of the Cardwell sisters. That's why I didn't want you to get in touch with me. Suffice it to say, we don't have to worry about it since she is gone. This may sound harsh, but after the things she did to Melissa and me, I can't feel sorrow about her passing.

The main thing I want to tell you is I met a wonderful man on my way to Texas to join Melissa. His name is Chet Randell. We had a quick and unusual courtship and I'm now his wife. As Rosemary used to say when she'd get a piece of candy or anything she considered special, I'm deliriously happy.

The first coincidence I'll mention is Chet had inherited a ranch near the town of Bell Haven. Before I elaborate, let me back up a little bit. As soon as we arrived, we were married in Bell Haven. It was a double wedding. Aunt Vernetta's maid, Annie, had escaped with me and she met a man she fell in love with. She was the other bride.

Chet and I spent our first night together at the Bell Haven Hotel. The next morning, we had no more than gotten down to the lobby to have breakfast when we came face to face with Weldon Wheaton III. He started yelling for me to get away from

Chet because I was his woman, and we were going to get married.

When Chet told him I was his wife, Weldon went crazy. He rushed up and grabbed me and said it couldn't be true. He'd paid ten thousand dollars for me, and I belonged to him.

In an instant, Chet grabbed the man and things started getting knocked down and breaking. It just so happened the sheriff was in the hotel dining room, and he came running out. As Weldon was about to stab Chet with a knife he produced from somewhere, the sheriff saw it and shot the man.

After we told him what had happened, he asked us to stay in town until he sent a wire to Philadelphia. Later in the afternoon, he came to tell us about Aunt Vernetta's death. He found out Weldon Wheaton had killed her then left town to follow me to Texas. I'm sure you'll be informed of all this soon if you haven't been told already.

Now for the good news. The same afternoon, but before going to the ranch Chet had inherited, he took me to see our sister. When we visited Melissa and her husband, we found out Chet happens to own the ranch adjoining theirs. See what I mean about coincidence!

Being able to connect with Melissa again was fantastic. She and Joe are happy, as are the children who look to them as their parents. Ruth Ann's mother-in-law is a dear lady, and she seems to love them all and considers them her family. The children were calling me Aunt Catherine before we left. I think they make a wonderful family and though she didn't tell me anything, I suspect Melissa is going to make us aunts again before cold weather arrives. It's so nice to know she and I will get to see each other often and we will go to the same church as soon as the town is able to find a preacher. The one who married us had to leave town because of a family problem. The town leaders have sent out a call for a replacement.

Remember Melissa saying she believed we'd all be living close together again someday? I don't think she was wrong, and I don't think it's a coincidence she said it. I have a feeling it's in God's plan for all of the Cardwell sisters to be close together again.

As she said in her letter, this one from me can serve as our Sister Circle until we're all together and can form our circle in person.

Please write when you can.

Love for ever, Catherine.

Bernadette sat back in almost disbelief, though she knew it was true. The aunt she only knew by name was dead and two of her sisters were married and now lived close together the way Melissa had predicted they all would someday. Maybe Catherine was right. Maybe they all would be near each other again.

"Oh, dear God," she muttered. "As we all prayed on the day of our parents' funeral, please let her prediction come true. I'd love nothing more than to live near my sisters again."

She then tucked the letter away, knowing she'd read it many times just as she had the one Melissa sent. She then stood. It was time to check on Elsa and to make sure Henry was settled and wouldn't bother her anymore this evening. Just in case, she picked up one of the extra fireplace irons stored in the attic to defend herself if necessary.

As she had hoped, she found Henry passed out on the sofa and Elsa seemed to be sleeping well. Knowing she was safe for one more night, she went to her room, locked her door, and pushed a straight-backed chair under the knob for extra protection. She then undressed and went to bed.

~ * ~

The next morning, as she always did, Bernadette stopped by Elsa's room to check on her. At first, she thought her aunt was sleeping peacefully, but on a closer look, she realized something was wrong. She hurried closer. Elsa looked pale, and she wasn't breathing.

Shaking her aunt, she cried, "Oh, no! Aunt Elsa, wake up."

There was no response and she yelled, "Henry, come here!"

Henry didn't come but Ginny did. "I heard you calling as I was coming in the back door, Miss Bernadette. What's going on?"

"It's Aunt Elsa. I can't get her to wake up."

Ginny hurried to the bed and after looking down at the woman, she grabbed Bernadette's arm. "I think she's dead."

"Oh, no! She can't be. She was fine when I went to bed." Bernadette began to cry.

Ginny put her arm around her shoulders. "Where's Mr. Henry?"

About that time, a sleepy, stumbly Henry came into the room. "What has happened to cause you to make all this noise?"

"I'll get Miss Bernadette out of here. You need to go get the doctor, Mr. Henry."

"Is Elsa worse this morning?"

"I think she's dead. We need the doctor."

"I need some coffee."

"I'm sorry, sir. We'll worry about coffee later. This has to be taken care of right now."

Through all this, Bernadette hadn't spoken. She wanted to but no words came. She was still in shock as Ginny led her from the bedroom. For some reason, she thought she saw Henry smiling as he quit arguing with Ginny and went out the door.

Surely not she thought. *Not with his wife dead or dying. Even he isn't callous enough to be happy about her death.*

It wasn't long until the doctor arrived and pronounced Elsa dead. In another short time, the undertaker came and took her body away. It seemed almost immediately the house filled with neighbors and friends.

~ * ~

When Bernadette's friend, Julie, and her parents showed up, they spent some time talking with her, then Mr. and Mrs. Rafferty struck up a conversation with a neighbor they knew. At this time, Bernadette was able to get Julia to the side for a somewhat private conversation.

The first thing Julia said was, "You're awfully nervous, Bernadette. I know you cared for your aunt, but since you knew she was dying, I didn't expect you to be so upset and scattered."

"Of course, I'll miss Aunt Elsa, and you're right. I knew her death was going to happen. It was still hard to accept when it occurred, but that's not what has me so upset."

"Then what is it?"

"I'm scared, Julia, and I don't know what I'm going to do."

"What are you afraid of?"

"I feel like I have to get out of this house."

Julia frowned. "Why?"

"I just am and if I can work up the courage to make the trip alone, I'm going to head to Texas after the funeral."

"Texas! Why would you want to go there?"

"I haven't had a chance to tell you, but I received a letter from Catherine yesterday. She went to Texas to visit Melissa. On the way she met a man, fell in love, and got married. And believe it or not, she now lives on his ranch which connects to Melissa's husband's place. If I can get there, I'd be close to two of my sisters and I'd love it."

"Oh, Bernadette. I'd miss you terribly if you went so far away from Atlanta."

"I'd miss you, too. But you know I can't stay in this house alone with Henry."

Julie frowned. "Don't you think he'll need you to help him through his grief?"

"I don't think he'll be grieving as much as you think he is."

"What do you mean?"

Bernadette looked around to make sure nobody could hear her. "I think he's glad Aunt Elsa is dead, Julia."

"Oh, Bernadette. Surely not."

"If you could see how he's been acting, you'd think the same thing. Not only that, but I'm also afraid to be here alone with him."

Julie stared at her friend. "Why?"

"He's made some remarks to me which have made me uncomfortable." She grabbed her friend's hand. "But please don't tell anyone I told you this. I could have misunderstood."

"You know I won't tell anyone. But you need to tell me what he has said to you."

Before Bernadette could answer, Martha Rafferty walked up. "I'm sorry to interrupt your conversation, but your father says we need to go, Julia. He has some kind of business to take care of with Michael. But of course, we'll come back tomorrow, Bernadette."

"I appreciate you coming, Mrs. Rafferty," Bernadette said. "Friends are such a comfort at a time like this."

"Yes, they are, and, as I said, Julia and I will be back tomorrow to support you. Of course, you know you're welcome to come stay with us if you need to get away for a while."

"I know, and I appreciate it. But I think I need to stay here. This morning, a relative of Aunt Elsa's first husband came in from Union City, along with her daughter. I think she said her last name was Jetter and they plan to stay until after the funeral."

"I don't remember the name, but I do remember Roger Blackburn. He was Elsa's first husband. He was a good man. I don't know Henry very well." Martha smiled at her and added, "I'm glad you'll have someone here with you besides him, Bernadette. What little I've seen of him today tells me he doesn't seem to understand everything that's going on."

"I'm sure he'll be fine in time," Bernadette muttered, though she didn't believe it.

"Then, we should go, Julia," her mother said.

"Yes, Mother." As she stood, Julie whispered to Bernadette, "We'll talk tomorrow."

Bernadette nodded, hugged her, then walked them to the door. As she turned back into the room, she headed to speak to a neighbor who had just arrived. On the way, she had to walk by Henry, who was chatting to some man she didn't know. If she didn't think it was impossible for him to do so at a time like this, she would have sworn he winked at her as she passed by him.

~ * ~

Martha Rafferty insisted Julia and her husband have supper at their house since they'd cooked plenty to not only take to Bernadette in the morning, but for themselves as well. Julia accepted the invitation.

Drake wasn't surprised when Julia took his arm and suggested they go to the sunporch and have a brother and sister talk while their mother busied herself in the other part of the house and they waited for their father and Willard to arrive.

After taking seats in the comfortable wicker furniture, he said, "Well, little sister, it'll be nice to have a chat with you as long as you're not trying to convince me to give up my life as a cowboy and move back to Atlanta."

She laughed. "I would like to see my big brother more often, but I have sense enough not to try to talk him into something I know he'll never do."

"Too bad others in the family don't see things the way you do."

"They'll eventually give up trying to persuade you to change the life I know you love." Her face grew serious. "I do have something I want to talk to you about, and since we're alone this looks like a good time."

"What is it?"

"Since you live in Texas now, have you ever heard of a town called Bell Haven?"

His eyebrow shot up. "How in the world did you hear about Bell Haven?"

"My friend, Bernadette's sister, lives there and she told me about it."

"I see. What do you want to know about the little town?"

"Nothing, I guess."

"You're confusing me, Julia."

"I'm sorry. I'm only worried about my friend and I don't know how to help her."

Still wondering where this conversation was going, Drake said, "Then why don't you explain to me what's going on and maybe I can help."

She sighed. "I hope I'm not breaking a promise about not revealing what she told me in confidence, but I feel I have to tell somebody. I think Bernadette is afraid of her aunt's husband, Henry. She told me today when he's been drinking he has said some inappropriate things to her and made her feel uncomfortable. She acted as if she was afraid to be alone with him since her aunt has died."

"Did she tell you what he had said?"

"No. She said we'd talk later." She shook her head. "If it hadn't been serious, she never would have mentioned it to me."

"Will you see her again soon?"

"Oh, yes. Mother and I will go back tomorrow and take food, then the funeral is arranged for Saturday morning. I'll see her then, too."

An idea came to Drake. "Tell you what. Since your husband and Dad will probably be busy, I'll take you and Mom over tomorrow and meet this friend of yours. I'm pretty good at understanding people and I might be able to help her out."

"Oh, Drake. How wonderful."

"You might want to think about inviting her to stay here until after the funeral."

"Mother invited her today, but she said some relatives of Elsa's first husband showed up and plan to stay there until after the burial. She felt obligated to stay with them."

"I see. Then, we'll go tomorrow, and I'll see what I can learn about the situation."

"You're so smart, Drake." She grinned at him. "I guess that is why you've always been my favorite brother." She quickly added, "But don't tell Michael, because I love him, too."

He laughed. "I won't say a word, especially since you're my favorite sister."

Julia shook her head. "If I recollect correctly, I'm your only sister."

Martha came out onto the porch. "There you two are. Mind if I join you?"

"Don't mind at all, Mom." Drake smiled at her. "No man in his right mind would ever think sitting here with two beautiful women is anything but heaven."

"Oh, my goodness. He's still the smooth talker he's always been, Julia. You know you have to watch a man like him."

"I know, Mother. But it's nice to hear him say these things, isn't it?"

"Absolutely."

Drake only grinned.

~ * ~

It was close to nine o'clock in the evening when the crowd began to thin and Bernadette wandered into the kitchen. She was a little hungry since she hadn't eaten any supper, and she knew some of the neighbors had brought in food.

She also knew she wasn't the only one who hadn't eaten when she found Minnie and Addie Jetter at the kitchen table. "Hello, ladies," she muttered.

"Hello, Bernadette," Minnie said. "There's some good food on this table. Why don't you join us?"

"Thank you." She picked up a plate and moved to the table. "I'm glad you came in here because I'm sure you didn't get a chance to eat either."

"No, we didn't." Minnie looked at Bernadette and said, "I wonder if Elsa's husband has had any food."

Bernadette shrugged. "I don't know, but I'm sure if he gets hungry, he'll come in here and find something to eat."

"Do you mean you don't make sure he is taken care of?" Addie asked.

"Of course not. My job was to take care of Aunt Elsa, not her husband."

She got a clue of what the two women thought of her when Minnie said, "I guess now that Elsa is gone, you'll take over the household and start caring for Henry."

Bernadette frowned. Why were these women questioning her about Henry? She couldn't help it if her voice sounded a little snippy when she said, "I most certainly will not. As soon as the funeral is over, I plan to leave this house as quickly as I can."

"But who will look after him if you leave?" Addie asked.

"I'm sure as long as he keeps paying her, Ginny will continue to come in to fix food and do the tasks she's been doing around here. I did tell her not to come today because I knew there would be plenty of food brought in."

Addie smiled and started to say something, but Minnie put her hand on her daughter's arm to stop her, then said, "Then I guess Henry may decide to accept our offer to come and stay here for a while after the funeral."

So that is it. For some reason they want to move in here with Henry. I hope they don't end up regretting doing it. But she didn't dare bring up Henry's faults, especially his drinking. All she said was, "I think he'd be wise to have you stay with him."

Addie grinned, and Minnie said, "I'm glad to see we're not interfering with your plans."

"Not at all. I think you staying here is a good idea."

Little else was said, though Bernadette felt as if both Minnie and Addie were watching her closely, if not suspiciously. As quickly as she could, she finished eating, stood, and said, "I'm tired, so I'm going to my room. I will see you ladies in the morning."

As she went out the door, she heard Addie say, "Oh, Mama. I don't think we need to worry about Bernadette any longer."

"I don't know. Maybe we should watch her for another day or so."

Not staying there to hear any more, Bernadette hurried toward the stairs. She hoped to miss Henry on the way to her room, but she didn't.

He came up behind her. "There you are, and I see we're alone. How about us having a little talk about our future before we turn in."

She hurried forward, saying, "No, Henry. I'm tired."

He would probably have said more, but she heard Minnie and Addie enter the room. She didn't slow down to see what they said to the man. Inside her room, she locked her door, then leaned against it and muttered, "Dear Lord, please help me through the next few days and then please help me escape here and get to Texas to be with my sisters."

~ * ~

When Bernadette came downstairs the next morning, she was surprised to find Minnie in the kitchen frying ham. "Good morning. Has Ginny not arrived yet?"

"Good morning to you, Bernadette, and nobody was here when I came down."

"I suppose she's running late today." Changing the subject, she said, "I hope you slept well last night."

"I did. In fact, the bed I slept in here was much more comfortable than the one I've been sleeping in at home. Elsa had a lot of nice things."

"Yes, she did, and I'm glad you rested well. I'm sure we'll have a busy day ahead of us with all the neighbors and the many people from Aunt Elsa's church who will probably drop by with food and to pay their respects."

"You're most likely right," she said, then changed the subject. "The coffee is ready. Do you want a cup?"

"Yes, I do. Thank you."

Minnie poured her a mug of coffee, handed it to her, then set a second one on the table for herself. "I hope you don't mind me making myself at home in the kitchen, but I need my coffee to help me get started in the morning. I decided to cook the ham but didn't plan to fix any eggs. There's plenty of bread and I thought the ham would be enough for us, since most of the food the neighbors brought in are cakes, pies, and vegetables."

"I don't mind at all. In fact, I want you to make yourself at home in the kitchen or any other part of the house. Of course, that goes for Addie, too."

"Thank you, Bernadette. Now, let's take a seat and eat our ham before the people start coming. I figure you're right about them arriving soon."

Bernadette took a chair at the side of the table. "Is Addie coming to eat?"

"She can get something when she comes down. She's taking advantage of being able to sleep later than she does at home."

"I see," she muttered and slid the piece of ham between the sliced biscuit Minnie gave her. She didn't mention Henry because she knew he was somewhere sleeping off the effects of all the whiskey he'd consumed yesterday, and though he was her least favorite person in the world, Bernadette had never liked to gossip about anyone.

She was surprised when Minnie asked, "If I asked you some questions, will you be honest with me?"

"Of course, I will."

She looked into Bernadette's eyes. "Does Henry get drunk often?"

After a shocked pause, she answered. "As I recall, he seemed to start drinking more after Aunt Elsa became sick enough to require bed care."

"So, he didn't drink much before then?"

"Well, once in a while, he'd come in staggering, but Aunt Elsa would take him out of the room. I was never around him often when he was drunk until lately."

"I see. Then..."

A sharp rap on the front door interrupted her, and she stood. "I guess that means our company has arrived, and we'll have to continue this conversation later."

"You're right." Bernadette stood, too. "I'll answer the door."

~ * ~

After the first visitor, several neighbors and some of Elsa's church friends came by, dropped off food, stayed for a little while to pay their respects, then left. Only a couple of them inquired about Henry. When Bernadette heard Minnie tell them he wasn't up to seeing company, she decided to use the same answer if anyone asked her about him.

Around ten o'clock, a group of five ladies, who said they were the food and sympathy committee from the church, arrived, donned aprons, and took over the kitchen. This left the family members to concentrate on the guests without stopping to deposit the food in the kitchen.

At ten-thirty, Julia Rafferty Bingham walked in with the best-looking man Bernadette had ever seen. She realized Addie must have thought the same thing because she rushed forward to greet them.

Knowing her friend, Julia, had always been able to handle most any situation, she stood back and waited. She didn't have to wait long.

Julia said a few words to Addie, took the basket from the man and handed it to Addie. Then, with a smile, she took the man's arm and steered him across the room to stand beside her friend. "Hello, Bernadette. I'd like you to meet my brother, Drake."

"Howdy, Miss Bernadette," he said in his acquired Texas drawl. "I'm pleased to meet you. Julia has told me what good friends you are."

Bernadette hoped she didn't blush when she held out her hand and said, "Hello, Drake. Yes, we've been friends since the day we met, and I'm pleased to meet you, too, though I almost feel I know you because of the way Julia brags about her big brother."

Not one to waste time, Julia butted in and asked, "Is there somewhere we can talk in private?"

Before Bernadette could answer, Minnie walked up.

Bernadette introduced them.

After they expressed their condolences to Minnie, Bernadette said, "Mr. Rafferty is leaving town in a day or two and they would like to discuss something with me concerning their family. It shouldn't take long, but would you mind if we step out for a little while?"

"Of course not, dear. Why don't you slip out on the terrace. You'll have all the privacy you need there."

"Thank you, Minnie. We won't be too long."

When they reached the terrace, Drake pulled one of the chairs to the side, giving him an unobstructed view of the door. The ladies sat on the bench facing the garden.

Drake spoke first. "So, Julia tells me you want to run away to Texas."

"Yes, it's exactly what I want to do."

"Well, Bernadette ... May I call you Bernadette?"

"Of course you'll call her by her first name," Julia butted in. "If you decide to pass her off as your sister, or your cousin, or even your wife, you can't call her Miss Cardwell."

Bernadette couldn't help smiling as she said, "Yes. You may call me Bernadette and I'll call you Drake."

"I will tell you right off, I have a train ticket to leave here on Saturday and I don't want to delay my trip. Since it's not a good idea for a woman to travel alone, I volunteered to see you get safely to Texas if you really want to go."

"I most certainly want to go and it's nice of you to offer to get me there."

"Then it's settled. Can you be packed and ready to leave by Saturday?"

Bernadette didn't blink. "The funeral service will be at eleven-thirty Saturday morning, and I can be ready any time after it's over."

He gave her a quick smile. "That will be fine. The train leaves at two. Then, if you're sure you want to go to Texas, I'll take care of getting your baggage aboard and purchasing you a ticket."

"I definitely want to go, and I'll give you the money for the ticket before you leave here today."

"That won't be necessary. We'll settle up later." Before he went on, he threw her his quick smile again. "How many trunks will you have?"

"I don't have a lot of things and I'm not sure I'll require a trunk. I may be able to get everything I own in two or three carpet bags."

Julia butted in. "Ladies don't travel with two or three carpet bags. I think you should use a trunk. Besides your clothes, you may want to take a few mementoes of your aunt."

"Since I don't want anyone to know I'm going out of town, how will I explain leaving here with a trunk?"

Julia patted her hand. "You'll tell anyone who asks it's too sad for you to stay in your aunt's house without her and you will be staying with me for a while."

"That should work."

Drake asked, "Can you have your trunk packed by four o'clock tomorrow?"

"I'm sure I can."

"Good. I'll come by then and get it to the station. If anyone asks why I'm doing this, tell them I'm leaving on Saturday and

Julia asked me to get it to her house before I left town because her husband is too busy to take time off to get it."

Julia added, "After the service on Saturday, Willard and I will take you to the station where Drake will be waiting to escort you to Texas. When people wonder why you aren't at the house after the funeral, we'll let them know you were too overwrought to face anyone."

Bernadette shook her head and said, "It looks like you two have it all worked out for me, and I thank you."

"All you have to thank me for is asking my brother to help. After I told him about you wanting to leave, his Texas Ranger training kicked in and he devised the plan." She nodded at Drake and added, "I think part of a ranger's job is planning escapes."

He grinned and winked at them.

~ * ~

As soon as she saw Julie and Drake to the door and bid them goodbye, she turned to see Henry coming down the stairs. He looked mad and she tried to hurry from the entrance back into the parlor, but she didn't make it.

Henry grabbed her arm and demanded, "Who was that man?"

She jerked her arm away. "What man?"

"The man I saw you with on the terrace."

"How did you see me on the terrace with a man? Are you spying on me?"

He looked a little contrite, but said, "I happened to go by my window and saw you grinning at him. Besides, I don't think it's a proper time for your friend Julia to bring some strange man here to meet you."

"You know Julia wouldn't do such a thing. The man with her was her brother."

"That's not so. Her brother runs the family business, and I know him. The man you were on the terrace with certainly wasn't Michael Rafferty."

"Of course, it wasn't. It was her other brother, Drake. He's home for a visit and Julia asked him to bring her over to meet me and to deliver a basket of food."

"Meet you? Don't you already know him?"

"No. He had left the area when I moved here to take care of Aunt Elsa." She glared at him. "Now, if you'll excuse me, I need to get back to the guests."

He grabbed her arm again. "Where does he live?"

She frowned at him and jerked her arm away. For some reason she felt she shouldn't tell him the truth. She bit her lip and said, "Somewhere in the west. Maybe New Mexico or Wyoming. I didn't pay much attention when they told me. I do remember he said he was some sort of lawman. A sheriff or marshal or something. Why does it matter anyway? He'll be leaving town soon."

He grabbed her arm again. "How do you know?"

"Because they said so." Again, she jerked free of his grasp.

He muttered, "I'm sorry, Bernadette. I can't help being jealous when I saw you with another man. You know I'm crazy about you. That's why I fired Ginny when she showed up yesterday. I figured we didn't need her around interfering in our lives."

"So, that's why she hasn't shown up today."

"Of course. As I said, I didn't figure we'd need her here any longer."

Bernadette's temper flared. "How dare you say such a thing to me when your wife has not yet been put in the ground!" Before he had a chance to answer, she fled through the door to the parlor and came face to face with Addie.

The young woman said, "You look upset, Bernadette. Are you all right?"

"No, I'm not and please do me a favor, Addie. When Henry comes through the door, stop him from getting to me. I can't explain now but come to my room before you go to bed tonight and I promise I will tell you everything." She hurried away as Henry entered the room.

~ * ~

That evening Bernadette was folding one of her three dresses when there was a soft knock on her door. She asked, "Who is it?"

"It's me, Addie."

Bernadette opened the door. "Please, come in."

"I brought Mama with me. I hope you don't mind."

"Of course, not. Let me move those things off the settee so both of you can sit there."

"Let me help you," Minnie said, then frowned. "What are you doing with your clothes?"

"I'll explain as soon as you're seated."

After transferring the clothes to the bed, the women sat on the settee and Bernadette pulled a chair up to face them. "Let me start by saying when you both arrived here, I wasn't sure why you had come since you hadn't visited during Aunt Elsa's illness. I decided I'd not say much to you until I knew what was going on but now, I feel compelled to tell you my plans."

The mother and daughter glanced at each other but didn't say anything.

Bernadette went on. "When I came here to take care of Aunt Elsa, she was sick but still getting around, though it wasn't long until her health worsened, and she was confined to bed. We then hired Ginny, the maid and part-time cook. I learned today Henry fired her yesterday." She looked at Millie. "That's the reason I saw you in the kitchen this morning instead of her."

"You did mention she'd probably come later, but she didn't show up all day, and we were too busy to question where she might be."

Bernadette nodded and went on with her story. She told them how she had become leery of Henry since he had started making inappropriate remarks to her after her aunt was bedridden. Then after Elsa's death, he had become blatant with his actions. She ended with, "That's why I've made arrangements to leave here as soon as the funeral is over. I want to get away from him, and my friends, the Rafferty family, have offered to let me stay with them."

"Oh, Bernadette. I never dreamed Henry made you feel so uncomfortable here." Minnie reached for her hand.

"Neither did I, though I noticed he drinks an awful lot." Addie turned to her mother. "Will I be safe here?"

"Don't worry, dear. I'll be here with you." She turned back to Bernadette. "Since you've been honest with us, I think it's time we told you why we showed up at this time since we hadn't visited during Elsa's sickness."

"I assumed it was because you're related to Aunt Elsa's first husband."

"Roger was my brother. There were only two of us and we were close. In fact, I thought a lot of Elsa because I know how lonely she was when Roger died so suddenly. Since they never had children, they doted on Addie. It didn't surprise me when she remarried in less than a year after Roger's death, but it did shock me when we stopped hearing from her. Then my husband, Bernard, passed away and she didn't show up for the funeral. I had written her shortly after my brother's death and told her we didn't have to carry out the requirements of his will since my husband was still alive at the time. When Bernard was gone, I wrote to her and told her it was time to make things right. A week later, I got a letter from her husband saying things had changed. He said she was a sick woman and there was no way he would let me upset her life by bringing up family business."

Minnie paused and Bernadette said, "I'm getting a little confused, Minnie. Did you have some sort of arrangement with Roger and Aunt Elsa?"

"You need to tell her the whole story, Mama."

Nodding, Minnie went on. "Addie is right. The arrangement I'm referring to is what was to be done with this house if something happened to Roger or me. Since it was built with the money our parents left the two of us, we agreed on either of our deaths, one of us would buy the other out or the place would be sold, and his share was to go to Elsa and my share was to go to Addie. But somehow things have changed, and I don't know if it was Elsa's or Henry's idea, but someone tried to fix it so Addie and I were left out of anything to do with the house."

"I see now." Bernadette thought for a minute. "I'm not a lawyer, but it looks to me like the most Henry would be entitled to is Aunt Elsa's share, and he may not be entitled to that."

"We were thinking the same thing. So, I guess we need to find a lawyer. Do you know any in town who would be willing to help us?"

"As a matter of fact, I do. My friend Julia is married to a lawyer and from what I understand he's a good one. I'll give you his name and address. Also, I'll mention it to them, so they will know who you are when you get in touch with him."

"Oh, Bernadette. You've been so helpful. Thank you!" Addie jumped up and hugged her neck. "Mama has been so worried because we didn't know how you fit in the deal."

"She's right, Bernadette." Minnie stood and gave her a quick hug. "But we know now. So, let's get you packed so you can get to your friend's house and away from Henry after the funeral on Saturday. Where are the rest of your clothes?"

"These are all the clothes I have."

Shocked, Minnie said, "Oh, no. This will never do. You need more since you'll be staying with your socialite friend. Come with me, Addie, and Bernadette, you start packing your other things. We'll be back in a few minutes."

Before she could answer, Minnie was out the door and Addie followed her.

By the time she finished folding her few clothes and had put them in the trunk, the two women returned. Addie had almost more dresses in her arms than she could carry, and Minnie had her arms full of women's necessities.

"Oh, my goodness, I can't..." Bernadette started to say.

But Minnie interrupted. "Now, don't argue with me. Elsa would want you to have her best clothes because I'm sure some of them haven't been worn in a long time."

"But Addie..."

Minnie shook her head. "Don't start. Addie is taller and heavier than you. She couldn't wear a thing because nothing here will fit her."

"What about you?"

"Most of these things are designed for a young woman. I'm much too old for them."

After a few other attempts to reject the clothes, Bernadette finally accepted them, and they all ended up in the trunk. Not only was she touched by this woman's generous offer, but she was delighted to get all the pretty dresses. She not only thought it would be nice to have them, but it was a wonderful remembrance of the aunt she had come to love.

~ * ~

The funeral went off without incident on Saturday. In the family receiving line to thank the guests for attending, Bernadette managed to put Minnie and Addie between her and Henry. She could tell from his reaction he didn't like it, but there was nothing he could do about it.

Near the end of the line to speak with them were Julia and Willard. After introducing them to Minnie and Addie, Bernadette leaned close and whispered in Julia's ear, "Is everything set?"

Julia nodded and said loud enough for all to hear, "We'll wait for you at the gate."

After the last guest left, Henry turned to Bernadette and asked in a sharp voice, "What did she mean, she'd wait for you at the gate?"

"For heaven's sake, Henry," Minnie snapped. "Bernadette is grieving the loss of her aunt, and she needs some time with her friend before going back to the house."

"I don't see..."

"Of course, you don't. It's almost one o'clock, so let's head to the house and partake of the wonderful dinner I'm sure the church ladies have prepared for us. Addie and I will be riding with you, and Bernadette will be along soon."

"That's right," Addie added. She then leaned over and hugged Bernadette. "Take care."

"You do the same." Bernadette returned the hug then reached to hug Minnie.

Henry reached to hug Bernadette, but she ignored him and hurried to her waiting friend.

As she climbed into the buggy beside Julia, Bernadette said, "Are you sure everything is set to pull this off?"

Julia patted her hand. "I'm positive. Your trunk is already on the train, and I have your small bag with the personal things you will need for the trip right there at your feet. Drake has your ticket and he's waiting for you at the station with a basket of food Mother insisted he take for the two of you. He said he'd wait outside and not get aboard until you got there."

"What if...?"

"Don't start creating problems, my friend. Try to relax. Everything is going as planned."

"Then why are we headed toward your house instead of the station?"

Willard chuckled. "I saw Henry Goddard watching us when we pulled out. I decided to head this way. We'll turn at the next intersection, then go to the train station the back way."

"Then I'm going to try to relax and think things will work out fine."

"You do that. Now, let me tell you, I saw you had put Mrs. Jetter's address in your satchel. I put our address in there, too. Just in case you forget it. I want you to write me as soon as you get to Bell Haven and let me know what's going on and what you think about the place and of your decision to go there."

"When I get settled, I promise you'll be one of the first people I write."

"I better be."

"I appreciate you telling me about Mrs. Jetter," Willard said. "I didn't say anything at the funeral, but I've done a little checking, and I think I'll have good news for her."

"Oh, how wonderful."

The friendly chat relaxed Bernadette and the next thing she knew, they pulled up to the station platform and she saw Drake Rafferty waiting for her. Her heart began to beat a little faster, though she didn't understand why. She decided it must be because of the excitement of heading to Bell Haven to see Melissa and Catherine again.

~ * ~

As she stepped on the platform, Drake smiled at her and said, "It won't be long before the train pulls out. Maybe we should hurry and get aboard."

She nodded, then turned to wave at Julia and her husband one more time. "I'm ready," she mumbled.

"Don't be surprised when the conductor greets you. I told him I was accompanying my fiancée to Texas to visit her family."

Bernadette was surprised. "Your fiancée?"

"I thought it would explain our different last names and still wouldn't surprise anyone when we're seen together." He offered her his arm and added, "Now, shall we get aboard?"

The conductor grinned when they walked up to the door. "Well, I see she didn't stand you up, Rafferty."

Drake returned the grin. "I never doubted she'd come."

"It's a pleasure to meet you, miss. I hope you enjoy your visit with your family."

Bernadette gave him a quick smile and said, "Thank you."

There was no more time for talk as Drake ushered her up the aisle to a seat near the middle of the car. He stood back and let her sit beside the window. He then sat the basket he had on the floor between them. "Mom packed us a lunch because she knew you didn't get to eat anything after the service."

"That was sweet of her."

He grinned. "I'm glad she sent it, because I'm getting hungry and I bet you are, too."

"I'm still a little nervous and I don't think I could eat anything for a while. Do you mind waiting for a bit?"

"I'm sure I won't starve, so I don't mind if we wait until the train pulls out."

It wasn't long before the whistle blew, and the train began to jerk. Bernadette's heartbeat increased and she glared out the window. Had she actually done it? Did she get away from Henry and the unthinkable plans he had for her? Could she now relax and appreciate the fact Drake Rafferty was actually escorting her to Texas to join her sisters?

She glanced at him and started to tell him to break out the food, but she didn't get a chance. The conductor came into the car yelling for everyone to get out their ticket.

For a moment she was taken aback. "I don't have a ticket," she muttered.

"Don't worry. I have it," Drake said as he took two tickets from his pocket.

The conductor stood beside their seat and Drake handed him the tickets.

"I'm glad your fiancée made it." He looked at Bernadette. "I have to admit, she was worth waiting for."

"Yes, she is, and as I told you earlier, I never doubted she would show up."

"You two, enjoy the trip." He nodded at Drake, smiled at her, then moved on.

Bernadette couldn't help blushing and to cover it, she said, "I know you're hungry, Drake, and now we're moving, I think I've relaxed enough I could eat a piece of the fried chicken I think I smell. How about you?"

"Oh my, Bernadette, if you're going to be this easy to get along with, this is going to be a pleasant trip to Texas."

She couldn't help blushing again.

~ * ~

The food had been served, the kitchen cleaned, the church group had left, and Minnie and Addie were relaxing in the parlor chatting in muted tones when Henry burst into the parlor and yelled, "Where the hell is Bernadette?"

"Watch your mouth, young man! We'll have no such language spoken here."

He frowned. "Unless I'm confused, this is my house, and I'll say anything I please."

Addie's eyes got big, but she didn't say anything.

Minnie went on. "As long as we're here, I expect you to have enough respect for us to at least try to use a few manners."

"If you don't like what I say in my house, why don't you leave. After all, the funeral is over and I'm sure Bernadette and I can take care of things without your help," he yelled.

With a smile on her face, she said in a calm voice, "We promised some of Elsa's friends we'd be here for a while, and they plan to visit us here. That means we'll be staying a while."

Still in a loud voice he said, "I ain't going to argue with you about it now. All I want to know is when is Bernadette coming home."

"She didn't tell me." Minnie shrugged and looked at Addie. "Did she tell you, honey?"

Addie shook her head.

Minnie went on. "Then if she didn't tell you, Henry, I would guess she'll come when and if she decides to come."

"What do you mean 'if'?"

"I don't mean a thing. It's just a figure of speech."

Henry opened his mouth to speak but must have changed his mind because he whirled around and began muttering curse words as he stalked down the hall.

Minnie looked at Addie and grinned. "I think that went pretty well, don't you?"

"I don't know, Mama. He scares me."

"Relax, honey. He can't do a thing except cuss and threaten us, hoping we'll leave. If we confront him, you see how he backs down. The best thing you can do is not let him know you're afraid of him."

"I'll try, Mama, but the truth is, I am afraid of him."

The next thing they heard was the front door slam.

Minnie laughed. "He's probably going to get drunk, which means he won't be back before suppertime."

"Thank goodness."

"I'm glad, too."

Addie turned her head to the side and looked at her mother. "When he does come back and he sees Bernadette is still not here, what do you think he'll do?"

"I don't know. Let's just hope he's so drunk he passes out and doesn't notice she's gone." Minnie stood. "In the meantime, let's go to the kitchen and have another piece of the strawberry pie Miz Rafferty brought. All this mess with Henry has made me hungry."

"Sounds good to me." Addie got up and followed her mama out of the room.

~ * ~

It was midmorning, a few days later, when the train's direction going toward Bell Haven, Texas ended, and Bernadette stood on the platform watching Drake help the wagon driver put their luggage inside to transport it to the stagecoach office. The train had been uncomfortable at times, but she had heard stories of how horrible stagecoach travel could be. She hoped most of these stories had been exaggerated, and she would find it wasn't much worse than the train.

Shaking her head, she told herself, even if it was unpleasant at times, it would be worth it to see her sisters again. Besides, she admitted, Drake had made the entire trip not only bearable, but somewhat enjoyable. He was a special man, and she could now understand why Julia was so proud of her brother.

After the last piece of their luggage was aboard, he turned, looked at her, and reached out his hand to help her from the platform. With a twinkle in his dark eyes, he said, "Your carriage awaits, Miss Cardwell."

She smiled back at him and took his hand. "Thank you, kind sir."

He then ushered her to the two-seated wagon and helped her to the seat behind the driver. To her surprise, he climbed in and sat beside her.

She whispered, "I thought you'd sit with the driver."

"No gentleman would leave his fiancée to ride alone. The driver knows where to go. He doesn't need my help."

"I thought the pretense of me being your fiancée was only until we were safely away from Atlanta," she whispered, since he'd kept his voice low.

"You never know what will happen, so I decided we'd just go with it for a while. That is, if you agree to it."

"Of course. You have everything so well planned. I'll go along with whatever you say."

He chuckled. "That's good to know."

She blushed but didn't reply.

~ * ~

Addie put her clean clothes away, came down the stairs and hurried to the kitchen where she knew her mother would have a good dinner waiting. Going through the door, she was surprised to walk in and hear Henry arguing with her mama. He was saying, "She's been gone a month. Somebody has to know where she is."

"It hasn't been a month, Henry. It's only been a few days," Minnie said as she sat a bowl of beans on the table.

"Well, it seems like a month to me."

"I admit it's strange she hasn't been in touch, but maybe she ran away because she doesn't want to be found?"

He frowned. "It can't be true. I know how much she was looking forward to starting a new life here with me. She wouldn't run away."

"I don't think you're seeing things clearly. Hasn't it ever occurred to you that maybe instead of sharing her life with you, she wanted to get as far away from you as she could?"

"No!" He seemed to become frustrated. "As I said, she was looking forward to our future as much as I am."

"Did she tell you she was looking forward to it?"

"She didn't have to. I could tell how she felt by the look in her eyes."

"You could have mistaken the look in her eyes."

"I'm tired of arguing with you, old woman." He whirled around and Addie jumped back.

He laughed and threw his arm around her shoulders. "Why, I could tell the first day you walked in here, this little girl had a hankering to get to know me, and if I didn't have plans for me and Bernadette, I'd give her a taste of my loving."

Though Addie had always shied away from Henry, this remark made her furious and the tension boiled to the surface. She grabbed a coffee mug from the table and slammed it against his head. "You're such a fool. No wonder Bernadette felt she had to get away."

Holding his head, Henry glared at her and roared, "What do you mean?"

"If nobody else will tell you the truth, I'm going to. Bernadette couldn't stand the sight of you, so she made plans to leave town right after the funeral and said she was going somewhere she would never have to see you again."

"Liar!" He screamed and lunged toward her. "I'll get you for saying that."

"Oh, no you don't!" Minnie grabbed the big dish of hot beans and brought it down on the top of Henry's head.

He crumpled to the floor.

Shocked, Addie said, "Oh, Mama. You may have killed him."

Minnie knelt down beside him, felt his neck, and shook her head. "He's not dead. He's still breathing."

"Good. I don't want my mother to go to jail for killing a man."

Minnie said, "To be perfectly honest, I wouldn't care much if he was dead."

"Mama!" Addie tried to show shock at her mother's words, but she couldn't hold back the snigger that slipped out.

Her mother grinned but said, "Hand me a towel. I need to get some of these beans off him. They were still boiling when I took them off the stove so I'm sure he's going to have some nasty burns."

An hour later, Addie and her mama sat down to eat a warmed-over supper. "Well, Mama. Things didn't work out the way I thought they would."

"You're right, Addie. I thought we'd have a sulking Henry to contend with."

"Instead, he's in jail for assaulting me, and the sheriff said you wouldn't be charged with anything because you were defending your daughter."

"And to top it off, our lawyer says he'll have everything cleared up about this house and it will be ours by the end of the week."

Addie smiled. "You know I need to listen to your advice more often."

Minnie lifted an eyebrow. "What advice?"

"You've always told me to do what I think is right in every situation and it will more than likely turn out to be the correct thing to do."

"Yep, I did say that, and I was right." Minnie grinned at her and added, "Honey, let's not let this food get cold again. Please pass me the corn."

Addie giggled and reached for the bowl.

~ * ~

When Drake helped Bernadette onto the stagecoach and ushered her to the middle of the seat facing forward, she couldn't help being pleased to see another couple already seated across the narrow aisle. The woman smiled and she returned it.

The man said, "I'm glad you have your wife with you, young man. My wife has been worried she'd be the only woman aboard this coach." He then added, "I'm Reverend Paul McGill and this is my wife, Helen."

"Drake Rafferty and this is my fiancée, Bernadette Cardwell." Drake sat beside the window. "I'll block some of the dust and it won't get on you," he explained."

Bernadette was surprised Drake had lied to a preacher about their circumstances, but she decided he must be serious about keeping up the pretense. She also decided there was nothing she could do but go along with it. She sure had no intention of pointing out his lie because he had been too good to her.

The clergyman raised an eyebrow but only said, "I misunderstood. I thought since you were traveling together, you were married."

"Oh, don't get me wrong. We plan to be married soon. Bernadette's two sisters live in West Texas. She wanted to have them witness our marriage, but I wasn't about to let her make this dangerous trip alone and me follow later. Being a lawman, I know how many bad things can happen to a woman traveling alone. I figured the best thing to do was come with her. We plan to get married as soon as we can get everyone together for the wedding ceremony."

"I can't help but say it's gallant of you to accompany her," Helen McGill said.

"There's truth in what she said," Paul added. "I firmly believe a man should always look after and protect his woman."

Drake nodded. "That's what my father always told me, and I agree with him."

Abe Welsh, the stagecoach driver, opened the door and stuck his head into the coach. He looked at Drake and said, "My partner, Jake, and I have your trunks and other luggage secured on top. We're waiting for two more passengers, then we'll be pulling out and I think I see one of them hurrying down the street now." He then backed away from the door before anyone could reply to his announcement.

Bernadette didn't want the talk to get back to her traveling with her fiancée. She glanced at the woman and asked, "Where are you folks headed?"

"To a small western town in the need of a preacher." She looked at her husband. "I can't ever seem to get the name of the town right. Tell me again the name of the place, dear."

"It's Bell Haven."

Shocked, Bernadette became strangled on the air she sucked in too quickly and began to cough violently. She knew she was turning red and unable to speak. But the only thing she had on her mind was *what in the world are we going to do about the lie now since we're headed to the same town?*

By the time she calmed down, a businessman got on the stagecoach and took the seat beside her. He greeted everyone, and said his name was Wade Neil. By the time introductions were over, a bearded cowboy climbed inside, glanced around, then sat beside the preacher's wife. He announced he was Nick Sherra, and he was tired and needed to take a nap. He then leaned back and put his brown hat over his face.

Bernadette bit her lip and noticed the others were also trying not to laugh.

The stage jerked and pulled away from the station. She forgot about the man under the brown hat and hoped the subject of her upcoming marriage wouldn't be mentioned again. For some time, it wasn't. Instead, the passengers learned Reverend Paul McGill and his wife had left Kansas to serve at Bell Haven Church because the town had been without a pastor for almost six months. They also learned Mr. Wade Neil was a businessman and was only going to the next town to a meeting. He seemed to be one not to talk much with strangers and also seemed to want to be left alone. The only thing he said making Bernadette a little uncomfortable was, "Well preacher, I must say you have a lovely wife to help you spread the gospel." And to Drake, he said as he pointed at her, "And you, Mr. Rafferty, have a beautiful fiancée. If you end up married soon, I wish you both much happiness in the future."

After they had been on the road for an hour or so, Nick Sherra made a blubbering noise, then removed his hat and sat up. "I'll shore be glad when we get to the first stop. I'm doing a job for another man, but this ain't no fit way to have to travel. I'm going to buy me a horse as soon as we stop. That's the way a man ought to be traveling."

Their first stop was in a small town called Crossroads and Abe Welsh said they had twenty minutes to use the facilities behind the general store. Ladies on the right and men on the left. He also said if they hurried and didn't waste time, they would probably have time to purchase anything they wanted in the store.

"Where can I buy a horse?" Sherra demanded.

"You can try the livery stable," Abe told him. "But don't take too long. I'll be pulling out in twenty minutes."

Ignoring him, Sherra headed down the street.

As the passengers returned to the stagecoach, the preacher said, "Looks like Sherra got a horse. There he goes.

They all turned to see the man riding away on a pinto pony.

"I must say, I'm glad he won't be riding with us any longer," Mr. Neil said.

Nobody replied but it was no secret everyone probably agreed with him.

After a few miles, Helen McGill dozed off on her husband's shoulder. Though Bernadette didn't understand how anybody could possibly go to sleep with all the shaking and rocking, she found herself feeling a little drowsy, too. She decided to rest and let the men talk if they wanted to. She soon drifted off and didn't know it, but she slept with her head resting on Drake's shoulder.

~ * ~

The sun was sinking in the western sky when they reached the way station where they were to spend the night. As they exited the stagecoach, Mr. Welsh said, "Take care of your personal needs, then eat a hearty meal. Miz Mason is a good cook but there won't be time for more than a quick breakfast of a biscuit and coffee in the morning."

Jake, the stage guard, laughed and added, "If we're lucky, the biscuit might have a piece of meat or a little jelly in it." He then pointed out the way to outside comfort stations.

The women's area was located to the left and the men's, to the right.

Helen said, "Bernadette and I will meet you men at the front door. Wait for us on the porch, please."

Drake nodded and Paul said, "We will, dear."

Bernadette and Helen rounded the corner and hurried toward the outhouse. They had almost reached the door when a shadowy figure appeared from the side and grabbed Bernadette. She didn't get a chance to scream because his hand covered her mouth, and she smelled something strange as she was being dragged into the woods behind the outhouses and the barn. She thought she heard Helen scream, but then it became quiet. She didn't realize anything else as she became unconscious.

~ * ~

Both Drake and Paul whirled around and headed toward Helen's scream. "Oh, my heavenly Father. What happened?" Paul cried out as he rushed to his wife who was lying on the ground. He dropped to his knees beside her and pulled her into his arms.

Drake knelt beside him. "Where's Bernadette?" he asked, though his practical mind told him Helen was on the verge of passing out.

He was a little surprised when she raised her hand and pointed toward the woods and muttered, "A man grabbed her."

Abe and Jake had followed and by this time had reached them. Both were talking, but Drake didn't pause to say anything more. He headed toward the woods on a run.

It didn't take him long to see where whoever had abducted Bernadette had entered the trees. The bent branches of the nearby bushes and the disturbed ground cover showed him the way. It took only minutes to reach the small clearing where he saw the cowboy tying a gagged Bernadette across a horse on her stomach.

It only took him seconds to recognize the pinto Sherra had been riding.

Drawing his gun, he eased close enough to see Bernadette didn't seem to be hurt but he wanted to make sure she was safe. Aiming his gun at the man, he demanded in a stern voice, "Step away from the horse with your hands in the air!"

The startled cowboy whirled around and fumbled for his gun. As soon as it cleared the holster, Drake fired. As the pistol hit the ground, the man screamed, "You shot me!"

"Be thankful I didn't kill you."

The drivers rushed into the clearing demanding to know what was happening.

"Hold that man," Drake said and rushed to Bernadette. Easing her off the horse and holding her in his arm, he removed the gag. Though he saw she was almost unconscious, he asked, "Are you all right?"

When he saw she couldn't understand, he held her close and whispered, "You don't have to be afraid any longer. I'm here now and you're safe."

Paul and Helen, who had followed the men at a slower pace, hurried to Drake.

Looking down at the woman in his arms, Helen said, "Oh, Bernadette. I'm so glad Drake found you."

"She can't hear you. She's unconscious." Drake looked at her. "Are you all right?"

"I'm fine. He just knocked me down when I tried to get Bernadette away from him." Again, she looked at the woman in Drake's arms and her eyes filled with tears. "Oh, the poor dear. What has he done to her?"

"He must have used some kind of knock-out drug to render her unconscious. She's breathing all right and she seems fine otherwise."

"You do realize the cowboy who grabbed her is the one who was on the stage with us, don't you?" Paul asked.

"I see it's him," Drake said, and added, "I also notice Wade Neil didn't come into the woods with the rest of you."

"I also noticed he didn't follow. I wonder why?" Paul said.

"We can find out later. I want to find out what the kidnapper has to say for himself." With Bernadette still in his arms, Drake turned toward the cowboy and walked the few feet to where the kidnapper stood with Welsh and his partner. In a stern voice, he said, "Nick Sherra, if that's your real name, why did you attempt to kidnap, Miss Cardwell?"

"It's none of your business. Besides, you shot my hand, and it hurts."

"Your hand is fine. It's not bleeding. Now answer the question."

"I ain't answering nothing,"

"In that case, you're under arrest for the kidnapping of Miss Cardwell and assault on Mrs. McGill."

The belligerent man laughed. "I know you said you was a lawman, but I know enough to realize some sheriff from some rinky-dink town doesn't have the authority to arrest me. Besides, when I get through telling them how you shot me and made the woman go with you, you won't have your job long."

"You could be right about a small-town sheriff not having any authority here, but you're wrong about everything else. I'm not a sheriff of any town."

"Then who are you?"

Holding Bernadette, a little away from him, Drake pulled the side of his vest from across his chest and revealed his badge.

"My word," Abe exclaimed. "He's a Texas Ranger and that gives him the authority to arrest you or anyone else breaking the law anywhere in Texas. Let's tie Sherra up, Jake."

"What about my sore hand?" Sherra complained.

"We won't hurt it any worse," Jake said.

Knowing the men would take care of the prisoner, he turned to his friends. "Let's get back to the station house. Bernadette seems to be trying to wake up and I want to get her taken care of."

Paul added, "I'm sure there are some curious people there, especially if they heard the gunshot and we need to let them know everything is all right."

"You and the Ranger inform everyone, and as soon as Jake and me eat a bite, we'll see if this fellow tells us what made him try to steal your woman."

"Thanks, Welsh. If Bernadette thinks she'll be all right, I might go with you to ask him those questions."

"I ain't telling you nothing. When the boss sees I didn't get her, he'll send somebody else to do the job."

"What do you mean?" Drake demanded.

Before anybody could answer, Bernadette muttered, "Where am I?"

Drake decided he could question the man later. He turned toward the station, and whispered, "Don't worry, sweetheart. I have you. You're safe now."

"Oh, Drake. I'm so glad." She then closed her eyes again as he hurried out of the woods, with his friends following.

~ * ~

Drake had been right—the manager and his wife and their twelve-year-old son were anxious to hear what was going on, but first Melba Mason had Drake put Bernadette down on the sofa in their quarters and her husband showed the men where they could tie up the outlaw in one of the sheds until they could decide what was to be done with him.

It was a little while before everyone settled down enough to eat supper, though Drake insisted on staying with the still upset and half-awake Bernadette. "If she comes completely awake, she will be scared because she won't know where she is, and I want to be here for her."

It wasn't long until Melba Mason brought him a tray of food. She assured him she would make sure Bernadette received something as soon as she was able to eat.

The food was surprisingly good and as he finished it, he looked at Bernadette and thought *Well, young lady, I knew I had grown to like you as a friend, but I never dreamed it would affect me the way it has to see you almost swept away. I've got to get control of these feelings before they get a firm hold on me. A serious relationship is not in the cards for me at this stage of my life. Being a free and happy Ranger is what I see myself being for a long time yet. Maybe until I'm ready to leave this world.*

He stopped thinking when she began to stir.

~ * ~

When Bernadette became almost completely conscious, she couldn't help herself; she threw her arms around Drake's neck and began to cry as she muttered, "I'm thankful to see you. I was afraid the man was going to kill me, and I didn't know why."

He held her close and whispered, "I'm here to make sure that doesn't happen."

"Is he ... I mean ...Where ..."

"Calm down. He has been arrested and you don't have to worry about him any longer." He eased her back to the sofa. "Now, you relax, and I'll go let everyone know you're awake."

"No. Don't leave me."

"I'm only going to the door."

"Are you sure?"

He smiled at her and stood. "Watch me and you'll see."

He stood in the doorway and announced Bernadette was awake and though she was still frightened, she seemed to be all right physically.

Helen and Paul jumped up and rushed to the door. They were soon followed by Melba Mason.

Mrs. Mason stood behind Helen who rushed to the couch and knelt. "Oh, Bernadette. It's so good to see you awake. I was afraid that awful man had almost killed you."

Bernadette smiled. "I'm going to be fine, Helen. Drake took good care of me."

"I know. We all saw how determined he was to make sure you were all right and then to see Nick Sherra was arrested. Shows how crazy your man is about you."

Bernadette blushed and muttered, "I kind of like him, too."

"Like, my foot! A person would have to be blind not to see how much in love you two are," Paul said.

Helen smiled at her. "I've only known you a short time, but it didn't take me long to see how much Drake cares about you. He made it clear to all of us he wasn't going to leave your side until you woke up and wasn't afraid any longer."

Bernadette blushed again, then whispered, "He takes looking after me seriously."

"I sure do," Drake said as he walked up. "I promised to get her to her sisters safely and I intend to keep my promise."

"Well, now since we see the lady is better, she needs to eat and I'm going to go make her a tray. Why don't you gentlemen go outside and let Miz McGill and me take care of her for a bit." When it looked as if Drake was going to protest, she added, "If you're still concerned about your woman, you can stay close to the front door, then come back in as soon as we get her fed."

After Paul said a quick prayer of thanksgiving Bernadette was awake and didn't seem to have any problems, Drake assured her he would be close by and if she needed him, all she had to do was call. The men then left the room.

~ * ~

On the front porch, Drake and Paul took the two chairs closest to the door. Paul looked at him and said, "I think you can relax now. Bernadette is in good hands."

"I'll relax when Sherra tells us who and why he was hired to kidnap Bernadette."

"I'd like to know myself, but we'll be moving on in the morning. We won't be here to find out."

"I'll be here until this is settled."

Paul frowned. "You don't intend to let Bernadette go on to Bell Haven alone, do you?"

"Of course not. She'll stay here with me."

The preacher shook his head. "No, Drake. She can't do that."

"Oh yes, she can. After what has happened, I don't trust anybody to take care of her except me."

"But what about her reputation?"

"Her reputation is fine."

"I know it is now." Paul raised an eye at him. "But everyone knows how you feel about each other. You don't want her to arrive to meet her sisters as a soiled woman, do you?"

Drake was becoming exasperated. "I don't know what you're talking about, Paul. Bernadette could never be considered soiled."

"I know you believe that and so do I, but it won't stop the wagging tongues." He shook his head at Drake. "Don't you realize how many people come through this stage stop on their way West?"

"I imagine plenty of them."

"Now think of how many times the story of Bernadette's kidnapping will be told, then retold and told again. How many times do you expect the correct version will survive."

"I assume you're right, but there's no way we can do anything about the gossip."

"There could be a way if you and Bernadette are willing to forget the wedding you're planning in Bell Haven."

Drake frowned and asked, "What are you talking about?"

Before Paul could explain, Wade Neil walked out onto the porch. "How is your fiancée?"

"She's feeling better. The ladies are taking care of her."

"I'm sorry I wasn't able to help when it happened. As I explained to the reverend, when I got off the stage, I felt violently sick. I was afraid I'd be in the way."

"We had enough help, but I did wonder why you didn't come with everyone else."

"I see. Did the cowboy say why he tried to abduct the woman?"

"No. But when I get a chance to question him, he'll talk."

A buggy pulled into the yard.

Wade looked relieved and headed to the steps. "There is my associate to pick me up to go into town. I plan on spending the night there instead of sleeping here. I have an early meeting in the morning, and it'll work better if I'm in town. I'm sure you can understand." Without saying anything else or waiting for a reply he stepped off the porch and headed to the buggy without looking back.

Paul spoke for the first time since Neil had joined them. "Kind of a strange conversation, don't you think?"

"Very strange. I have my doubts Wade is what he claims to be."

"You may be right." Paul took a deep breath. "Now, to get back to the suggestion I have about the way to save Miss Cardwell's reputation."

"Yes. I'm anxious to hear what you have to say about it."

"It's simple. I'm saying you and she could get married right here. I'm sure Mr. and Mrs. Mason would not object to a wedding taking place here."

For the moment Drake was speechless. He forgot all about his suspicion of Wade Neil and he wondered if the reverend had lost his mind. There was no way in the world he and Bernadette were going to get married here.

He was saved from answering the preacher because the stage driver and his guard walked up to the porch.

~ * ~

When Bernadette and Drake were alone again, and he explained the idea of their getting married to her, she stared at him as if he had two heads. "Why in the world would we want to get married here this evening?"

"As Paul said, it's to protect your reputation."

"I don't understand. I thought marriage was for two people who love each other and want to share the rest of their lives together. Not to protect a woman's reputation."

"You're right. But in this case, if we go through with it here, when we get to Bell Haven, we can have it annulled and nobody will be the wiser."

She cocked her head to the side. "What do you mean?"

"What I mean is, only you and I will know the marriage is in name only and it will make it easy for us to get an annulment."

Bernadette frowned. "So, we go through with a real wedding, but we won't really be getting married, though everyone here will think we are?"

"That's right."

"It seems to me we could just go on pretending to be engaged. It has worked well so far, and then when we get to Bell Haven, as we planned, we'll tell everyone we had a fight and called the whole thing off."

"We can do that but if we do, it'll mean I won't be able to keep you with me all the time until we reach Bell Haven. I know you don't remember the kidnapper saying if he didn't get you somebody else would."

With a look of fright on her face, she asked, "He said that?"

"He did."

Taking a deep breath and without looking at him, she whispered, "Then I agree. If you think we should do it, we will pretend to get married. I guess it won't be a much bigger lie than pretending we're engaged."

Drake shook his head and laughed. "You're right there. Should we tell the folks to get ready for a fake wedding?"

She shook her head at him. "I think we should leave the word fake out of the announcement."

He laughed again.

When they announced they were getting married and everyone at the way station was invited, they all seemed to get into the spirit of the wedding. The men washed up and the women rushed Bernadette into a private room to help her get ready. Melba Mason even insisted the men get Bernadette's trunk so she could wear her prettiest dress for the nuptials.

She then left Helen to take care of dressing the bride. Going out the door, she whispered to Helen, "I'm going to see if I can whip up a cake to celebrate the ceremony."

~ * ~

After washing up and putting on a clean shirt, Drake headed to the shed where Nick Sherra was tied. On the outside he saw young Willie Mason standing. He had a plate of food in his hand, and he looked scared.

"What's wrong, young man?"

"Pa is working in the barn and Ma said for me to bring the outlaw a plate of food."

"Then, what's the problem?"

"I took it to him, and he said I had to untie his hands so he could eat. I know he can't eat very good with his hands tied but I didn't think I should untie him without asking Pa or somebody telling me what I should do. When I told him this, he yelled at me."

"You did the right thing by getting out and not untying him. It'll not be easy, but his hands are tied in front of him. It'll be messy, but he can manage to eat. He was just trying to get you to untie him so he could escape."

"I was afraid it was something like that, so I told him again I couldn't do it. He then started yelling and cussing at me. He even told me he was going to kill me when he got loose. It kind of scared me and I run out." He looked down at the plate. "I didn't leave this, but I don't want to go back in there to give it to him."

"I understand why you feel that way." Blake nodded at the boy. "Why don't you give me the plate and I'll take it in for you?"

"Thank you, mister." He handed Drake the plate. "I ain't never had to feed a mean man before, and I shore appreciate you doing this."

Drake took the food and watched Willie take off in a run toward the house. Then he turned and went into the shed.

~ * ~

Helen smiled as she pulled several dresses from the trunk. "You have some beautiful clothes, Bernadette."

"All but three of them belonged to my aunt. I was the only female relative who was the same size as she and Miz Minnie insisted I take them. Of course, I'm grateful. I loved my aunt, and I'm sure it will make me feel close to her when I wear her clothes."

"That's a wonderful way to feel about it. Is there any particular dress you would like to wear to get married in?"

Bernadette thought a minute. "Maybe the blue one. It was new and Aunt Elsa told me she only wore it one time. I kind of think it was one of her favorites."

"Then I agree. It should be your wedding dress." Helen began shaking the garment to get the wrinkles out.

Melba Mason walked in with a tray in her hand. "Well, I had Willie take some food to the outlaw, and I decided to make us a cup of tea to sip on while we get Miss Bernadette ready to marry the handsome man of hers."

"What a good idea, Melba," Helen said. "Our bride seems to be a little nervous. Maybe it will help settle her down."

"Maybe I am a little nervous," Bernadette said. "But I can't help it. In only minutes, I went from being a fiancée to forgetting about the wedding we had planned in Bell Haven to getting married here in this way station where only my new friends will be attending."

"I'm sorry we don't have a fancy room for the nuptials, Miss Bernadette."

"Oh, please, don't think I'm complaining, Miz Mason. I'm grateful you are letting us have the ceremony here."

"It's an honor for us to have it. In the five years we have owned this stop, we've had many people stop to eat and sleep and I admit, a few unusual things have happened during these stops. But this is the first time we've had the pleasure of something as special as a wedding take place."

"Then this will be a pleasant memory for both parties." Helen turned to Melba. "Do you happen to have an iron I could use to press this dress?"

"Of course. Come with me to the kitchen. I'll put it on the stove to heat and you can press it in there."

"Great." She pointed her finger at Bernadette. "You keep working with your hair. I know you want it to look especially pretty for Drake."

Bernadette only nodded as they left the room. Turning to look at herself in the mirror, she wanted to shout *"What difference does it make? This wedding you two are so excited about isn't a wedding at all. It's just a farce so Drake can stay with me to make sure I get to my sisters' places safely."*

For some reason, this made her sad inside, though she knew she couldn't explain it or let anyone else know how she felt. Sighing, she picked up the brush and went to work on her hair.

~ * ~

Inside the shed, Drake said, "Since you didn't accept your supper from the kid, I decided to see if you'd take it from me." He sat the plate of food close enough for the prisoner to reach it.

"It'll be hard to eat with my hands tied."

"It might be a little, but since you're attached to the pole by the chain on your leg, you can get it to your mouth with your hands tied. Of course, if you prefer, you can go hungry."

Nick muttered a curse and reached for a chicken leg. He bit it, glared at Drake, and said, "It's cold."

"If you had eaten it when Willie brought it, it would've been hot."

There were a few minutes of silence, then Nick broke it. "Are you just going to stand there and glare at me while I eat?"

"I intend to ask you some questions."

"Ask what you want to, but I ain't telling you nothing."

"Why did you try to kidnap my fiancée?"

"'Cause he wanted her."

"How did you know he wanted her?"

"He pointed her out to me and he paid me good to grab her for him."

Ignoring his remark, Drake asked, "Who paid you to grab her?"

"I ain't saying."

"You better say. If you don't, you'll have to be tried for the entire incident as if you planned it alone. That means you'll spend many long years in prison."

"I ain't going to prison."

"How do you think you can avoid it? The witnesses against you will impress the judge."

"What do you mean?"

"Think about it, Sherra. A stage driver and his partner helped capture you. A preacher and his wife, who you knocked down, witnessed your capture, and to top it all, you were arrested by the

Texas Ranger who happened to be engaged to the woman you kidnapped."

Nick frowned. "But there won't be no witnesses here to testify against me. The stage leaves in the morning and you'll all be gone."

"It doesn't work that way, Sherra. The law requires us to be here. We'll all either stay and wait for the trial or we'll come back for it."

"Are you sure?"

"Positive. Now, why don't you decide to tell me who else is involved so it won't go so hard on you."

"You ain't going to catch him. He's long gone from here."

"It doesn't matter where he is. When I get more of my Ranger friends involved in the hunt, it won't take long to find him. Then I'm sure he'll deny having anything to do with you and you'll have to take all the blame."

Nick Sherra looked as if he was thinking. Finally, he muttered, "Maybe I'll think about it."

There was a noise outside and Drake nodded and said, "Somebody is coming, so don't take too long to think."

The door opened and Rob Mason stepped inside.

"Willie said this outlaw tried to get him to untie him. I thought I better come check on things. I don't like his kind trying to intimidate my boy."

"I can understand you wanting to check, but Willie played it smart. He left the shed and took the food with him," Drake said.

"I'm proud of Willie and told him so."

"All I wanted was my hands untied so I could eat better. I weren't gonna hurt the kid," Sherra said with a growl.

"Looks like you're managing to get it down with your hands tied," Rob said.

"Well, it ain't easy," he muttered and stuck a handful of mashed potatoes into his mouth.

Rob ignored him and turned to Drake. "How about you. You getting nervous?"

Drake shook his head. "Maybe a little bit, but I'm more looking forward to it."

"Man, I was a nervous wreck when I tied the knot with Melba."

"Who's gettin' married?" Nick Sherra glared at them and asked.

"Not that it's any of your business, but the Ranger and his woman have decided to get hitched right here in this way station and we're all invited. All of us except you, that is."

"The boss ain't gonna like her getting married."

Drake whirled on him and demanded, "What do you mean by that?"

"He wants all the women to be pure and she won't be pure no more."

Drake jerked the plate out of the man's hand, set it aside, grabbed Nick's shirt collar and yelled at him, "Explain what you're talking about and do it now."

"What are you going to do to me if I don't talk?"

"If you want to take the chance, you'll see."

Nick Sherra must have believed him because he started talking. He told them the man wanted Bernadette because she was beautiful and untouched by a man. He said his boss's goal was to start a bordello, not with working girls but with virgins because he knew men would pay any price to be the first with the women. He also told them where the bordello was to be located and where five of the six women he wanted to start his business were being held prisoner. In fact, he told everything except the name of the man who was behind it all. No matter how Drake prodded, he wouldn't give up the man's name.

Finally, Drake and Mason left the shed telling him to think about it tonight and they'd talk with him again in the morning.

"Don't matter. I ain't gonna tell you," were Nick Sherra's last words on the subject.

~ * ~

Though simple, the wedding ceremony turned out to be a rather festive occasion. Melba Mason had decorated the room with wildflowers and candles, and with the help of Helen McGill had cooked a special wedding supper, plus a small wedding cake. The men, including the stage driver and the guard, had washed up and put on clean shirts.

A room located off to itself was made up especially for the newlyweds. When they retired, Bernadette's emotions ran in all directions as they entered the private room. She was nervous and somewhat relieved when, without saying anything, Drake took a pillow and a blanket from the bed and made a pallet on the floor at the foot of the bed.

Bernadette didn't say anything either, but she gave him a timid smile.

He smiled back. "I intend to keep my promise to you," he said.

He didn't have to explain because she fully understood. Their marriage, which wasn't a marriage, would be over as soon as they reached Bell Haven. She nodded at him and went behind the screen to put on her nightgown and to fold her wedding dress and put it in the carpet bag she'd brought to the room earlier. She glanced at her blue traveling suit hanging across the screen knowing she'd dress in it in the morning. As soon as the light was blown out, she slipped from behind the screen and got into bed. She didn't understand why she felt a little sad.

~ * ~

A fully dressed Drake bent over the bed and smiled at the sleeping Bernadette. He couldn't help noticing how pretty she was. Shaking the thought away, he patted her cheek and said, "You need to get up and get your traveling clothes on, Bernadette. The stage is readying to pull out."

She opened her eyes and in a sleepy voice, she whispered, "Isn't it too early?"

"Must not be because Abe told me we had only a few minutes, and you know it wouldn't look right if I left my new wife behind.

I'll have you a cup of coffee ready when you get downstairs." He rose up, though there was nothing he wanted to do more than to crawl into bed and hold her in his arms and let her drift back to sleep. Knowing this was impossible, he headed for the door without giving her time to answer.

When he got downstairs, Abe asked, "She about ready to go?"

"She will be."

"Good. I want to get to town and have the prisoner put in jail. That's gonna throw me behind schedule enough without having to wait for her to get prettied up."

Before Drake could answer, Melba Mason said, "I knew you'd be in a hurry, so I sent Willie to take the prisoner a cup of coffee and a biscuit. I didn't want anybody saying we didn't feed the man while he was here."

Before anyone could answer her, Willie's voice could be heard screaming for his dad as he ran toward the house. The door burst open, and a breathless and scared Willie yelled, "Pa, the man has blood all over him and I think he's dead!"

The men all jumped up from the table and headed for the shack where Nick Sherra had been tied. Entering, they saw what Willie had seen – a bloodied corpse still secured to the post in the corner. When they all acted as if they didn't know what to do, Drake's Ranger training kicked in and he took over. "Since I'm the only lawman here, I guess I'm in charge," he said.

There was no argument as each man nodded his head. They all looked relieved to let him tell them all what to do.

It didn't take as long to get things in order as everyone thought it would. Jake, the guard, went to town to get the sheriff and to go by the office to tell them what was going on so they could inform the main stage line.

Rob Mason and his son, Willie, were told to go ahead and take care of the stock and any other chores that had to be done so the women wouldn't have to come out of the house.

The preacher was to stay with the women and try to keep them calm while Drake and Abe, the driver, looked around the shed to see if there were any clues to be had.

"You know, Drake," Abe said. "I thought I'd encountered about anything a man could imagine making these runs, but this beats all."

"I know what you mean. I keep playing the conversation I had with Sherra over and over in my head. I can't help but think I missed something."

"How could you have missed anything? He just kept saying things like the man he worked for was gone, though he did explain what the capture of your woman was all about. He even told us where he had the other women stashed."

Drake frowned. "I just wish it would come together in my thoughts. I know it's there. If I could just..." He stopped in mid-sentence and turned to Abe. In an excited voice he almost shouted, "I've got it. I know who is behind the whole thing."

Abe looked startled. "Who?"

"Never mind. I'm going to borrow a horse. I need to meet the sheriff. This man has to be arrested before he leaves town again."

"But first tell me who..." Abe didn't finish his sentence because Drake was halfway to the barn.

While Willie saddled a horse for him, Drake ran into the house and told Bernadette he had to go after the criminal, and he wanted her to stay at the way station until he returned.

She tried to argue with him, but he shook his head, pulled her into his arms, and kissed her passionately. He then let her go and hurried out the door before she could say anything else.

~ * ~

Two nights later, Bernadette, who had stayed at the way station when the stage pulled out the next day not because Drake had asked her to, but because of the kiss he'd given her, was awakened by a hand covering her mouth. Though she couldn't see anything in the heavy darkness, her eyes flew open, her heart began to beat wildly, and a surge of panic descended on her. Her heart slowed down a little when a gentle whisper said, "Don't be afraid, Bernadette. It's me. Drake."

She nodded and he removed his hand. "I knew it would scare you when I came in and I didn't want you to scream and wake up everyone in the house. I knew they'd get up and start asking me questions and all I wanted to do was sleep a little before I told them what had happened. It's been a rough couple of days."

"Are you all right?"

"I'm exhausted but otherwise, I'm fine."

She glanced around the room and still couldn't see anything. "What time is it?"

"I think it's around three o'clock."

"In the morning?"

"Yes."

"Will you answer one question before you go to sleep?"

"If you'll let me sit down on your bed before I fall down."

"Of course."

He sat. "What's your question?"

"Did you catch him and who was he?"

"Yes, I caught him, and it was Wade Neil."

Bernadette shot up to a sitting position. "Who did you say?"

He didn't answer.

"Drake," she said, but he still didn't answer.

Frowning, she moved to the other side of the bed and lit the lamp on the table. Looking around, she saw Drake was no longer sitting on the side of her bed. He was lying down with his upper torso on the bed and his feet and legs hanging toward the floor. He was fast asleep.

Though she wanted more details of the arrest, she knew she didn't have the heart to pressure him to wake up and tell her about it tonight. She reached down, removed his boots, then eased his legs to the bed. Though she knew he'd probably be more comfortable with his clothes off, there was nothing she could do about it. She did manage to get his gun and holster off him and hang it on the bed post.

When she had done all she could do to make him comfortable, she went back to the other side of the bed, blew out the light and got into bed beside him. "After all," she mumbled into the darkness, "he is my husband, though he might not realize it yet. It doesn't matter what he thinks because the kiss he gave me when he left me here made up my mind about what's going to happen between us. Though it might take him a while to accept the fact, I intend to stay his wife from this day forward and we're going to have a long and happy marriage together."

She then snuggled close to him and grinned. "In fact, when he wakes up in the morning, he's going to wonder what went on between us tonight." She almost giggled aloud. Then added, "Maybe after we've been married several years, I'll tell him the truth, but until then I'll only grin and tell him it was a wonderful night."

She then put her arm around his waist and snuggled closer. It wasn't long until she went back to sleep with a smile of happiness on her lips.

Five

Rosemary

It was Monday and a few weeks before her seventeenth birthday, and as she had done every Monday and Thursday between ten and eleven o'clock in the morning since she was fifteen years old, Rosemary Cardwell left the orphanage to walk the little over a mile to the small post office in the East Texas town of Weatherson, to collect the mail for The Clanton Orphanage. She had been going to fetch the mail since she was fourteen, though for the first year she only went with Velma, a girl whose regular chore it was. When Velma left the orphanage, Mr. Clanton said Rosemary was now trained well enough to handle the job alone. He also said as long as she followed the strict rules Velma had taught her, the job would be hers.

Only once had she verbally questioned one of those rules. On the last week she accompanied Velma to town, there had been a letter addressed to her and she saw it was from Mitch O'Donald, a friend who had promised to keep in touch with her when he had left the orphanage because Mr. Clanton decided his services were no longer needed. The fact he was twenty and had worked there since he'd aged out as a student a few years earlier, made no difference to the owner. He replaced Mitch with Mr. Watson, an older man, whom many of the adults complained didn't do the job as well as Mitch had. Those complaints fell on deaf ears because Mr. Watson was still employed there.

Rosemary was excited when she saw the letter from her friend and reached for it so she could rip into it. Velma jerked it out of her hand. "No, Rosemary. It doesn't matter if you see a letter addressed to you, you are not allowed to open it. The rule is, all mail goes to the orphanage owner, Mr. Clanton. If he isn't in his office, you're to give all the mail to his sister, Miss Gladiola, whose office is down the hall from his." Rosemary frowned. "Why? If a letter is addressed to you, you should be able to open it."

"I think so, too, but the rules are not up to you or me. Mr. Clanton put this rule into effect the year Millie, the girl who was training me for the job, opened a letter addressed to her. I'm not sure what was in the letter, but Mr. Clanton was so upset, he took the job of getting the mail away from Millie and told me I was to do it alone from then on."

"I still don't understand."

"Neither do I, but I know having this job is a privilege and to keep it you need to obey all the rules. So, if you ever find a letter addressed to you, don't open it. Give it to him and if it's something you should see, he'll pass it back to you."

Shocked, but not sure what to say, Rosemary muttered, "I understand."

Although she didn't understand at all. Rosemary decided then and there when she was doing this chore alone, she'd probably break this rule if she were ever faced with a letter addressed to her.

When she started getting the mail on her own, there was a letter from her sister, Melissa. Since there was nobody to stop her, she hid the letter in her chemise and read it alone in her room. She did the same with the letter from Catherine. In the meantime, she managed to write to each of them and tell them she was happy they had met and married their husbands, but it would be better if they didn't write to her often. She hadn't heard from Bernadette, but since Catherine had given her all of their addresses, she sent Bernadette a letter, too.

It was some time before she heard from Mitch again. He seemed upset she hadn't answered his letter. She wrote to him and explained the situation and he immediately replied he wouldn't write often, but she had his address, and she was to get in touch with him if she needed him for anything between letters. This thrilled her and though he was three or four years older than she, she knew they still had the special bond they'd had when he lived and worked at the orphanage.

Another special bond she had made in the orphanage was with little Benny Neven, who was going on three-years-old and whose father sent him to live at the orphanage because his mother had died, and he either couldn't raise him alone or didn't want to because of the child's disabilities. He had two missing fingers on his left hand and three missing toes on his left foot. Though Benny coped with the hand, the affected foot interfered with his walking. Also, when the little boy began to speak, he had a hard time pronouncing words.

Because Benny had what some people considered physical defects, few of the older children wanted to play with him and some made fun of him. The teachers and other adults simply ignored him. This upset Rosemary and she treated the child as if he were family. It wasn't long until she felt as if they were related.

Later she learned Mr. Clanton wouldn't have taken the child as a pupil in the orphanage if his father hadn't agreed to send money monthly until Benny turned three or was adopted.

Nobody knew what was to happen to the child after his third birthday. But all agreed it probably wouldn't be a good thing since it was a well-known fact the child's father was also ashamed of the boy because he was born with what he considered uncorrectable defects.

To top it off, the woman the father planned to marry refused to raise Benny as her stepson. Rosemary had learned all of this by eavesdropping on Dwight Clanton and his sister.

None of these things mattered to Rosemary. She was crazy about the sweet little guy who had attached himself to her on his first week at the orphanage and was beginning to try to say her name, though it came out as *Osemary*.

~ * ~

When Rosemary arrived at Weatherson's post office, she saw a poster on the side of the adjoining buildings advertising a small animal circus coming to town in a couple of weeks. As she paused to study the picture, she knew it would thrill Benny to be able to see these wild exotic animals in real life instead of on the pages of the books she read to him over and over again.

Though he had made it clear his favorite animal was the bear, she knew the elephant and the tiger they pictured on the advertisement would excite him. Besides, they might have a bear because under the tiger's left paw were the words '*and many more exciting animals not seen in everyday life.*'

It then crossed her mind, no matter how nice he'd been to her lately, Mr. Clanton would probably never give her permission to take Benny to town to visit this circus. It was the thought of the word '*probably*' which gave her the idea to think about approaching him when she caught him in one of his rare, good moods.

Moving away from the poster, she hurried up the steps of the post office and went through the front door. "Hello, Mr. Sykes," she said to the balding man behind the counter.

"Good morning, Miss Cardwell." Without either of them having to explain why she was there, he added, "We haven't been busy this morning, so I have the Clanton Orphanage mail sorted and ready for you."

"Thank you, Mr. Sykes." She took the mail he handed her across the counter and slid it into the orphanage mailbag. She didn't have to say anything else because two men came through the door behind her. She gave the postmaster a quick nod and left the building.

As was her custom, she hurried out of town to the small grove of trees beside the road on the way to and from the orphanage. She went to the downed log she always used, sat, and began thumbing through the mail. Though she didn't expect to find anything addressed to her, she knew if she missed a day of checking something could slip by.

She was shocked and delighted to see a letter to her from her sister, Bernadette. She couldn't wait to know what her sister had said. Ripping open the missive, she began to read.

My Dearest, Rosemary,

Melissa and Catherine told me I would be taking a risk by writing to you since the mail to the orphanage is checked and enclosures such as money may be confiscated. Still, they encouraged me to try to get through to you. So, I decided to take the chance you would receive this letter, and I am writing to you with hope.

I feel you deserve to know what has happened in my life since Aunt Vernetta separated us on the terrible day of our parents' funeral. I also thought you'd like to learn our older sisters are both still extremely happy with the way their lives have turned out with their cowboys and their new homes near the small town of Bell Haven, Texas.

As you may or may not remember, when Aunt Vernetta separated the four of us, I was sent to be a companion to an ailing aunt in Atlanta. I didn't know the woman, though they told me her first husband was a good man, and her second husband wasn't nice at all. At first everything was fine, and it turned out I not only liked the woman, but I loved her.

Then she grew sicker and eventually became bedridden. It was at this time that her husband began to say inappropriate things to me, but I was able to elude him most of the time. It changed when she eventually passed away. He became aggressive toward me. He kept saying things like 'Since Elsa is finally gone, we can admit our feelings for each other.' I assure you I never had the least interest in the man and couldn't wait to get away from Atlanta and from him.

When some of Aunt Elsa's first husband's relatives came to the funeral, they soon saw how he was treating me and helped me avoid him until I could escape.

I also had a good friend in Atlanta whose brother, Drake Rafferty, is a Texas Ranger and was in town visiting his family. Knowing he was soon heading back to Texas and how much I wanted to get away from Atlanta and Aunt Elsa's husband, my friend enlisted him to accompany me to the area where Melissa and Catherine live.

I won't go into the details, but he and I became good friends on the trip, and when we encountered a ruthless businessman, he saved me from a terrible situation I could have been forced into. I know it was meant to be because before we reached Bell Haven, Drake and I fell in love and were married.

Since being a Texas Ranger would take him away from home so much, he made the decision to only help the Rangers in local and surrounding areas when he is needed.

The sheriff of Bell Haven was hurt, and he asked Drake if he'd serve as the local sheriff until he recovered. Of course, Drake said he would. In the meantime, the sheriff decided to retire and only work part time in the office. Drake is now the main sheriff. We have a lovely little house on the street behind the jail, and we both love it.

But don't think since I live in town, and our sisters live on ranches with their husbands, we don't get to see each other often.

We all attend the same church and most Sundays we go to one of our homes for Sunday dinner and enjoy being together. All our husbands have become good friends, too.

I know Melissa's prediction that the four of us will all be together again someday has almost come true. When you are able to leave the orphanage and come here, it will be a reality. A reality which could happen when you reach your next birthday, since you said you planned to leave there when you turn seventeen, or eighteen at the most. When you get here, we will no longer have to have our Sister Circle by letter, we will be able to have it in person.

If you can, please try to let us know your plan for this year. We will send you money or anything else you need and help you make any arrangements necessary to get here. In the meantime, know we love you and speak of you often.

Your loving sister,
Bernadette

Rosemary hugged the letter to her chest and whispered, "Oh yes, Bernadette. I want to come to Texas to be with my sisters and as soon as I can, I'll write and let you know. It may be next year, but it's all right. Things aren't as bad for me here as they have been in the past. When I was younger it was hard, but in the last couple of years both Mr. Clanton and his sister have been nicer to me. As long as I know I can be with my sisters again someday, I don't mind waiting to have our Sister Circle in person again."

She read Bernadette's letter once again, then folded it and stuck it in the top of her chemise as she had done with her previous letters. She knew as soon as she was alone in her room, she'd read it again then hide it under the false bottom of her heavy wardrobe. That was where she hid other things she knew she wasn't allowed to have, such as the paper and envelopes and the few stamps she'd been able to get for her own use, as well as the small amount of money she'd been able to save from what she'd been given to buy necessities or treats when she did something to please Mr. Clanton.

She'd found the secret place the day they'd moved the wardrobe into the small private room she'd been allowed to use after Velma had left. She didn't know if anyone else knew about the false bottom, but she didn't think so. Though the owner's sister, Miss Gladiola Clanton, opened the wardrobe now and then and peered inside, the woman had never indicated there was anything she'd missed, or that she knew about the false bottom.

Rosemary stood, stretched, then left the woods, and headed toward the orphanage with a happy heart. She knew if anyone questioned her about being especially happy today, she'd tell them the brisk walk into town had made her feel invigorated. She knew she was always good at thinking of replies everyone believed whenever she needed them.

~ * ~

When she got to the home, Rosemary decided to go in the back door because if she used the front Mr. Clanton might decide to invite her into his office to have one of the chats he'd been having with her lately. Though they often talked about the orphanage, or some of the children, or even the weather, she didn't want to take the time to visit with him now. She wanted to get to her room, read her letter again, then hide it.

She went through the back hall leading to the owners' private dining room not expecting either Dwight Clanton or his sister to be there this early for lunch. But she was surprised when she heard Gladiola Clanton say, "My dear brother, I tend to think you have lost your mind."

"Don't be foolish. I'm sure you've guessed I've been grooming Rosemary for this since she became such a pretty budding teenager. Since she's almost a woman now, I consider her beautiful and I suppose others think the same thing."

"I never had a thought of her being especially pretty, Dwight. She's only sixteen years old, you know."

"She'll be seventeen in a few weeks. By anyone's standard, that's considered a young woman of marriageable age."

"Maybe if the groom is as young as twenty or so, but you're almost fifty. Much too old to consider marrying a child such as Rosemary."

Dwight's voice rose an octave. "I don't want to hear such words come out of your mouth. If you don't back me in this, I'll have to do something about it."

"What can you do?"

"A lot, my dear sister. A lot."

"Such as?"

"If you must be reminded, Father left this orphanage solely to me. You only work here because of my benevolent nature and as long as you do my bidding, your job is secure. Otherwise, be prepared to find another place to live and start seeking employment elsewhere, which I'm sure wouldn't be very easy at your age. You do remember you are only a few years younger than me, don't you?"

In a hesitant voice, she said, "Of course, now I understand. If you want to marry Rosemary when she turns seventeen, I will help you achieve that goal any way I can."

He chuckled. "I thought you'd see things my way, Gladiola. Now, ring the bell. I'm ready for our earlier than usual lunch to be served. We need to get finished before the trustees show up for our afternoon meeting."

"May I ask you one question before I summons the food?"

"If you must."

"You know how much Rosemary loves little Benny Neven. Do you plan to adopt him?"

"Of course not."

"Then what....?"

"Don't worry about it, sister. I only expect one more payment. You know his father will quit sending money for his care when he turns three this month and I won't have to put up with him any longer."

"But…"

"Forget about the little nuisance. You know children his age have accidents they don't recover from." He emitted a vicious chuckle and added, "Just as a sister who hasn't learned not to ask foolish questions can have an accident to take her out of this world without anyone ever knowing what caused her demise."

When she said nothing, he laughed and said, "Now, ring the bell. I'm getting hungry."

You can't panic now. Rosemary grabbed her mouth and kept repeating the phrase to herself silently as she slipped back down the hall. She knew she had to get away before they discovered she had overheard their conversation.

She reached the side door leading to the main part of the building. Hurrying through it, she kept silently talking to herself. *If you possibly can, you have to act as if everything is normal. Go put the mail on Dwight Clanton's desk since he isn't there to engage you in a conversation. You then have to go to the lunchroom to make sure the younger children eat, then are put down for their naps. Afterward, you must join the older ones for your lunch and theirs. It'll then be their play time before they go to their afternoon classes. It won't be easy, but once the children are taken care of, you can take refuge in your room and try to digest what you overheard and decide what you have to do to foil Mr. Clanton's evil plan and not only save Benny's life, but yours as well.*

By the time night fell and she was ready to go to bed, Rosemary had the beginnings of a plan to escape the life Dwight Clanton had planned for her, but she knew she would have to have help to pull it off. Her first step in acquiring this help was to write a letter to her friend, Mitch O'Donald, and put it in the mail the next day she went to the post office. She only hoped he was still at the same address since she hadn't heard from him in several months. If not, she didn't know what she'd do because she didn't think she had time to contact her sisters for help.

Rosemary didn't let her mind linger on this long as she tried to come up with a plan to make sure Benny would be safe. The more she thought about it, the more she realized the only answer was to take the little boy with her when she left, though she didn't have a clue as to how she was going to accomplish this.

~ * ~

On Thursday Rosemary tried not to let anyone see how anxious she was to make her trek into town to get the mail, though it seemed fate brought in all kinds of situations to delay her trip.

First, Gladiola called her into the small office down the hall from her brother's larger one. "I need you to go to the general store and buy a pack of hair pins for me, Rosemary. I've lost so many lately I'm having a hard time keeping my hair put up in the way my brother insists I wear it."

"I'll be happy to get them for you, Miss Gladiola," Rosemary said and forced a smile. She knew this would delay her in beginning the steps to carry out her escape plan.

"Also, buy a peppermint stick. I'm out and I need it to settle my stomach when the cook puts too much spice in the food."

"Yes, ma'am," Rosemary muttered, though she knew full well the real reason for the candy was because Miss Gladiola loved it and used the upset stomach as an excuse to buy it. Most of the other residents at the orphanage knew it, too, and often laughed about it behind her back.

Gladiola counted a certain amount of money. Then counted it again and slipped it into an envelope and handed it to Rosemary. "This is the exact amount it will cost. Don't lose it."

"I won't," she replied and turned to leave.

Finally, she thought she was on her way to get the mailbag. But it didn't happen. She was at the door when a teacher came running into the office. "Miss Clanton, Becky Dearing, one of the eight-year-old girls in my class, fell on the steps and twisted her ankle. It's swelling awfully bad, and I can't find Mr. Clanton. I'm not sure what to do."

Gladiola caught Rosemary going out the door and told her to come with her to check the girl because she might need a doctor. Of course, Rosemary obeyed.

Because the ankle looked bad, Gladiola told Rosemary to go by the doctor's office in town and tell him to come check to make sure the girl's foot was only a sprain and not broken.

Finally, Rosemary was able to get the mailbag and head toward Weatherson. But she encountered one more delay.

Dwight Clanton met her at the gate as he returned from his morning ride and informed her there was something he wanted to discuss with her as soon as she returned. Though chatting with him was the last thing she wanted to do today, she bit her tongue and nodded.

He grinned and headed to the stable, leading his horse.

At last Rosemary was on her way to get the mail, though she knew her main goal today was to send the letter to Mitch. She also knew she had to be careful doing it. Her entire escape plan depended on him getting the letter and nobody knowing she sent it.

She had so much on her mind when she got to town, she paid no attention to the posters advertising the coming circus which were still up on buildings and posts. She decided the first thing she needed to do was to go to the doctor's office because she felt Becky's injury was top priority. She then decided her next stop should be the mercantile to pick up the hair pins and candy for Miss Gladiola.

When she got to the post office, she would do the most important thing. She would slip the letter she'd written to Mitch into the outgoing mail slot when Mr. Styles wasn't looking. She realized this was being overly cautious, but she wanted to make sure when she made her final escape there was no way she could be traced, and knowing how devious Dwight Clanton was, he would probably question everyone she had any contact within Weatherson.

Elsie Martin looked up when Rosemary entered Martin's General Store. "What can I help you with, young lady?"

"I want to purchase a pack of hair pins for Miss Gladiola Clanton at the orphanage, please, ma'am."

"Did she send any money?"

"Yes ma'am." Rosemary laid the money on the counter. "She said this was the correct amount with a penny left over to buy a peppermint stick."

"Good. I told her last time she came in, her brother had informed me she couldn't add any more of her purchases to the orphanage account. Therefore, I've decided if she doesn't bring the money with her or send it, I can't let her have the merchandise."

Rosemary didn't know what to say, so she only nodded at the storekeeper.

Elsie got the hair pins and a peppermint stick, wrapped them, and laid them on the counter. She then picked up the envelope, counted it, then nodded. "She told you right. This is the exact amount, but I can't believe she didn't give you enough so you could get a piece of candy, too."

"It's my job to get only what they tell me to get," Rosemary mumbled.

"Do you want to buy anything for yourself?"

"No, ma'am, but thank you for helping me." She picked up the package and smiled.

"Well, in that case, why don't I treat you to a piece of candy?" She opened the lid on the big jar and pulled out another peppermint stick.

"I don't think they'd like for me to accept it, but I do thank you for offering."

Elsie laughed. "Then, don't tell them. Besides, if you don't want it, I bet there's another person at the orphanage who would appreciate a surprise."

Rosemary hesitated, then said, "There is a little boy I read to. He's almost three years old and I doubt he's ever had a piece of candy."

"Then take him two pieces, and when you're in town again, please stop in." She handed Rosemary two peppermint sticks and turned to wait on the customer who had come into the store. Rosemary hurried out the door and headed to the post office. She had gone only a short distance when she noticed a man getting out of a wagon parked in front of the gun shop. An almost squeal of delight escaped her throat, but she pushed it down, and with her heart racing, she rushed forward to catch him before he went into the shop.

Reaching him, she exclaimed, "Mitch O'Donald! I can't believe I actually ran into you. I was on the way to mail you a letter."

"Hello, Rosemary and what is this about you sending me a letter? I thought you weren't allowed to get in touch with me."

"Oh, Mitch! I'm not supposed to write you but something terrible has happened and you were the only person in the world I thought might be able to help me."

"Well, why don't we go into the café down the street, and you can tell me all about it?"

"I can't. I have to go to the post office and get the orphanage mail." She reached into her pocket. "Everything I need to tell you is in this letter. Go ahead and take care of your business, then if you can meet me where I left instructions in the letter, please do so."

"I don't understand."

"I'll explain everything if you can meet me. In the meantime, if anyone says anything about us talking here on the street, just tell them you remembered me from the orphanage and stopped to speak."

"I still don't...." He didn't finish his sentence because Rosemary had hurried away.

~ * ~

Puzzled, but knowing he'd have to read the letter to find out what Rosemary was talking about, he stuffed the missive in his pocket and went into the gun shop to pick up the rifle he'd saved up to buy. After getting his purchase, he headed to Martin's General Store to pick up a few more of the supplies he was collecting for his trek to the Colorado mountains in search of gold, though the trip was beginning to look as if it might not happen.

"Hello there, Mitch," Elsie said as he entered. "I'm guessing you're here to add to your supplies for your big trip."

"You've guessed right. Got to be prepared. It's a long way from here to Colorado."

"So, when is this trip planned or have you changed your mind about going?"

"We'll finish with the work on the ranch at the end of this week and then they won't need those who were hired for the roundup. We planned to leave here shortly after we get our final pay." He grinned at her. "And why did you think I might change my mind about going?"

"I went out to sweep the walkway in front of my front door and saw you talking to the pretty young woman who had just been in here."

For some reason he didn't want to admit the plan to search for gold in Colorado might not happen. She'd have too many questions. "Just ran into her and remembered I knew her from when I was working at the orphanage and she recognized me too. Her name is Rosemary something or other. I can't remember what. Do you know her?"

"No but she came in to buy hair pins for Miss Clanton."

"Yeah. I remember the Clanton siblings often made the students run their errands." Not wanting to get into a discussion about the orphanage or about Rosemary, he added, "I hope you still have those canned peaches I got here the other day because I want to buy five more."

She laughed. "Of course, I do. But you're going to have to stop eating your supplies or you won't have enough food for the long trip to Colorado."

He grinned. "I'll do my best not to eat everything, Miz Martin."

After finishing his shopping, Mitch stowed his purchases in the back of the wagon. He then headed to the blacksmith shop to have the left front wheel, which had been wobbling, checked. He figured then would be a good time to read the letter Rosemary had given him.

~ * ~

Mitch let Rosemary out of the wagon before it could be spotted on the road leading to the orphanage, and she hurried away with hope in her heart. After he met her in her usual stopping place in the woods and she explained more fully about the plan Dwight Clanton had for her, he was furious. Not only did he want her to leave with him, but he didn't even want her to go back there to get her meager possessions.

It took him a while to calm down, but he did when she explained about Benny. After thinking it over, he agreed the only thing she could do was bring the little boy along when she made her escape. He agreed to meet her again when she came for the mail on Monday. He also agreed to keep their relationship a secret from anybody in town since he knew Dwight Clanton would probably come to town in search of her when she left.

The only thing concerning her now was the fact he had told her he planned to go to Colorado with a couple of friends to search for gold. Now, she wondered if he'd expect her to go with him or was his plan to get her out of town then let her find her way to Bell Haven on her own.

These thoughts filled her mind as she entered the gate to the stone building which had been where she had lived for several years. She always thought of the Clanton Orphanage as the place where she lived. She had never let it cross her mind to consider it home.

Entering the front hallway, she headed to the owner's office. As she expected, Miss Gladiola was at the desk in her office and the door was open. "Did you get my hair pins?" Gladiola barked without saying hello.

"Yes, Miss Gladiola. I did. I also got the peppermint stick you wanted." She took the package from the mailbag and handed it across the desk.

The door to his private office opened and Dwight Clanton stepped out. "Gladiola, go to the lunchroom and make sure our food will be ready in twenty minutes. I have a few instructions for Rosemary, then I'll come to eat."

Gladiola didn't hesitate. "Yes, brother," she said as she got out of her chair and left the room without saying anything else.

He turned to Rosemary. "Come into my office, my dear."

She knew she couldn't refuse, so she went through the door he held open for her. Without being told where to sit, she hurried to one of the plush pull-up chairs in front of his desk. She then placed the mailbag on the desk. "There wasn't a lot of mail today," she volunteered.

He gave her one of the smiles she often thought of as sneaky, then asked, "We don't usually get as much on Thursday, but did you happen to see if there was anything from Mr. Neven?"

"I wouldn't know, sir. You know I'm not allowed to look through it." She wasn't about to tell him she had looked but hadn't seen a letter from Benny's father.

He smiled again. "You are so dependable, Rosemary, my dear. It never occurs to you to break a rule, does it?"

Not knowing what he was getting at, she mumbled, "Of course not, sir."

He flipped through the mail. "Well, it's not here. Maybe it'll come next week."

"Maybe so, sir."

He looked directly at her. "Since there wasn't much mail, I must ask why you were later than usual in getting home?"

"I'm sorry, Mr. Clanton. I guess it was because of my other errands."

He raised an eyebrow. "What other errands?"

"Miss Gladiola told me to go tell the doctor to come and check on Becky's ankle because she thought it might be broken. It took me a little while to find his office. Then I went to the general store to get the hair pins and candy Miss Gladiola wanted. By the time I got the mail, I guess I was a little tired and walked back here slower than I usually do."

He frowned again. "I can't believe she sent for the doctor without telling me. Also, why should you have to do her shopping for her?"

"I didn't mind."

"Of course, you didn't. You're too nice."

Before she could answer there was a knock on his door and he growled out, "Yes? Who is it?"

The door opened and Gladiola stuck her head inside. "Dwight, the doctor is here, and he says Becky's ankle is broken. He wants to take her to his office to treat it. I think you should come and see him."

"You're right. I'll be right there." He stood to leave and added, "We'll talk later, Rosemary."

She only nodded, and hurried away before he could change his mind and tell her to wait. She wanted to get to her room, hide the candy Miss Martin had given her and think about what she could do to get Benny away without anyone knowing. She also wanted to think about what she should tell Mitch on Monday. If he had his heart set on going to Colorado, would she agree to go with him and forget about going to Bell Haven and her sisters? She hoped this wasn't a decision she'd have to make.

After she went to bed, Rosemary didn't think she'd be able to sleep. There was too much on her mind. Yet, when she was about to doze off, she sat straight up in bed. It had come to her in a flash, and she knew exactly how she could get away from the orphanage with Benny. Now all she had to do was figure out how to convince the orphanage owner to unknowingly help her pull off her scheme.

~ * ~

On Monday, Rosemary was able to hide two changes of outfits for Benny and a few of her personal items in the mailbag. It would have held more, but she knew the bag had to look flat when she left the building. She didn't want her plan to be discovered since she had it all worked out in her mind.

Making sure it looked fine, she headed to Dwight Clanton's office to see if he had anything for the outgoing mail. Now was the time to approach him about Benny. She only hoped she would be able to pull it off.

As she stepped through the office door, he looked up and smiled. "Hello, Rosemary. I knew I could count on you to be right on time this morning."

"Good morning, Mr. Clanton."

He handed her a letter. "I have just this minute sealed this missive because I want you to mail it for me today."

"I'd be glad to, sir." She took a deep breath. "If you're not too busy, do you mind if I have a short talk with you?"

His eyes lit up. "I'm never too busy to talk to you, Rosemary. Have a seat.

"Thank you." She sat in one of the chairs in front of his desk and tried to hide her nervousness. "I guess what I really want is to ask you a question."

"Then by all means, ask it, my dear."

She took another deep breath. "I don't know if you've seen the advertisements in town or not, but there is a small animal circus coming to town later this week."

He grinned at her. "Are you telling me you want to go see it?"

"Not at all." After another breath, she blurted, "I wanted to get your permission to take Benny Neven to see it."

He frowned. "Oh, no, Rosemary. I could never permit you to do such a thing."

She glared at him. "But..."

"There's no need to argue with me about it. My answer will still be *no*. As I said, I would never permit it."

Rosemary couldn't hide the hurt and disappointment she felt. She didn't say a word, but she gave him a look of pure hatred, grabbed the mailbag, and stalked out the door.

~ * ~

Gladiola walked into his office. "What in the world did you say to Rosemary? She looked ready to kill somebody."

"The young lady had the audacity to ask me to permit Benny Neven to go with her to some sort of circus which is coming to town this week. Of course, I refused."

His sister raised an eyebrow. "You made a big mistake, brother."

He frowned. "I don't see why you would say that."

"It's simple, Dwight. The look she had on her face told me I have a better chance of getting little Benny Neven to seriously consider marrying me than you do in convincing Rosemary to marry you."

"Don't be ridiculous. She'll realize what a good life she'll have with me."

"You're wrong, Dwight. If she had felt disappointed or been somewhat upset with your refusal to let him go, you could probably overcome it. But I saw in her eyes, when you told her Benny couldn't go, she had nothing but pure hatred for you. There's no way you can overcome such a hatred in the weeks left before her birthday."

He frowned. "I'm sure she understands why I had to refuse such a thing."

Gladiola shook her head. "No, she doesn't. She saw it as a mean thing for you to do. She's crazy about Benny and she now sees you as a heartless and cruel headmaster of this place. She'll never trust you again."

"I don't believe you."

Gladiola got up and went to the door. As she opened it to step outside, she said, "You'll see I'm right when she gets back with the mail." She then closed the door behind her.

~ * ~

Parked and sitting in his wagon near Rosemary's stopping place on her way to the post office, Mitch wasn't sure what he was going to tell her. He thought he had it all planned out but the more he went over the words in his mind, the more he wondered if he should or could say them to her. Maybe he should drive off before she arrived and just make sure she didn't see him again before he left town. Of course, this would make it easier for him, but would she be able to work out her problem without his help? Before he could make up his mind about what to do, she appeared around the curve in the road. His heart began to beat faster than it should when he saw her, and he couldn't help smiling, though he didn't understand why.

As she drew closer, he noticed how she had matured into a lovely young woman since he'd befriended her when she was still a young girl while he was at the orphanage. It had been fine to help her when she was young, but the last thing he wanted to do was get involved in another pretty woman's problem. He took a deep breath and let the thought cross his mind that he already knew the right thing for him to do, and it was to tell her he'd see she got out of town with the little boy, but there was no way he was going to give up his plan to go to Colorado to take her to the other side of Texas.

He had the offer of another job in this area and since the trip to Colorado with his friends was about to fall through, he'd decided to take the job, save up more money, and then head to

Colorado later. That way he wouldn't have to tell her about Marcie or how she had treated him and left him leery of getting involved with another pretty woman's problems. He knew the incident with Marcie had taught him a lesson enough to last a lifetime.

He didn't ponder these thoughts long because as Rosemary drew nearer, he could see she was walking in such a way as to make him think she was mad. She was walking faster than usual, and her shoulders were slumped.

When she was within a few yards of the wagon, the smile she sent him didn't cover the evidence she'd been crying.

As soon as she muttered a 'hello' to him, without greeting her back, he jumped from the wagon and blurted, "What's wrong, Rosemary?"

Rosemary almost fell into his arms. "Oh, Mitch. I don't know what to do."

"What has happened?"

"He won't let me take Benny to see the animals and I don't know any other way to get him away from the orphanage." She began to cry. "I can't leave there without him. I couldn't live with myself knowing I left such a sweet boy there to die."

In an instant, all the notion he'd had about not helping Rosemary get away with the child fled from his mind and he said, "You won't have to leave him. We'll think of something to do to get him away from there."

~ * ~

After making a tentative plan, Rosemary would only let Mitch drive her to the edge of town. She insisted it would be better if no one saw them together and realized they knew each other. "I'm sure when we leave, Mr. Clanton will come to town and ask questions."

"You're right. Which means we better plan to leave next week."

"If I don't get him to relent and let me take Benny, I'll get him away from the orphanage somehow. I have to. I won't leave without him."

"In the meantime, I'll think about getting in touch with Benny's father and see what we can work out with him."

"I don't think you should do that, Mitch. He might tell Mr. Clanton."

"You're right. It'll be better if we wait util we get to Bell Haven. Since you say he doesn't want his son, it shouldn't be a problem if we wait."

"I think that's wise. I'll try to find out how we can reach the man. On Thursday, I'll bring as much of our things as I can get away without anybody knowing." She smiled at Mitch. "I'll love you forever since you've been so good to help me."

He gave her a strange look and mumbled, "What are friends for?" Then added, "Now let's get started on this plan of ours and the first thing you need to do is get the mail, then go back and try to talk to Clanton."

"I'm ready." She got out of the wagon and headed into town as Mitch drove away toward the country.

Rosemary made a quick stop at the post office then headed back to the orphanage. Since Mitch had asked her to do so, she had agreed to try once more to talk to Dwight Clanton about taking Benny to see the animals, though she doubted it would do any good. She knew how stubborn and mean the man was.

When she reached the owner's office, the door was closed. Taking a deep breath to prepare herself to face Clanton, she knocked. She then heard him say, "Come in."

Working up the courage by taking another deep breath, she opened the door and stepped inside. Walking up to his desk and putting the mailbag on the side, she glanced at him, and muttered, "Here's the mail."

"Thank you, Rosemary," he said with a grin. "You are such a dependable lady."

She did not return his grin. Instead, she nodded and turned to leave without saying anything about Benny. She wanted to think about what to say a little longer, and knew she had time to do it before she went for Thursday's mail.

He stopped her exit by asking, "Was there anything interesting in the mail today?"

Knowing full well she'd seen probably the last letter from Benny's father, she said, "I'm not allowed to go through the mail." She wasn't about to tell him she had seen the letter and had copied the return address. Again, she started to turn, and added, "I need to go help the children with their lunch."

"Just a moment, Rosemary." She paused and he went on. "I can't help but notice you seem to be a little out of sorts today. Did something happen in town to upset you?"

"No."

"Are you sure? I have a feeling you're upset. Is it something you don't want to tell me? You are special and I think the world of you. You should know I would want to help you if somebody did something to hurt your feelings in any way."

She couldn't help the small *"Humph"* that left her throat. But she said nothing.

He frowned. "Rosemary, you need to tell me what the problem is. I don't like seeing you in such a downcast mood."

Before she could stop herself, she muttered, "You know full well what my problem is."

He looked puzzled. "How can I know if you don't tell me?"

She put her hands on her hips and glared at him, and before she could stop herself, she said, "Mr. Clanton, haven't I obeyed all the rules around here? Haven't I run errands in town for you and Miss Gladiola without complaint? Haven't I made the trek to get the mail every Monday and Thursday for almost two years, no matter how bad or good the weather? Haven't I helped the teachers when they needed it? Haven't I helped look after little

Benny because nobody else around here cares what happens to the precious little boy?"

She stopped to take a breath, then went on. "Then when I ask for the favor of taking little Benny to see some animals because I know how much he'd like them, you give me a flat *NO,* and that, Mr. Clanton, is what I'm upset about."

He frowned. "But Rosemary, you should know I can't let a student take another one off the orphanage grounds. If something were to happen, it could cause a lot of trouble for us. As the responsible person you are, I'm sure you can understand why I had to say no to your request."

Rosemary glared at him, and it took her a minute to respond, but when she did, she couldn't seem to control her temper or her words. Instead, all the resentment of her forced stay at the Clanton Orphanage rushed into her mind and her usual timid voice came out with words that seemed to drip with disgust and hate.

"No, Mr. Clanton! I don't understand at all, and furthermore, as long as I'm a prisoner here in your orphanage, I'll do the jobs I'm assigned, but I will never forgive you for being so horrid to me when I asked you for the first favor I have ever asked of you. In refusing me this one request, you told me that no matter how many of your ridiculous rules I follow, or how I do my other duties, or how I feel about the unfairness of things around here, I will never be good enough for you to permit me to have one thing I want because it was something you didn't think of. In fact, when I leave here, and let me assure you I'll be leaving as soon as I get in touch with my sisters, I will look back on this place as a hellish prison. A prison I couldn't escape from and you as the evil warden who controlled every aspect of my life." Without giving him time to say anything, she whirled around and ran out the door with tears running down her cheeks.

Hurrying as quickly as she could, she knew she had messed up the tiny hope she'd had of changing his mind about letting Benny go to town with her. But at that moment, it felt good to at last say the things she had wanted to say to him for a long time.

~ * ~

Stunned, Dwight Clanton sat back in his chair and stared at the closed door. His first thought was *she was so upset she had no idea what she was saying.* There was no way he believed Rosemary was this distressed about not getting to take the little boy to town to see animals. Especially a child who wasn't going to be at the orphanage much longer. Didn't she realize the amount of time she wasted with the kid? Time she should be using to support him in all the decisions he enacted around here, not only for the company's benefit, as well as hers, when she became his wife.

He frowned and stood. He knew he had to confront Rosemary, but maybe he should give her a little time to cool off, which he had no doubt she'd do before the day ended. Besides, it was time to meet Gladiola for lunch. Though she wasn't very smart, she was a woman. Maybe she could tell him what was going on in Rosemary's head. Then when she had time to settle down, he would have a talk with the young lady again. After all, she was the young woman he planned to make his wife soon. She had to be made to realize outbursts such as this one couldn't be permitted. After all, he would be the head of their family as a man should be.

~ * ~

The next day Mitch parked his wagon in front of Martin's General Store and went inside.

"Hello there, young fellow," Elsie Martin called out. "Have you eaten up all your peaches and come for more?"

"Not this time, Miz Martin. But I did come to get a couple of things I need before I leave on Saturday."

"And what would do you need?"

"A camp chair, a Dutch oven, a coffee pot, and a couple of things I'll look for because I'm not sure of what they are yet."

"Well. Come along and help me gather these things." As she pulled a coffee pot off the shelf, she said, "I thought one of the other fellows was supposed to bring those items."

"Bobby was supposed to, but his pa got gored by one of their long-horned cows the other day and Bobby had to go home to help out his mama. I bought some of the things he didn't want to take home with him."

"Oh, my. I've heard those long-horned cows can do a lot of damage to a person."

"I've heard it, too."

"Are the other fellows still going with you?"

"I reckon Dutch will and maybe Herb. We're going to pull out Saturday morning."

She frowned. "What do you mean, you reckon?"

"I'm pretty sure Dutch will go. Anyway, he said this morning he was. But I don't think Herb will. He is in love and is trying to talk his girl into going with us, but I don't know if she will or not." Mitch shrugged. "Personally, I don't think this is a trip for a woman, but I told him it don't matter to me whether she goes or not."

"Why is that?"

"Because I still intend to go, even if I have to go part of the way alone."

"What do you mean, part of the way alone?"

"My cousin, Luke, works on a ranch in southern Colorado and we're going to meet up with him."

"I see."

"I know a lot of men have done the trip alone, so I don't see why I can't. I sure wouldn't think of taking no woman."

"That's the spirit, Mitch. With your determination, I'm sure you can do it even if you end up going alone. You'll probably strike it rich when you get there, too."

"I hope so, Miz Martin." He laughed. "If I do, I'll come back to town and share some of my gold with you."

"Now, ain't that sweet of you?" She handed him a Dutch oven. "I might even throw in a couple of extra cans of peaches, so you won't forget to come."

"It's a deal."

They both laughed as they continued to gather the supplies he was sure they would need.

When he finished shopping, he got into his wagon, knowing he had everything ready. He then headed out of town toward Rosemary's stopping place.

He was glad he'd chosen it to camp until Rosemary showed up on Monday because he felt relaxed and safe there. Very few people came down this road unless they were headed to the orphanage, and there were ample trees to hide his wagon if someone did happen to come by.

After his shopping with Elsie Martin, he knew it would never occur to the woman to tell whoever searched for Rosemary and the little boy there was any possibility he had anything to do with her disappearance because she would tell them he left on Saturday. So would the other merchants he had told about his pending trip to find gold.

The guys he'd planned to go with in search of gold would tell them he was determined to go, so he'd left to find it on his own. As far as they both would know, he left on Saturday and was on his way to the Colorado mountains.

Now, all he had to do was set up a temporary camp and wait until Rosemary showed up on Monday. Then they would take the back road out of the area and head to the Texas town where Rosemary's sisters lived. He didn't make any plans afterward because he had no idea what he'd do after getting her and the little boy to their destination, though the vague idea of striking out for Colorado was in the back of his mind.

~ * ~

With one of his beloved books hugged to his chest, Benny sat in the child's wagon with the mailbag and all the belongings

Rosemary was able to hide inside. He giggled and babbled as she pulled him toward her stopping place on Monday morning. Since everything had gone so smoothly this morning, she only hoped nothing would prevent Mitch from meeting her there, as they had planned. She then chastised herself for having the negative thought. Of course, he'd be there because he had said he would be, and she had no reason to doubt him.

Sure enough, when she rounded the bend, she saw his wagon. Or at least she hoped it was Mitch's wagon. This one had a canvas top over the bed.

She hastened her pace. If it was really him, she couldn't wait to tell him how things had gone with her getting permission to bring Benny along. If it was a stranger, she'd ignore him and go on into town.

Then she saw Mitch working with the horses and her heart began to beat faster.

When she reached the wagon, she greeted Mitch with a smile. "I'm glad to see you."

"Didn't think I'd leave without you, did you?"

"I hoped you wouldn't."

"I see you have the young man with you." He smiled at the little boy who was glaring at him. "Looks like my suggestion of asking Clanton again to bring him worked."

"It didn't work in the way you thought it would."

"What do you mean?"

"I'll tell you later. But first, I want to put the extra supplies I have in the wagon, which I see you have put a cover on."

"I thought we might run into some rain or other bad weather, and we needed to protect yours and Benny's things. It's a long way to Bell Haven."

"That was thoughtful of you."

"What do you have to take today?"

"If you have room, I want to take everything I have with us. I don't want to leave anything here that could be traced to us. Just be careful with the bundle in the back of the wagon on the mailbag. It has our dinner in it."

"Dinner?"

"Yes, dinner, and yes, there is enough for you. The cook actually let me pack it myself, so I was able to get you a man-size portion."

"Great."

"I figured you'd like that."

"Of course, I do. I just hope the cook was making something good today."

"She was. Now let's get this stuff packed."

"I've got all my camping stuff arranged because I knew we would need to leave here as quickly as possible, and I've already put everything you had hidden here in the woods in the wagon along with the supplies, but there is plenty of room left for Benny's wagon, and all its contents."

"Good." She reached for Benny. "Come with me, honey. Mitch needs to put your wagon in the back of his. We're going to ride in the big wagon now."

He nodded and reached his arms for her.

It wasn't long before they sat on the wagon seat and Benny was in her lap, still hugging his book and stealing glances at Mitch, whom he hadn't yet spoken to.

In a soft voice, Mitch asked, "Is he afraid of me, Rosemary?"

"Maybe a little but don't worry about it," Rosemary explained. "He hasn't had many reasons to trust men. When he gets to know you better, he'll warm up to you."

"I hope so."

"Now, it's my time to ask a question. Why have you headed down this back road? Aren't we going to go through town?"

He grinned at her. "From what you said, I gathered you're determined to keep anyone from Clanton's place from being able to follow you. I thought it best if we weren't seen together, so I led everyone to believe I left for Colorado on Saturday. Therefore, I camped out at your stopping place until you arrived. I also decided we'd use this road around town. It'll take a little longer, but nobody will see us this way."

"You're so smart, Mitch."

He grinned. "Thanks."

Benny leaned against Rosemary and yawned.

"Looks like you're getting sleepy, sweetheart. Why don't you let Rosemary take your book and you snuggle down in my arms and take your morning nap?"

He nodded, handed her the book, cuddled closer to her, and in a matter of minutes, he was so relaxed he fell asleep.

She looked at Mitch. "I promised to tell you how my talk with Mr. Clanton got him to relent and let me bring Benny to town with me. I just didn't want Benny to hear me talking about it. He's terrified every time the man's name is mentioned."

"The talk with the man seemed to have worked, so I'm glad I suggested it."

She laughed. "Well, my friend, it didn't work the way we both hoped it would."

He gave her a puzzled look. "What happened?"

"I planned to be calm and beg him if I had to, but I didn't get a chance. As soon as he saw me, he began to go on and on about how I wasn't the bright happy young woman I always was, and he wanted to know what my problem was. I tried to get away from him, but he kept pestering me and I couldn't hold it in any longer. I completely lost control of my emotions, and I started yelling at him. I told him he was the reason for my downcast mood, and I told him why."

Mitch gave her a surprised look. "You didn't."

"Oh, yes, I did. I told him that no matter what I did for his precious orphanage, nothing was good enough to be rewarded with the one request I'd asked him for in all the years I'd been there. I told him the place was nothing but a prison to me and he was the evil warden. Once I finished my tirade, I didn't give him a chance to say anything. I ran out of his office, slammed the door behind me and hurried out the front door. I don't know if he followed me or not because I stayed hidden for a while."

Mitch laughed. "I can't imagine you getting so mad, Rosemary and now I'm confused. How in the world did you get away with Benny?"

"That's the ironic part. I was sure I had blown getting him to change his mind and I was trying to think of how I could get away from there with Benny."

"How did you do it?"

"After my outburst, I helped get the younger children fed, then I slipped in the back door to go to my room and get everything together. When one goes in that way, the hall to the students' rooms goes by the private dining room where the Clanton siblings eat. As I went by, I heard voices. He was telling Gladiola about my outburst, and it surprised me when she told him he'd better rethink Benny's trip to town if he ever expected to marry me. He resisted at first, but when I realized he was going to give in, I hurried to my room to wait for him or her to come to give me the good news."

Mitch laughed. "So, to get your way when you want something, you throw a little girl fit."

She laughed. "Here I am, so it worked, didn't it?"

"Go on and tell me the rest."

"It was about an hour later when his sister came to escort me to his office. She stayed to listen to his apology to me, and of course, I apologized to him for my actions, though I had meant everything I had said to him, and my apology was all pretend. They believed me. Then the three of us planned how Benny and I would head to town this morning. It was even his idea to take him in the wagon in case he got tired, and I wouldn't have to carry him."

Mitch reached over and touched her shoulder. "I'm glad it worked out, and I must add, I'm proud of you."

"Thank you, Mitch." She gave him a big smile, then leaned and kissed the top of Benny's head, and added, "I'm pleased you're proud of me, and of course, I'm thrilled it worked out. I could have never left the place without Benny."

"I understand. I see how devoted to you he is."

"I'm the only person in the world who cares about him."

Mitch shook his head. "No, you're not. I've already started to like the little fellow, and I don't understand why his father doesn't want him. I thought parents always loved their children, no matter what happened. I know my folks loved me until they were killed. I bet if my mama had been the only one to die in the accident, my papa would have never let me go to Dwight Clanton's orphanage. Of course, with my mother being a half-breed, none of the relatives on either side wanted me."

"When my parents died, an aunt I had never met took over and decided where each of us four sisters would all go. I was in Shreveport for a while, then when they closed, I was sent to Clanton's orphanage."

He winked at her. "I guess it worked out best for us. I can't imagine having to take you and Benny from Louisiana to West Texas in this wagon."

Rosemary laughed. "You always had a way to pull me out of thinking of the bad things, so I'm not going to talk about that place anymore. As a matter of fact, I'm getting a little hungry. Do you think we'll be far enough away from Weatherson to have our lunch when Benny wakes up from his nap?"

"My dear Rosemary, you've just made my day. I'm going to speed up a little bit, and I'm sure by the time Benny wakes up, we'll find the perfect place to eat."

~ * ~

The sun was going down when Dwight, as he always did, walked into Gladiola's office without knocking. "I finally got rid of old Mr. Beeson. You know, he'll never leave until all the other trustees have gone."

"I'm not surprised."

"Well, where is it?

"Where is, what?"

"The mail. I told Rosemary to leave it with you because I'd be tied up when she got back from town."

"I haven't seen Rosemary or the mail, Dwight. I figure she's staying at the circus as long as she can."

He frowned. "But it'll be getting dark soon."

"I'm sure she'll be back at any time now."

"She better be!" He turned and stalked out of the office.

Gladiola glared at the closed door and a horrible thought crossed her mind. *What if Rosemary doesn't come back?* Immediately, another thought followed. *What if she's run away because she somehow found out what Dwight planned for her future or what he intended to do with Benny? But it was impossible for her to know, wasn't it? Nobody knew he planned to marry the girl except me, or he planned an accident for Benny as soon as he got the last check this month. An accident I'm trying to figure out how to prevent.*

Her thoughts continued in this vein because she knew if the girl had run away, Dwight would somehow make it her fault, and heaven only knew what he'd do to her then. She knew how vicious he could be when things didn't go his way. Gladiola couldn't help it. In a matter of minutes, her heart was pounding, and tears were sliding down her cheeks as she was trying to think of a plan to get him before he got her.

~ * ~

When Dwight found out Rosemary had not returned to the orphanage, he was furious. His instinct was to confront Gladiola again, but on his way back to her office he changed his mind. He turned toward the back door and headed for the stable. He intended to saddle his horse, go into Weatherson and if necessary, bring Rosemary and the kid back himself. That was, unless he could think of a way to leave the kid behind without Rosemary knowing he'd deliberately done so. He'd gotten the last check from Benny's father, along with a note telling him as far as he was concerned, his son was dead, and he never wanted to hear from the orphanage again, not even if some unfortunate accident did happen to the child, he no longer considered the kid his son.

When he reached town, he went directly to the post office and found it was closed. Frowning, he looked around and saw the posters advertising the circus tacked around on walls and posts. Thinking maybe he should check there, he headed toward the field on the edge of where they had said they'd be set up. On his way through town, he noticed most of the stores had closed, except Martin's General Store.

Making a quick decision, he reined his horse up in front of the store, dismounted, tethered his mount, and went inside.

"Hello, mister. How can I help you tonight?"

"Are you Mr. Martin?"

"Yes. I'm Reese Martin."

"I'm Dwight Clanton from the orphanage. I met your wife when I was in here some time ago, but I don't recall meeting you."

"Probably haven't met me. My wife usually opens up and works here in the store until mid-afternoon. Then, I come in so she can go home, rest up a bit and cook supper. As a matter of fact, I came in just before noon because we were awfully busy today. I should have closed an hour ago, but because of the crowds I couldn't. I'm getting ready to close and go home shortly."

"I won't keep you long. I only came in on the chance you may have seen one of the young ladies from our home. She brought a little boy to visit the animal circus when she came to get the mail this morning and they should have been home a long time ago. I was concerned something might have happened to them."

"There were some women in here with kids today, but I'm pretty sure they were all local because I knew most of them.

Before Dwight could answer, the door opened, and Elsie Martin came inside.

Ignoring Clanton, Reese asked, "Is something wrong, wife?"

"I just walked up to ask you the same question. Supper has been ready for almost an hour, and I was worried about you."

"It has been busy this evening, but I'm about ready to close."

Dwight decided he better say something nice to the woman because she might know something about Rosemary. "I'm sorry I held your husband up, Mrs. Martin, please forgive me. I was asking him if he'd seen two of our missing students."

"Oh, that's terrible. What happened?"

He explained about Rosemary taking Benny to the circus.

"I know Rosemary. She came in here to buy hair pins for your sister just last week. She was a delightful young lady and seemed to be one you could count on to do the right thing. I'm sure I would have noticed if she was in here today."

"You're right. She is one of the most dependable ladies at the orphanage. That's why I'm so concerned about her."

"I wish we could help, Mr. Clanton," Reese said. "Maybe you should check with some of the other merchants when they open in the morning. You might want to go out to where the animal circus is set up and check this evening."

"There's no need to do that," Elsie said. "I've been told they close at sundown because the animals get restless and have to be fed and bedded down for the night. Besides it is mostly young children and their mothers who come to see the animals, and a mother doesn't keep her children out late anyway."

Dwight said, "I'll go by there just in case Rosemary was held up."

"If I were you, I'd make a stop and talk with the sheriff."

Dwight frowned. "You don't think someone has kidnapped her, do you?"

"Not at all," Reese said. "I suggested the sheriff because he usually knows when anything strange happened around here."

Without saying anything else, Dwight rushed out the door, mounted his horse and headed to the sheriff's office.

~ * ~

As Rosemary and Benny sat on the blanket Mitch had spread on the ground for them, he watched as she opened the bag containing the food she'd brought from the orphanage and placed a piece of fried chicken on each of the three plates he had given her. It gave him a strange feeling to watch her act as mother to the little boy.

Shaking his head as he looked at the plate, he said, "I can't believe they were serving this at Clanton's place today. I don't remember having anything this good when I was there."

Rosemary laughed. "They don't do this often. They were having the state board and somebody who inspects orphanages to make sure the place is run properly for dinner and for meetings and inspections this afternoon. I'm sure this was to impress them. Otherwise, you may have had to settle for cold potatoes and dry corn bread."

He chuckled. "I would have been used to it if it had been what you brought. It was often what I ate while I was there."

"We are used to it, too, aren't we, Benny?"

"I like nickin," Benny muttered and picked up the chicken leg.

"Well, *nickin* is not the only good thing we're having. There are some green beans, corn, and roasted potatoes to go with it. They were so busy in the kitchen they let me get the food for us. I was able to get extra when they weren't looking." She filled the first plate and handed it to Mitch. "I'm sorry you have to eat the vegetables cold, but I'm sure they will still be good."

"I was afraid to build a fire, so we could warm things up," Mitch said. "When we get farther away from Weatherson, we can have heat to cook and make coffee to drink. I'm not yet ready to take a chance on us being caught."

"I've never had a whole cup of coffee and I'm looking forward to it."

"Why haven't you had a whole cup?"

"None of the students are allowed to have it."

"Then how do think you'd like a cup?"

She gave him a mischievous smile. "I know because when I had to get coffee for one of them, I'd take a sip before I got where they could see me."

"You keep surprising me, Rosemary. I never thought you had a streak of rebellion in you."

"Well, I do have. Now let's eat. I'll help Benny, then we probably need to move on, don't you think?"

"Yes, I do. The horse will be rested, and I think we should put in as many miles as we can before it gets dark."

"You're taking such good care of us, Mitch."

His heart fluttered again, but he concentrated on his food and wouldn't let himself look at her until they were ready to pack up the leftovers.

~ * ~

The next morning, Dwight Clanton went into the sheriff's office before noon. "Have you found out anything?" he demanded without greeting Sheriff Jess Peeks.

The sheriff, who was standing at the potbellied stove pouring himself a cup of coffee, took an instant dislike of the man but kept it well hidden as he said, "Nothing yet, though I've been looking," he said as he turned and sat his coffee cup on his desk. "Would you like a cup?"

"No," Dwight snapped. "All I want is to know if you've found Rosemary."

"Have a seat and I'll tell you what I found out." He took his time moving to his desk and sat in the swivel wooden chair behind it. Taking a sip of his coffee, he asked, "First, have you heard anything from the young lady?"

"If I had, I wouldn't be here."

The sheriff still didn't let it show Clanton's rude manner bothered him and made him wonder about the man and his relationship with his student. "Nobody around here has seen or heard from her either."

"I did go by the post office, and they said she didn't pick up the mail yesterday."

"I see. It means she never made it to town."

"It could mean she's been kidnapped."

Jess nodded. "Let's not jump to conclusions. I will tell you I learned some boys who did some temporary work on a nearby ranch have left for Colorado in search of gold in the mountains there."

"Do you think they would have kidnapped her and made her go with them?"

Peeks shook his head. "No, I don't."

"Why not?" Dwight acted excited over this news.

Jess noticed the man's excitement but continued in his usual relaxed way. "For several reasons. First, if they took her, what happened to the little boy she had with her? They wouldn't want a little child along. Second, why would they want a young girl, who they would also consider a child, to go with them to search for gold? But the most compelling thing is, I went out to talk to one of the guys who stayed behind to get married. He told me the others left on Saturday and you said your students came here on Monday, so she couldn't be with them."

Dwight didn't seem to want to admit it couldn't have happened the way he suggested. "But are you sure they left on Saturday?"

"I am because the guy who stayed behind had no reason to lie, and because I talked to Elsie Martin about it, and she verified it."

"How could she do that?"

"You don't trust anybody, do you Clanton?" He didn't wait for the man to answer but went on. "She said one of the guys came into the store on Thursday or Friday to pick up a few extra supplies and told her they were pulling out early on Saturday morning. She even said they planned to hook up with one of their cousins who lives just over the line in Colorado."

Dwight's face fell. "Then I guess she's not with them."

"Clanton, I have to ask you, why do you seem to only be interested in the girl's disappearance? You have talked about her a lot and only mentioned the little boy a few times. Looks like you'd be concerned about the child."

For an instant Clanton looked flustered. Then he said, "Of course, I'm concerned about Benny. I knew when we found Rosemary he would be with her."

The sheriff didn't believe a word of it, but he knew the orphanage owner didn't have any idea he thought this. To keep the man ignorant, he said, "I'll tell you what I think my next step in this situation will be. I'll send wires to the towns around and ask them to be on the lookout for your students. If somebody did take her, they'd stop someplace where they'd be seen. Now, how about giving me a detailed description of each of them."

After Dwight gave the sheriff the descriptions and left, Jess poured himself another cup of coffee and took his chair to look over what Clanton had said about each student.

He thought *You may fool some people, Mr. Orphanage Owner, but you don't fool me. You gave a concise description of Benny Neven but the one you gave of Rosemary Cardwell could only describe a beautiful, desirable, grown woman who most any man would dream about. Not of the young girl who is on the verge of becoming a woman.*

He shook his head again and his thoughts continued. *I'm sure she's like my fifteen-year-old daughter, Suzanne, who is beginning to attract young fellows who are on the verge of becoming men. You want the girl back for some nefarious plan of your own, you old coot, and I don't intend to help you do it. Oh, I'll send the wires to the nearby towns just like I said I would. Of course, I won't send them today. Three or four days from now will be soon enough. As for Miss Cardwell and little Benny, I'll find out as much about them as I can. If I discover she has run away, as I suspect she may have done, I'll make sure you never find out when or where she and the boy went.*

~ * ~

The next morning as Rosemary climbed out of the wagon, she saw Mitch bent over a small fire with a coffee pot in his hand; her heart leaped when she noticed how handsome he looked. Pushing the thought aside, she concentrated on knowing he was making coffee. She smiled to herself as she reached back inside the wagon. Benny jumped into her arms.

"Good morning," she said as she walked toward the fire. "Looks like you're making us a special treat."

"I thought we were far enough away to chance a fire, and I needed my morning coffee." He grinned at her. "How did your sleep in the wagon go last night?"

"I slept fine, thanks to your thoughtfulness of putting a mattress back there for us."

"I thought you and Benny would be more comfortable on it than in a sleeping bag."

"We were." She changed the subject. "If you'll look in the food bag I brought, you'll find some biscuits and cooked ham I was able to grab while I was getting yesterday's food. In the meantime, I'll make a quick trip behind those bushes and let Benny do his business and take care of my needs."

"Sounds great. I even have a pan we can warm up the ham in."

When they returned, Mitch had the food warming. He looked at the little boy. "I guess you'll have to drink water if Rosemary thinks you're too young for coffee, Benny. We'll stop in the next town we come to and get you some milk."

Benny looked at him and whispered, "I wike milk."

"That's good. It'll help make you grow up big and strong."

Benny didn't say anything, but he did give Mitch a shy smile.

Rosemary smiled, too. "I told you he'd soon see you weren't like the other men he's been exposed to. Before you know it, both of you will have a new friend."

"Great. I think the food is hot. Let's eat."

As they began to eat, Rosemary looked at him and said, "I know you had no way of knowing, but this is a special day for me and I'm getting to have a good breakfast and my first cup of coffee with two of my favorite people."

Mitch grinned. "What is special about today, the fact we are away from Weatherson?"

"It does make it special, but that's not what I'm talking about."

"Then what is so special about it?"

"It's my birthday, Mitch. I'm seventeen years old today."

Mitch stared at her for a moment because it hit him full force; Rosemary was no longer the young girl he'd known and befriended in the orphanage. She was now a young woman. A beautiful one.

Finally, he found his tongue. He lifted his cup of coffee and said, "Happy birthday.

"Thank you, Mitch. Do you know you're the first person to wish me a happy birthday since I was separated from my sisters?"

"I'm glad I was here to say it today."

"I'm more than glad. I'm overjoyed. Especially when I think of what would have happened to me if you hadn't gotten us away from Dwight Clanton."

"Bad man!" Benny said and turned to Rosemary.

She put her coffee down and put her arm around him. "Please don't be afraid, sweetheart. We are far away from the bad man. He can never come near us again because the good man has saved us."

He looked at Mitch. "Good man?"

"Yes, Benny. He's a wonderful man and I know he'll take good care of us."

Mitch didn't say anything, but it crossed his mind she could be right. Maybe he was destined to take care of them. At least until they got to Bell Haven.

As soon as the meal was over, Mitch made sure the fire was out, they then climbed on the wagon seat and headed west. This time, instead of sitting on Rosemary's lap, Benny sat on the seat between her and Mitch.

~ * ~

When Sheriff Jess Peeks walked into the reception area of the Clanton Orphanage, he walked up to the desk and spoke to the teenaged girl there. "I'd like to see Mr. Clanton," he said to her.

"I'm sorry, sir. Mr. Clanton left almost an hour ago and hasn't come back."

"Then, could I speak to his assistant?"

"I don't know if he has one, but when he's not here, he always tells us to go to his sister, Miss Gladiola Clanton."

Jess was a little irritated he'd made the trip to see Clanton and missed him. But as he always did, he didn't let this feeling show. He simply said, "Then, may I see her?"

"Of course, sir. Follow me." She stood and headed down the hall beside the desk.

They passed a couple of closed doors, then she knocked on the third one they came to. From inside, a woman's voice called, "Come in."

The girl opened the door and said, "Miss Gladiola, the sheriff of Weatherson is here to see Mr. Clanton but he's not here, so I brought him to see you." She then stepped aside, and Jess walked in.

Gladiola seemed surprised the lawman wanted to see her since Dwight wasn't there, but she nodded at the girl, and she hurried away, closing the door behind her.

"Hello, Mr. Sheriff. Please have a seat."

He did. "By the way, my name is Jess Peeks, and as the young lady said, I'm the sheriff of Weatherson. As you probably know, I've been working on the case of your missing students."

"Then Sheriff, maybe you should speak with my brother instead of me.

"I intended to, Miss Clanton, but I was informed he had left the orphanage earlier. I figured since I'd made the trip here you would be willing to talk with me."

"Of course, I will. I just don't know how much help I'll be."

"You may know more than you realize. People often do, so do you mind if we start our discussion by you telling me what you remember about the day the students disappeared?"

"I'll try to remember as best as I can." She took a deep breath and said, "As I recall, it was on Monday of last week, which is one of our regular mail pick-up days. The other pick-up day is Thursday. The only thing different on Monday was Mr. Clanton had given Rosemary Cardwell permission to take little Benny Neven with her to visit some sort of animal circus which had come to town."

She then described Rosemary and Benny's close relationship. She went on to explain the board of directors, some state officials, and an orphanage inspector had come for lunch and how the meetings lasted until late afternoon. She ended with the fact no one knew Rosemary and Benny hadn't returned until then and, though they were concerned, they decided they were having a good time at the circus and were running late. But after waiting until dusk, Dwight Clanton went to town to search for them.

The sheriff sat back, looked at her, and his instinct told him she was probably more open and honest than her brother. He decided to see if he could get more information from her. He decided to push her a little to see if he was right.

"Your brother thinks Miss Rosemary has been kidnapped. Do you think this could be true, Miss Clanton?"

"I don't know, Sheriff, it could have happened that way, but I think her disappearance could be something else."

"Such as?"

She hesitated, then blurted, "She may have run away."

This surprised him but he didn't let her see. Instead, he asked, "Did the girl have a reason to want to run away?"

Gladiola seemed to be choosing her words carefully when she said, "She and Mr. Clanton had a disagreement the day after she got back from getting the mail on Monday and she was very mad at him."

"Do you know what they argued about?"

"Oh yes, and by the next day everyone at the orphanage knew and were talking about it. Rosemary had asked him for permission to take Benny Neven to visit the animal circus in town and he refused to give her permission to do so. It really upset her, and they had heated words. Now, I don't know if she told anyone about the fight or if someone overheard the argument, but soon everyone here knew about it."

"Did you hear it, Miss Clanton?"

"I was coming down the hall when I saw Rosemary come running out of his office and she looked mad enough to kill somebody. When I asked Dwight what was going on, he told me."

"Thank you for telling me this, Miss Clanton. It gives me something more to look into. I'll check the stagecoach and train schedules and see what I can find. Now, is there anything else you can think of which might give me other leads?"

By the time Jess left the orphanage, he not only knew about the fight, but he also knew Benny's time at the home was limited to the end of this month, Rosemary had family in Texas and Dwight Clanton did have a plan for Rosemary Cardwell's future, but she didn't know what, though he had his own idea of what it could be.

He also knew he had given Gladiola Clanton his word he wouldn't tell her brother who had told him all these things. He felt sure he would be able to keep this promise.

As he climbed on his horse to return to Weatherson, he felt it had been a productive day. Much more productive than it would have been if Dwight Clanton had been at the orphanage when he came to question him.

~ * ~

As they stopped for supper the next afternoon, Benny looked at Mitch and gave him a shy grin, then looked down at the cup of milk in his hand. "Good milk," he said in a timid voice, "I dink?"

"I'm glad you like it, Benny, and yes you can drink all of it if you want, and if you want more, we have it. A growing boy should drink lots of milk."

Benny looked around at Rosemary. "Can I?"

"Yes, honey. You can drink. Mitch is a good man. He wants you to have all you want."

Benny turned up the cup and began to take big gulps.

Rosemary reached over, took his arm, and pulled the cup away from his mouth. "Don't drink so fast, honey. You could choke. Nobody is going to take your milk away."

He looked at her as if he didn't believe her. "Bad man did."

"I know he did, but Mitch is a good man. He won't do that."

Mitch frowned. "Did somebody take milk away from him at one time?"

"Bad man did," Benny said.

"What's he talking about, Rosemary?"

"Benny, do you want to tell Mitch about the bad man?"

Benny shook his little head. "You tell."

"All right, I'll tell. Sometimes when the younger children were having their meals, the bad man, as Benny calls him, would come into the lunch area, and watch them. If they were having some difficulty feeding themselves, he would scold them. As you can see, Benny sometimes has trouble holding his cup with his missing fingers, and one day the man was there when he spilled some milk. It made the man mad, and he walked over, grabbed Benny's cup out of his hand and poured his milk on the floor. He then told him if he couldn't do better, he wouldn't be allowed to have milk again."

"I can't believe he'd do such a thing to a child."

"He never did it when I was helping the little ones, but I was told it happened several times when I wasn't there."

Mitch turned to Benny. "Well, little fellow, you don't have to worry about me getting mad when you drop something. I drop things myself and I don't have the excuse of missing fingers. So, if you spill some of your milk, we'll just have to put more milk in your cup for you."

Benny's eyes got big, and he looked at Rosemary as if he was asking her if Mitch was telling the truth.

"I told you Mitch was a good man, Benny. As we travel along, you're going to see for yourself. In the meantime, let's finish our supper. If I'm not mistaken, the good man said he was going to open a can of peaches for our dessert tonight. Do you like peaches?"

"Don't know."

"You probably don't, since you've probably never had them, but my guess is you will like them when you get a taste. I'm sure I will, too."

After they finished eating, Rosemary put Benny to bed in the wagon and since it was getting too dark to read one of his books, she told him a couple of stories from memory.

When he drifted off to sleep, she kissed his forehead and climbed out of the wagon and saw Mitch sitting by the dying campfire drinking a cup of coffee.

Walking over to him she said, "Mind if I join you?"

"I have the other camp chair waiting just for you."

She sat. "I appreciate it."

Before she had a chance to say more, he said, "Has Benny always had it so rough in his short life?"

"From what I've learned, his mother loved him, but she died when he was only a few months old. His father hired a woman to look after him who quit before his second birthday. By then his father was getting ready to marry again and his bride refused to be a mother to the child, so he was sent to the orphanage. He's been there for about a year, but his father said he would only pay for his keep until he was three years old. After that, he told Mr. Clanton to do whatever he wanted to do with the child because he never wanted him back."

"Do you know what Clanton planned for Benny's future?"

She nodded and bit her lip. "The same day I found out he planned to marry me, I learned he also had a plan to get rid of Benny."

"What was the plan?"

"He said kids his age often had accidents they didn't recover from. I knew then he intended to kill Benny. That's why I insisted on bringing him with me. There was no way I could leave him at the orphanage."

Mitch reached over and touched her hand. "You no longer have to think you have to protect Benny alone, Rosemary. I'm here now and together we will make sure he never has to see Clanton again."

"Oh Mitch, thank you. Somehow, I always knew I could count on you."

Mitch didn't say anything else, but he squeezed her hand before he let it go.

~ * ~

Nina Peeks sat across the kitchen table from her husband, and said for the third time, "Where in the world is your mind tonight, Jess. I've asked you twice if you're going to be off Saturday so you can take Suzanne and me to the barn dance on Saturday night."

"Yes, Daddy. Will you?"

"I'm sorry, ladies. I guess I have a lot on my mind tonight, and to answer your question, I plan to be off. The deputy said he'd work. Of course, I might have to keep my eyes on things at the dance."

"Why, Jess? Do you expect trouble?"

"Not really, but there's a strange fellow who has been showing up in town at odd places. It wouldn't surprise me if he came to the dance."

"Why would he go there?"

"As I told you, a couple of students have disappeared from the orphanage, and he's determined to find them."

"But doesn't he realize they've probably left Weatherson by now?"

"I'm not sure if he's thinking about it logically." He pushed back his plate. "That was a good supper, Nina. You always seem to know when I need a good beef dinner."

"I guess it's because I've been married to you so long."

"It was good, Mama." Suzanne smiled at her. "When we finish washing the dishes, can we work on the dress you're making for me to wear to the dance?"

"Of course, we can." She stood. "Let's see how fast we can get these dishes washed."

Jess was glad his girls, as he called them, had something planned for the evening. It would give him plenty of time to go back to the office and go over the information he'd gathered.

When he got back to the office, Jess found Deputy Alvin Moore looking at the answer to a wire he'd sent. "What in the world is this?" Alvin asked.

Jess moved to the desk chair Alvin vacated. "Pull up a chair. I think it's time I told you what I'm doing about Dwight Clanton's claim his students have been kidnapped."

When he finished, Alvin asked, "So you think the man wants to get the girl back, but he doesn't care a whit about the boy."

"That's right. From what I've been able to gather from the rumors I've heard, he wants to marry the girl as soon as she turns seventeen."

Alvin frowned. "Why would he want to do such a thing? I've never met the man, but the Dwight Clanton I've heard about is old enough to be a seventeen-year-old-girl's grandfather."

"You've got that right. My thinking is the girl found out his plan and has run away."

"If this is true, the girl was smart to take off. I just can't help wondering why she would take the little boy with her."

"It puzzled me for a while, so I slipped back to the orphanage today and talked with some of the older students. I learned the rumor is Clanton plans for the kid to have an accident he doesn't recover from because his father will no longer send money for his upkeep."

"Are you kidding me?"

"No, I'm not. Everything I've told you is the truth." He sat back and looked at his deputy. "Would you like to help me prove it?"

"I sure would. I've heard some strange things about the man. You can never tell what we'll dig up."

Jess grinned. It felt good to know he was going to have help with this confusing case, and before he returned home, they had a tentative plan for the next few days. Jess was going to check with the young men again to see if Mitch O'Donald had left for Colorado, and Alvin was going to pose as a rich businessman who was interested in buying Clanton's orphanage.

When he got home, he even told his wife about their plans. She was in full agreement and said, "You must do all you can to see he doesn't find her, Jess. That girl is only a couple of years older than Suzanne."

~ * ~

It had become their habit to sit at the dying campfire after Rosemary put Benny down to sleep each night. As she moved over and took the cup of coffee Mitch held out to her, she said, "Thanks. You sure seem relaxed tonight."

"I am, and it's because I'm extra happy."

She turned her head to the side. "And why are so extra happy tonight?"

"I'm happy because Benny seems to accept me now. Did you notice how he ran and hugged my neck when you told him it was time to go to bed?"

"Yes, I noticed and if you remember, when we first started out, I told you it wouldn't be long until he warmed up to you."

"I do remember but I didn't expect it to happen so quickly."

"To be honest, neither did I." She grinned at him. "But on the other hand, I've always known you're the type of person people trust immediately. I knew the first time I saw you at the orphanage, I did."

"I couldn't keep myself from helping the little lost girl who was struggling to carry those heavy buckets.

"I guess that's the time you became my knight in shining armor."

A little uncomfortable with the conversation, Mitch changed the subject. "I figured when we get to Bell Haven, you'll think it's time I left you with one of your sisters and headed to Colorado in search of gold."

Rosemary's heart began to beat faster, and she bit her lip. She didn't want to face the fact they'd separate because she wasn't sure she'd ever see him again. She managed to mutter, "Is that still your plan?"

"Well, you do know I postponed my Colorado trip to get you away from Clanton."

She looked at her coffee cup. "I know you did, and I appreciate it more than you know. I'll miss you."

He smiled at her. "Well, it's not like we're going to get to Bell Haven tomorrow. We don't have to say goodbye yet."

She suddenly jumped up.

"What's wrong."

"I thought I heard Benny. I better check on him," she whispered. The truth was she didn't want Mitch to see how upset she was at the thought of him leaving them or the tears which had formed in her eyes because she couldn't stop them.

It took her longer to calm down than she thought it would, but finally she felt she could face him again.

"Was Benny all right?"

She nodded and told Mitch the lie she thought up while she was in the wagon. "I think it was a bad dream. He's sound asleep now."

"Good. Maybe when we get further away, he won't have bad dreams."

"I hope none of us will, Mitch."

It wasn't long before they decided they'd better get some sleep, too.

~ * ~

Two days later, Dwight Clanton walked into his sister's office. "Is everything ready for Mr. Fitz's visit, Gladiola?"

"Yes. We're all set." She eyed her brother. "Why is this man so important, Dwight?"

"From what I've been able to learn, he's some millionaire businessman from Houston."

"Why in the world would a millionaire businessman from Houston be interested in visiting our orphanage?"

"Seems he was raised in an orphanage somewhere up north and it was a great experience for him, and he wants to buy an orphanage in the area, since Texas is now his home."

Gladiola looked frightened. "You're not going to sell this place to him, are you?"

"Depends on what kind of offer he makes me."

"You can't do that. What'll happen to me, Dwight?"

He laughed. "You'll be fine, sister, dear."

"What do you mean?"

"There's something about this place I've never told you."

"What?"

"You're actually my silent partner. If I sell the place, you get a portion of the profits."

She stared at him. "Why hadn't you told me this before?"

"Because I knew you'd be down my neck trying to help run the place."

"If I could...."

"See what I mean? You know nothing about how to make money with a place like this, so I knew I had to do it all myself, and when I find Rosemary and make her my wife, I intend to buy you out."

Before she had time to answer, Millie came into the office. "Mr. Clanton, you wanted to know when we saw a visitor coming and he's on his way. He's in some kind of fancy buggy and it looks like the sheriff is riding his horse alongside him."

~ * ~

That evening the deputy went into the sheriff's office, hung up his hat, and dropped into the chair facing Jess who was shuffling some papers. "I'm finally back and I'm glad to report I learned a lot more about the man and his business than I expected to, Sheriff."

"Good, then you'll be excused for being so late in getting back to town."

"I didn't think I'd ever get away from him, but it was worth it. He even let me look at some of the books and records he keeps on running the place. They told me right away he was a greedy man who'll do almost anything for money. It didn't take me long to see where he was taking most of the money families are sending to keep their kids there or where he was cutting the programs the students were supposed to receive as well as money supposed to be used to feed them. I even made a few suggestions about where he could cut more money out of what's coming in. He made notes and told me I'd make a good supervisor for an orphanage."

"Did you make him an offer on the place?"

"No. I told him I'd have to check with my attorney and my banker before I made a firm offer, but I dropped a figure, and it made him look as if he was going to hug me."

Jess laughed, then said, "After I introduced you to him and left you two alone, I took advantage of my trip there, too. I spent some time with his sister. I'm almost convinced she has no idea of what he's doing. In fact, she told me she only realized recently she owned part of the place. That led me to think he's been taking from her share, too."

"When we arrest him, do you think she's capable of running the place?"

"It's possible, especially if we get some knowledgeable people behind her."

"Good."

"I also found out something from her I'm going to check out. It seems a former student there was a good friend of Rosemary Cardwell, and they stayed in touch after he left. It turns out he was one of the men who had planned a trip to Colorado in search of gold. Since the trip fell through, they said he left alone the Saturday before Miss Cardwell disappeared. Now I'm wondering if he did or if he led them to believe he left."

"Are you saying you think he helped the woman get out of town?"

"I'm saying there's a good possibility he did." Jess raised an eyebrow. "If this turns out to be the case, I think he must be a good man to do it for her. In fact, I'll go so far as to say I hope he cares enough for Miss Rosemary to marry her before they get to Bell Haven."

Alvin frowned. "Why do you think they went there?"

Jess grinned. "That's where her sisters live, and I found out they're only waiting for her to get old enough to leave the orphanage and join them."

"Then, Sheriff, when we get all this sorted out, I figure you'll have enough evidence to arrest Dwight Clanton and I'm sure he'll be going away for a long time."

Jess began to fold papers. "You're right. Let's call it a night. I'm ready to go home and have a good supper with my family."

The deputy only nodded and in a matter of minutes the two men headed for their respective homes.

~ * ~

Though they were making good time on the trail, Mitch couldn't help noticing Rosemary had been especially quiet today. Then when he thought about it, he realized she hadn't had much to say since the evening he'd brought up the fact he'd be leaving her soon after they arrived in Bell Haven. But he didn't think this would keep her from talking with him. Would it?

Surely, she knew he couldn't stay in such a little town. What could he do? He didn't have a lot of skills to make employers look at him with favor in the few businesses existing in such a small place. As for working on a ranch, the odd jobs he'd done there weren't what most ranch hands did. Mainly he looked after the horses, wagons, and other ranch equipment, where he used his limited blacksmithing skills. He really liked that type of work and knew if he could get more training and could buy his own equipment, he'd like to set up a shop of his own. But this was another dream he felt he had to put aside until he managed to get his hands on some money. One of the first lessons he learned when he left Clanton's place was nobody was anxious to hire or work with a man who had obvious Indian blood. But they wouldn't hesitate to let him use his skills to shoe their horses, fix their wagons, or make anything they wanted or needed from the metal plates he forged.

Before he could think further, they rounded a curve and came upon a man working with the wheel of the wagon he'd pulled to the side. The wagon was full of bags of feed and what looked like smaller bags of seed.

Mitch pulled backward on the reins, and the horses came to a stop. "Got some trouble?"

"Shore have." The bearded older man glanced at Mitch. "Looks like I'm about to lose a wheel and I shore hate to do it. I'm affeered if I can't fix it, I'll lose my feed and my wife's seed to the coming rain."

Mitch wasn't sure if it was going to rain, but he said, "I'll pull my wagon over behind yours and see if I can help you."

"I'd appreciate it, young man. I can do some things when the equipment breaks down, but I ain't so sure I can fix a wheel."

As he pulled his wagon over, he glanced at Rosemary, who had a sleeping Benny in her lap. "You don't mind me stopping to help the fellow, do you?"

"Of course, not. It's the kind of man you are, Mitch. Always ready to help those in need."

"I'll do my best to park where you'll be under the shade of one of these trees on the side of the road. If you get too hot, you can climb in the back."

"We will."

She said nothing else as Mitch jumped out of the wagon to help the stranded man.

~ * ~

Rosemary's conscience nagged at her a little for being so standoffish with Mitch for the last couple of days. But she couldn't help it, and knew it wasn't fair, but every time she looked at him, all she could think about was the fact he'd be leaving them soon. Though she knew it was the way things would happen, it broke her heart every time she thought of it.

Benny stirred and looked up at her. "Why we stop?"

"Mitch is helping a man fix his wagon."

He rose up. "I help?"

"No, honey. He'll get it done and we'll be going on our way."

Benny wiggled and she let him get off her lap and sit beside her in the wagon seat. "I read book?"

Rosemary sighed. "Honey, your books are back in the wagon. Why don't you look around here? You might see some wild animals if you do."

"See bear?"

"I doubt you'll see a bear, but you might see a deer, or rabbit, or even a snake."

"Go catch one?"

"No, Benny." Her words came out sharper than she meant them to, and she was immediately sorry.

Before she could say anything else, Benny looked up at her. "Why you mad?"

"Oh, Benny. I'm so sorry. I didn't mean to sound mad. I just have a lot on my mind." He didn't answer and she wondered what she could say to ease his mind. Then she saw an eagle flying overhead. She grinned and said, "Look up at the big bird, Benny. Isn't it pretty?"

Benny looked where she pointed. "Not big."

"It might not look big but if it was closer to us, you'd think it's big."

"We get closer?"

Rosemary laughed and at the same time, she heard Mitch chuckle.

He winked at her and said, "I'm anxious to see how you explain this to him."

She shook her head at him and smiled at Benny. "Honey, the bird is up in the sky. We can't go there because we can't fly."

"Why not?"

"Because God didn't make us with wings."

Before Benny could ask her why not, Mitch said, "Benny, I see an animal up ahead you might like. I'm going to stop the horses, and you look over there at the edge of the road."

Benny leaned over Rosemary and looked. "Is it bear?"

"No. It's called an armadillo."

"I go see?"

"No, son. You need to stay in the wagon."

"Bite me?"

"I don't know, but it looks like it might." He shook the reins, and the wagon moved forward. "I think we better move on and let it go home. Its mother might be waiting for it."

Benny nodded and leaned across Rosemary's lap. "I still see dilla."

She put her arm around his shoulders. Smiling at him she said, "I don't want you to fall out, so I'm going to hold you."

When Benny settled down, she glanced at Mitch and mouthed a 'thank you' at him.

He winked at her again.

~ * ~

After they ate supper, and Rosemary put Benny to bed, she wasn't sure if Mitch would expect her to come to the campfire for their usual evening talk. Though they'd talked very little on the trip today, she decided she'd head in his direction. She couldn't help smiling when she saw the empty chair beside him.

As he always did, he handed her a cup of coffee as she sat. "I may have to turn over the making coffee to you. This is extra good tonight, and your pan bread was good as it always is."

"I thought making the coffee was the least I could do after you went off to hunt the delicious food we had for supper. I also wanted to thank you for cleaning it before you got back. I don't know how Benny would have acted if he'd seen the dead rabbits."

"I understand, but you know he's going to have to eventually learn much of the food we eat are animals we hunt."

She sighed. "I know, but I guess it's the mother instinct in me. I want to protect him as long as I can."

"Can I confess something to you, Rosemary?"

"Of course, you can."

"I sometimes forget you're a young woman, not the cute little girl I used to kind of look after when you came to the orphanage. I don't think I'd ever seen anyone as lost and unhappy as you were that day."

"You're right, Mitch. I was miserable and in need of someone who seemed to care. I'd been torn away from the only people who loved me and sent away. Then when I kind of adjusted to the awful orphanage in Louisiana, I was jerked up and sent to a worse one in Texas where I was even more lost. You came into my life at the time I needed someone the most, and I'll always love you for that."

"You're special to me, too and I care for you." He gave her a smile. "I guess that's why I don't understand why you've suddenly seemed to want to be anywhere except around me. I thought we were getting along fine, then all of a sudden, you're almost not speaking to me."

She sipped her coffee, then decided to tell him the truth. "I'm sorry, Mitch. I guess it hit me hard when you said you were going to look for gold after we get to Bell Haven."

"I'm sorry it upset you, Rosemary. But what other choice do I have? I'm running out of money, and I don't have a job. I have to do something, and I figure Bell Haven is like the other towns I've been in. None of the businesses I've been to are anxious to hire a man with Indian blood. Going to Colorado seems to be the best answer for me."

"I suppose you're right." She sighed and a tear slid down her cheek. "It just breaks my heart to know I'll never see you again."

He grabbed her hand to keep her from running away. "We need to talk this out."

She didn't answer him, but she did relax in her chair.

"I'll come back someday, Rosemary. There's no way I could live the rest of my life and not know what happened to you and Benny. Though it'll probably break my heart when I do return and find you've grown up and married a man who little Benny is calling daddy."

She looked at him for a long minute. Finally, she said, "You still think of me as a little girl, don't you?"

"I know you turned seventeen, and some people consider it grown, I guess. It's just hard for me to separate you as a woman from the little girl I always knew."

"Well, I am a woman, Mitch. I became one the day I left the orphanage with Benny, who I intend to raise as my son. It was before my birthday, but it didn't matter. I was a woman. A woman who knew she had to somehow make a life for my little boy and me. As for that marriage you mentioned, it'll never happen unless I meet a man who will love Benny as his son, no matter how many other children I give him. If you had ever loved a child the way I love Benny, you'd understand." She started to stand again, but his words stopped her.

"I loved my little sister like that."

She was shocked to hear this. "You have a sister?"

"Not anymore."

"I'm so sorry, Mitch. What happened?"

"She was about Benny's age when she got sick and died."

Rosemary reached over, took his hand, and told him again she was sorry.

"It's all right, Rosemary. I accept I'm different from other men. I know it's not meant for me to ever love anyone again."

She frowned. "You're not talking about your little sister now, are you?"

"How did you know?"

"A woman can tell."

"I shouldn't have said anything." He dropped her hand and this time he started to stand.

Her words stopped him. "Tell me about her."

~ * ~

He had no intention of ever telling her, or anyone else, about Marcie Brown, but he found himself saying, "I met her last summer, and we had some wonderful weeks together. I loved her and thought she loved me because she'd said so several times. It got to the point where I worked up the courage to ask her to marry me. It was then when once again my world came crashing down on me."

He paused and she asked, "What happened?"

"She laughed in my face, then told me our time together had been fun because it was exciting to be with a man who was part Indian. Then she went on to say there was no way she'd ever marry me because her father would never accept a man like me into the Brown family, and the thoughts of grandchildren from such a union would be a curse."

Rosemary gave him a horrified look. "Mitch! How in the world could any woman do such a thing to a wonderful man like you?"

He chuckled. "Everyone in the world is not open and honest like you are, Rosemary. After living at Clanton's orphanage, you should understand."

"Oh, I know it happens. I simply don't understand why. I would never tell a man I love him unless I loved him with all my heart and would love only him for the rest of my life."

"I would have to say he would be a lucky man."

"And I'd be a lucky woman because he'd love me the same way."

"Have you met such a man?"

She jumped up. "Enough talk about love. I think it's time I turned in."

Mitch caught her before she reached the wagon. He turned her around to face him and looked into her eyes. Though it was a shock, it dawned on him who Rosemary loved or thought she did. He smiled down at her. "I think I know who the man is, and I know you'll always be truthful with me."

"Oh, Mitch. How could you know?"

He ignored this question and asked, "Is the man me or is it somebody else?"

She didn't answer but instead, she dropped her head against his chest and her body began to shake.

In spite of everything he thought about love for him in his future, his heart soared. "Don't worry, sweetheart. You don't have to answer, because I'm pretty sure what your answer is, and it pleases me more than you can know."

When she didn't answer, he went on. "As for me, to fight the grownup feelings I've had about you ever since we left Weatherson, I've been telling myself you're still the sweet little girl I knew in the orphanage. The one who didn't care I had Indian blood. The one who liked me for who I am, not somebody who cares who my parents were. I kept saying you and Benny and me were a temporary family."

She looked at him. "Temporary family?"

"Yes, but I know it's no longer a true statement. I can now accept you are a woman, and I can also accept our family is no longer temporary. I don't know when or even why, but I know in my heart we're turned into a real family. You, Benny, and me, and to put your mind at ease, I'll not be going to Colorado. I think I've come up with another plan."

She pulled back and looked up at him with a happy mist in her eyes. "What plan?"

"I'll try to find a job in Bell Haven so I can stick around with you and help you raise Benny. He's becoming special to me, and I want to see if he continues to be special when we're not together all the time. That is, if you don't mind me hanging around."

"Oh, Mitch I'd love for you to stay in Bell Haven, but I'm not sure where I'll be. As you know, two of my sisters live on different ranches. Only one lives in town."

"I guess they would object if I hung around you too much since we're both single."

"They might."

"Then maybe we should do something about that, too."

"What do you mean?"

"I might as well admit it. I love you, too, Rosemary."

"Are you sure?"

"I'm positive. I suggest we see if we can find a preacher in the next town we come to."

She didn't answer because his mouth covered hers and she couldn't speak.

But nothing more had to be said. Their heartbeats said it all.

Six

Bell Haven

The first few days in Bell Haven and the nearby ranches were not only exciting for the sisters as they once again were able to have their Sister Circle in person. The first one was held on the day Bernadette and Drake escorted Rosemary, Mitch, and Benny to the Jenson ranch. Rosemary was as excited to see her oldest sister, Melissa, as she had been to see Bernadette. She didn't even bother to ask how Catherine knew they were coming when she saw her and her husband waiting on the porch.

As soon as the buggy stopped, Melissa came off the porch, hugged Rosemary, and her family, then called out, "Sister Circle."

The men all ended on the porch and watched as the four women formed a circle, put their arms around each other, and in a tearful voice, Melissa said, "Dear Heavenly Father, we come to You to thank You for answering our prayer that we would all be together again. We never gave up, and we're so thankful it has finally happened. Thank You from the bottom of my heart, and I'm sure my sisters all feel the same way."

Each one then voiced their thankfulness, and once again they hugged. Then Melissa said, "Catherine, my mother-in-law, and I have cooked dinner for everyone, and if your husbands are like mine, I'm sure they're ready to eat."

"I'm sure Drake is. He mentioned food on the way out here," Bernadette said.

"Mitch always seems to be hungry," Rosemary added.

"Then let's head to the backyard where we've set up tables." Melissa took Rosemary's arm. "Then young lady, you can explain to all of us how our baby sister disappeared, then turned into such a lovely young married woman with a baby already."

Rosemary laughed. "I can't wait to tell you all about it."

By the time they left for Bell Haven, not only had Rosemary told her story, but her sisters had elaborated on theirs.

Mitch had been surprised and almost shocked to find they accepted him completely and without question, simply because he was Rosemary's husband. He even had had job offers from both Joe Jenson and Chet Randell before they headed back to town.

As for shy little Benny, who was cuddled on Rosemary's lap, he surprised them all when he raised his head and said, "I wike Dabid. He say I special. I come back to play?"

"You sure will, honey." Rosemary kissed his cheek.

It turned out Mitch didn't take a job on either ranch because the next day there was a drunken outlaw riding down the street shooting at all the business signs. At Asaph's Blacksmith shop, he not only hit the sign, but it fell on the lone owner, knocking the man into the hot fire and burning a large portion of his right hand and arm and breaking it as he fell.

Being the gentle and generous person he was, Mitch offered to help out until the only blacksmith in town was able to come back to work. Since Regis Asaph had lost both his sons in the army and his wife had died three years earlier, he accepted the offer and paid Mitch well.

When the blacksmith saw he was going to be laid up for a good while, he asked Mitch if he would move his family into his house so Rosemary could do the cooking and help him with his medicine. He assured him this would take place without them paying any rent. After talking it over with Rosemary, they agreed they should accept the man's offer.

~ * ~

Almost two months later, Rosemary had given Regis his dinner and his medicine and returned to the kitchen to set the table for Mitch to come inside to eat, when there was a knock on the back door. She opened the door and was surprised to see Melissa and David.

"Well, hello, you two. What brings you to town in the middle of the week, and where is baby Joey?"

"Joe had some business at the bank, so David and I decided to ride into town with him and come visit you and Benny. We decided to leave Joey with Althea."

"I'm so glad you're here. Please come in."

They followed her into the kitchen.

"Is Benny here?" David asked.

"Go through the door and you'll find him in the parlor. He's playing with some animals Mr. Asaph gave him."

Benny must have heard them because he ran toward the kitchen calling out, "Hey, Dabid. Come see animals."

"Sure." David followed him back into the parlor.

"Do you mind sitting in the kitchen, Melissa? I'm finishing up dinner for Mitch."

"I don't mind at all. Matter of fact..."

"You don't have to say it. I bet you'd like a cup of coffee or tea?"

"Tea would be great."

"Then take a seat and I'll make us a cup."

After Rosemary finished checking the pots on the stove, she put two cups of tea on the table and sat. "I'm so glad you came. Will you and Joe join us for dinner when he comes to pick you up?"

"I don't want to intrude. He said he'd take us to the café."

"What do you mean, intrude? You're family. Besides I have plenty of food cooking. Mr. Regis is a big eater and so is Mitch." She laughed. "Of course, Benny is trying to keep up with them both."

"Then I'm sure Joe will want to stay. So, as soon as we finish our business, I'll help you finish up dinner."

Rosemary looked puzzled. "We have business?"

"I guess it is business. That's another reason I came to see you. I got a letter from the sheriff of Weatherson. He sent it to me because he was able to get my address from the woman at the orphanage where you were. He had enclosed a letter for you and asked me to get it to you, so I have it." She looked in her purse and pulled out a letter. "Here it is. As you can see, I didn't open it. It's still sealed."

"I wonder why in the world the sheriff of Weatherson would send me a letter."

"I have no idea, but there is one way to find out."

"You're right." Rosemary broke the seal, unfolded the missive, and read:

Miss Cardwell,

Since I didn't have your address, I'm sure your sister will get this letter to you. Things have happened in Weatherson and in the orphanage and I was sure you would like to hear about them, so let me begin at the beginning.

When Dwight Clanton first came to me about missing orphans from his place, I was shocked and vowed to help him find them as fast as possible. But it wasn't long before I began to see a contradiction in the man's actions. It happened when I asked him if he thought something could have happened to them or if they ran away for some reason. When he kept insisting you had been kidnapped, I began to wonder if he actually wanted to find his missing orphans, or if he had some other plan for them. I then visited the orphanage and had a long talk with his sister. She hinted you had a good reason for running away and eventually told me why.

Being the father of a daughter a couple of years younger than you, the fact this old man intended to marry you made me furious. I decided then and there I'd never permit him to find out what happened to you.

Because I learned Mitch O'Donald had plans to leave for Colorado in search of gold, I had a talk with his friends. They were under the impression he had left the Saturday before you disappeared.

At first, so was I. I later learned he didn't go in search of gold, though I never informed Clanton of this fact. It was then I realized this Good Samaritan had helped you escape. I never told Clanton of this either.

But I did think the man's ability to run an orphanage needed to be looked into. My deputy and I devised a plan, and he posed as a millionaire who wanted to buy the orphanage. Clanton fell for it, so we were able to get the board members and state officials to delve into the case by confiscating the books and records.

It didn't take long to not only arrest the man for embezzling money from the children's guardians and parents, but we found a book where he'd worked out different plans he'd made to intimidate the children and eventually we found he'd written down a plan to murder Benny Neven because there would be no more money from his father.

Since she was the major help in the arrest of her brother, his sister has been allowed to stay and work at the orphanage under its new management. It is now a wonderful place for children who need to be there, and I thought it would make you feel better to know this.

I've also sent the name of Mr. Neven's lawyer because the man wants him to handle everything concerning his giving up his child. I have a feeling, and my feelings often come true, I think you intend to adopt Benny.

Another feeling I have is you will end up married to Mitch O'Donald. I hope this comes true, if it hasn't already, because from what I hear, he's a fine fellow.

Please write when you can and let us (my wife and daughter want to know, too) how things are going for you in your new home in Bell Haven.

Sheriff Jess R. Peeks
Weatherson, Texas

~ * ~

It was two months later when the O'Donald family and Regis Asaph left the church, went to the Randell ranch in the two-seater buggy for Sunday dinner, then headed home.

"I can't believe I'm doing this," Regis complained from the back seat.

Rosemary looked around at him. "Why not? You're getting much better and you're even going into the shop to help Mitch at times now."

"That's different."

"What do you mean different? You've decided to accept us as your family and Benny is even calling you papaw."

"I think of you as my family, but does it mean I have to go with you to church every Sunday, then have dinner with one of your sisters and her family? I've done it twice now, and I ain't used to this sort of thing."

"You might as well get used to it, Regis," Mitch said. "I was shocked at first, too, but it didn't take me long to realize I was welcome, and you'll soon understand you're welcome, too."

"But until you folks came into my life and took over the shop, I hadn't been in a church since Mamie died. Didn't never plan to go back till I went in a pine box."

Benny looked up at him. "Why you in box, Papaw?"

He put his good arm around the boy. "I weren't in no real box, sonny."

Benny frowned. "Why you say box?"

"That was just one of Papaw's expressions, honey," Rosemary said.

Benny didn't say anything else, but Regis said, "There's something else. Why do you sisters always get in a circle and talk every time you meet up? I ain't never seen nobody do such a thing before."

Rosemary explained the reason for the sister circle.

"I guess that makes sense," Regis said.

A deer suddenly darted across the field and Benny let out a happy squeal. The rest of the ride was spent with Benny asking Papaw to find more animals.

Rosemary looked at Mitch. "Honey, I have written a letter to Sheriff Peeks. I want you to read it before I mail it tomorrow."

"I don't have to read it."

"I know. But there might be something you want to add to it."

"Then if you want me to read it, I will."

She moved closer to him. "Since our son now has all of his papaw's attention, may I sit closer to my husband?"

He took the reins in his one hand and put his free arm around her. "You can do it, as long as I get to hold you like this."

"You can hold me like this anytime, my love."

Mitch leaned over and kissed the top of her head.

"Benny, I guess we better keep looking for animals. Looks like your mama and daddy have forgotten we're here in this back seat 'cause he just kissed her."

"Dat fine. Mama kiss Daddy, too." Without taking a breath he added, "Look, Papaw. There a rabbit."

Rosemary looked up at Mitch with a tear of happiness trickling down her cheek. He didn't say anything, but he grinned and pulled her tighter against him. They were both thrilled because it was the first time Benny had called them Mama and Daddy.

~ * ~

A few days later, as they sat on the front porch after supper, Sheriff Jess Peeks took the letter from his pocket and handed it to his wife. "I got this at the office today, and since you know how this all started, I want you to read it. It will tell you more about what has happened than I could ever tell you."

"Will I like it, or will it make me cry?"

He chuckled. "Maybe both."

She gave him a quizzical look and took the letter. It said....

Dear Sheriff Peeks,

I was thrilled to get your letter and I'm sorry it has taken me so long to write back to you, but I wanted a couple of things to happen before I wrote.

I was delighted to hear the students at the orphanage are now being treated as they should be, and Dwight Clanton got his comeuppance. Though I always knew he was a terrible man, I never guessed he was as evil as you discovered he was. No wonder Miss Gladiola seemed to back him in everything because it's now clear what could have happened to her if she didn't obey and help him carry out all his wishes. As I can now recall, I think I remember times when she would help the orphans behind his back. I'm pleased to know he never found out.

As for your intuition about Mitch O'Donald, you had him figured out right. He not only helped Benny and me escape the fate Clanton had planned for us, he took care of the entire trip. Needless to say, I have loved the man since I was a young girl. The trip to Bell Haven only showed me how much. In fact, when he finally accepted the fact I was no longer the little girl he'd befriended at the orphanage, he confessed he loved me, too. We were married three days before we reached Bell Haven.

My sisters received us with open arms, though it was also hard for them to realize I was no longer the baby sister they had to take care of. It took a little while for them to see me as a grown woman with a husband and child she considered their son. But they have finally done so.

As for us, we've added to our family, but I must back up a little to tell you how it happened.

Mitch always dreamed of being a blacksmith but didn't have the money to buy the equipment to start a business. A few days after we got to Bell Haven, their blacksmith's sign was hit by a stray bullet. It fell on the owner of the shop, knocking him into the fire, burning his arm, then breaking the arm as he fell. He was unable to work, and Mitch volunteered to help until he was better.

Since his wife had died and his two sons were also deceased, he invited us to move into his house so I could take care of him. I wasn't sure how it would work out because Benny was afraid of him at first.

But it didn't take long for the two of them to work things out. He won Benny's heart when he presented the child with a box full of animals he'd made in his shop for his sons. Benny won his heart when, on his own, he started calling the big man Papaw.

As for Benny, his name is now Benny O'Donald. It only took a week for Mitch and me to adopt him, thanks to the telegraph. We had no contact with the father. Everything was done through the lawyer, which was fine with us.

Both Mitch and I were thrilled the other Sunday when Benny called us Mama and Daddy for the first time.

Another thing pleasing us, though we hope we won't be taking advantage of it for a long time, happened just this past week. Papaw, as we all call him now, came in from a mysterious trip into town and handed Mitch a piece of paper.

It was a copy of his will. He has left everything he owns to his new family, as he called us. Of course, I cried, and it was hard for Mitch not to tear up.

We never dreamed our lives would be so wonderfully blessed when we got to Bell Haven. This is something I'll have to share in our Sister Circle this coming Sunday.

Thank you again for your letter and please tell your wife and daughter how much I appreciate them supporting you in keeping our "disappearance" a secret.

Blessings to you and your family,

Rosemary O'Donald (With a little input from Mitch, Benny, and Papaw).

"Oh, Jess. You're right, It is a wonderful letter, and I can't stop the tears that are about to leak out of my eyes."

"I told you."

"There's only one thing I don't understand."

"What's that, honey?"

"What in the world is a Sister Circle?"

"I don't know, Nina. Maybe she put it in there so we'd write back and ask."

She smiled at him. "I have a feeling we'll be doing just that."

Meet Agnes Alexander

Agnes Alexander is the name Lynette Hampton uses for all her books now, though a few written under her Hampton name are still in print. She is a multi-published author with over 60 published books. She writes in different genres, but her favorite to write and to read are Western Historical Romances. A lifelong resident of North Carolina, she has visited 48 of the 50 states and particularly enjoys vacationing in the western US.

She is the mother of one daughter (a first-grade teacher) who is married to the best son-in-law (a contractor) a woman could want. She is a grandmother of two grown grandchildren (brother and sister) who both graduated from college this year—a boy, Trent, who received his master's degree in grief counseling and is pursuing a job with hospice, and a girl, Blaire, who majored in dance and minored in business and has an offer to work at Disney World. Agnes lives within a mile of her family in a townhouse she shares with Victoria, her long-haired black and brown cat, who is the actual ruler of the house.

Other Works From The Pen Of

Agnes Alexander

Valissa's Home - Her brother loses her home in a poker game and Valissa is given two weeks to vacate. When the menacing new owner shows up early, is she safe to stay in the house until she finds a place to go?

Ulla's Courage - Finding out her relatives intend to confiscate her share of the family mercantile, then claim the money her father left her, does Ulla have the courage to marry a stranger who needs a wife to help him take his two children to Oregon?

Opal's Faith - Opal's faith in her father is tested when he moves his family from Memphis to a rundown ranch in Arizona where they discover a half-breed cousin and a murderer who intends to have the ranch if he has to kill the entire family.

Zelda's Guilt - A storm takes the live of Zelda's father and leaves her stepmother an invalid, who blames Zelda, leaving with the responsibility of her stepbrother and half-sister. Only the intervention of a passing stranger helps to unravel the mystery.

Nelda's Homecoming - Nelda is convinced her husband has a mistress, so she runs home planning to get a divorce. She doesn't count on him leaving the army and following her, trying to convince her he's innocent. She doesn't believe him because he won't explain who the woman in Cheyene is.

Wilma's Outlaw - Wilma watches her friends marry and start families and she figures she's doomed to spinsterhood. Then a man, who had run away from home as a youngster, shows up with five orphans he has rescued and her whole life changes.

Isabella's Baby - Isabella is tricked into a false marriage, but before she can confront the man, he is killed, then she discovers she is pregnant. Her family tries to force her to marry a terrible man, and she runs away. When she meets her false husband's brother, will he help her or will he help her family force her to marry the awful man.

Dear reader,

I hope you've enjoyed reading this heartwarming tale of the
love of sisters.

Your opinion is valuable to other
readers like you,
who may be looking for books like mine.

Please consider taking a few minutes to post a review,
however brief,
on the site where you purchased this book
or on the Wings ePress web page.

You may also want to visit my author page
at the Wings' website where you can find the rest of my
books.

Thank you!
Agnes Alexander

Visit Our Website

For The Full Inventory
Of Quality Books:

Wings ePress, Inc

Quality trade paperbacks and downloads
in multiple formats,
in genres ranging from light romantic comedy to general
fiction and horror.
Wings has something for every reader's taste.
Visit the website, then bookmark it.
We add new titles each month!

Wings ePress, Inc.
3000 N. Rock Road
Newton, KS 67114

www.ingramcontent.com/pod-product-compliance
Lightning Source LLC
Chambersburg PA
CBHW070455300726
48975CB00007B/2181

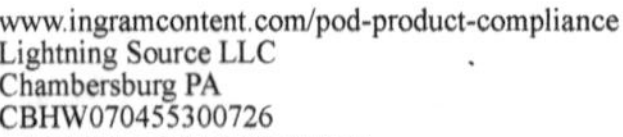